THE
REPORTER

Kerry B. Boerst

PublishAmerica
Baltimore

At the specific preference of the author, PublishAmerica allowed this work to remain exactly as the author intended, verbatim, without editorial input.

ISBN: 1-4241-1200-1
PUBLISHED BY PUBLISHAMERICA, LLLP
www.publishamerica.com
Baltimore

Printed in the United States of America

Dedication

For my husband Bill.
You believed in me when I did not. I love you forever.

For Brianna.
Without you, this book would have no title. Always follow your dreams.

For Crystal and Becky.
I love you both and, contrary to popular belief, we *are* a real family.

For the Nerbonne's everywhere.

Acknowledgments

Thank you to everyone who took the time to read through my manuscript, especially my husband, Bill, and my friends who work for Isabella County in Michigan. You know who you are. Your input was invaluable!

I would also like to thank all of my friends in and around the Southgate Mall in Missoula, Montana. Your support through this whole process has meant the world to me.

Isolation

You can drown in the
hate that it brings or
wrap yourself in the silence
and empower your
soul.

Chapter 1

The evening heat was oppressive and the countryside dry and dusty from a long July drought. Even the weeds in the ditches bordering Highway 70 in southwestern Arkansas were withered like an old balloon that has lost most of its air. Yet none of that mattered to Effie St. Martin. As she gripped the steering wheel and pressed the accelerator to the floor, it didn't even register that she was about to cross into Oklahoma. The only thing on her mind was the work that she was missing while she was on this so-called vacation and the man who was responsible for it all. Rich Hale. The name would forever bring her blood to a rapid boil.

At thirty-two, Effie was five years into a career with the *Lansing Sun Press*. She had started out as a part-timer and worked her way up to a full-time position writing for the *Community* section. And right from the start, Rich Hale was there whispering to her when everyone was out of earshot.

The very first time was just a few days after she had started at the paper. She was in the break room by herself, mixing a bit of cream into her coffee, as Rich walked in. Effie knew who he was before they had ever been introduced. Everyone knew who he was. You don't cover as many major stories or write for as many years as Rich Hale had without getting a little bit famous.

"Hello," she said, raising her coffee mug.

He gave her a quick look up and down then whispered, "Moo."

Had she really heard what she thought she had? "Excuse me?" she questioned. It couldn't have been. He was a professional.

"Just trying to speak your language," he said.

Effie's face went red. This could not be happening to her. Her eyes darted around the room and her mouth opened then closed.

Rich's mouth spread into a wide, toothy grin. "Listen, er—" His eyebrows arched expectantly.

"Effie," she breathed.

"Right, Heifer," he went on as he poured himself a cup of coffee. "You just stay out of the way of the real reporters, such as myself, and we will try to expand enough to accommodate your girth around here."

When he left the room, Effie stood there gaping after him. It just wasn't possible. This was a big newspaper and Rich Hale was a well respected reporter. How could that type of harassment still be happening to her? In grade school she had been known as butterball blimp and it was suddenly like nothing had changed since then.

She had spent her entire life hiding behind baggy clothes and long hair. It was as penetrable a defense then as it was now. Loose clothes and flaming red hair that hung to the middle of her back did nothing to safeguard her 253 pound body from the cutting words. In her heart, she knew there was no stopping the insults no matter what she hid behind. Rich Hale's nasty comments hurt just as much as the comments she endured growing up.

Over the years, it became a sport for Rich to ridicule Effie at every turn. Each time she was alone and he came near, her breath caught in her throat. The nasty comments would spew forth and Effie would just keep holding her breath, praying to God that no one had heard them. Maybe if she ignored them, they would go away and it would be like the words had never been uttered. The only problem was that the words had been spoken and no matter what she did, they echoed in her head. But still, her instinct was to keep her lips sealed. She always hoped that Rich would get tired of it and it would all stop one day.

Then again, everyone has a breaking point and on the 25th of July, five years after it all began, Effie knew she was getting close to hers. It didn't matter if Rich was being mean or if he was verbalizing what everyone else thought, it hurt just the same. She loved writing for the paper more than anything else in the world. Even that was not enough to keep her from contemplating leaving the paper, though.

Effie had just returned to her desk from the copy room where she'd had another run-in with Rich. She was sitting with her elbows on her desk and her face in her hands, trying to keep the tears from coming.

Sandra Bertram had called the desk next to Effie's home and had seen her come back and do the same thing on more than one occasion. She leaned over and spoke to Effie in a hushed voice. "He's going to keep doing that as long as you let him," she said.

Effie looked at Sandra and shook her head. How could she know what went on? And even if she did know, there was no way she could understand how it felt. Sandra was thin and stylish. As far as Effie was concerned, she was her exact opposite.

Sandra nodded, raising her right eyebrow slightly. "I know who it is and I know what kind of things he's been saying." Effie shook her head again. "Yes, I do know," Sandra whispered. "I overheard him saying something to you once a couple of years ago—before I moved over to this side of the newsroom."

"You don't understand," said Effie.

"What don't I understand?" asked Sandra. "I don't understand that the guy is a jerk? I don't understand that you are afraid to stand up to him because he is a big shot here? I don't understand that his words cut deep? Please, tell me what it is that I can't possibly conceive because I can't figure out what that is." There was a deep crease between her eyebrows as she shook her head in wonder. "What I do know is that I'm sick of watching you let him dance all over you and if you don't do something to put an end to it, I'll make sure that Mr. Ludgreen does!"

Effie gave her a despairing look. It was like Sandra could read her thoughts. Was she that transparent? "You just don't understand," she cried as she rushed off toward the ladies room with Sandra trailing after her.

"I'm sorry, Effie," she said, bursting through the door. "Maybe I don't understand but I can't watch you take that crap anymore. You have to fight back. At least say something back to him—"

Tears welled up in Effie's eyes and began to flow onto her cheeks. She raised her hands to her face and sobbed into them.

Sandra dropped her voice to a whisper and shook her head. "In all the times I've seen you hurry back to your desk and cover your face with your hands, I'll bet you've never once said anything back to Rich. You probably never stand up for yourself." She cautiously placed a hand on Effie's back and began rubbing it in small circles. "You have to let him know that you are not a doormat and it is not OK for him to treat you that way or he will never stop. The only person to blame for letting this go on so long is you."

Effie looked up at the woman next to her. "You have no idea what it's like. You can't even begin to know what it's like to walk in my shoes."

"And you have no idea what it's like to walk in mine," Sandra said, lifting one of her spiky heeled shoes slightly.

The woman shared a small smile for a moment then Sandra's expression became serious again. "Tell me, Effie, what makes it so hard to tell him to stop? They're only words. You're a professional journalist for Christ's sake. You put your words out there every single day," she scoffed. "We're talking about letting one person know how you feel. If you can't at least tell Rich that it isn't OK for him to treat you that way, you have no right to call yourself a journalist. Our job is to get the facts straight and let them be known. Set things straight with Rich or get out of the business, honey."

Effie stared at Sandra as she turned to leave. She pulled the door open then paused for a moment. "You're going to be hiding in her forever if you don't figure out a way to defend yourself, Effie," she said then let the door fall closed behind her.

Effie stared into the mirror for several minutes, searching for an answer. Maybe Sandra was right. Not once had she ever said anything back to Rich. Maybe she *should* say something to him. After all, he was just one person. And what made it OK for him to say such terrible things to anyone?

The weight of Sandra's words began to sink in. Effie had every right to stand up to that beast. But as Effie thought about confronting Rich, a shiver ran up her spine. What could she say to put an end to the awful words. Effie took a deep breath and straightened her clothes. She would have to worry about that when the time came.

A little while later, while staring at the words on her computer screen, Effie's concentration was broken. As Sandra cleared her throat, she nodded toward the far end of the room, drawing Effie's attention in that direction. Rich was talking with a group of co-workers but every once in a while he would glance in her direction.

Effie nervously shuffled through the papers in front of her, trying to look as busy as possible. Maybe that would keep him away. When she glanced up at Rich, the mischievous glint in his eyes told her otherwise. She braced for the cutting remark as he continued toward her.

"Hello Heifer," Rich murmured as he perched on the corner of her desk.

Oh God no! Why couldn't he leave her alone this one time? Effie's breath caught in her throat. It was like her airway had closed altogether. It was an effort to even fill her lungs. Her heart was beating so hard and for a moment, she thought she was having a heart attack.

Effie knew she had to calm down. Sandra was right! She had to stand up for herself and part of that meant not letting that bastard see how upset he made her. She counted to ten to calm her nerves and suddenly the air came rushing into her lungs. Her heart was hammering as fast as a hummingbird's but she knew she could not let the harassment go on any longer.

Effie's eyes darted from the blinking cursor on the desk in front of her to the man perched next to her. Sandra looked back at her for a moment and mouthed, "Say something back."

Rich was looking around the room to make sure that no one was listening. He chuckled then leaned over so close Effie could feel his breath on the side of her face. "I was just wondering something, Heifer," he whispered. "When you were baptized, did they have to do it at Sea World?" He laughed at his own joke. "I'm just asking because, you know, you're as fat as the whales that they keep there!"

Effie squeezed her eyes shut then sucked in a deep breath. When she opened her eyes again, Rich was getting up to leave. Before she even realized what she was doing, with a quivering voice, she said, "Um, Rich."

He did not hear her.

"Rich," she repeated louder. He stopped in his tracks then turned to look at her. "I—I was wondering if you could answer a question for me—I mean because you're such an expert."

He laughed and looked around. "Of course I'll answer a question— because I'm such an expert." Several people near them stopped what they were doing and turned their attention toward Effie and Rich.

"Well," she said, "I was just wondering—I mean I hear that excessive masturbation shrinks your dick. Is that really true?" With every word, she gained a little more confidence. "I mean that I would guess it is true because you know what they say about guys who drive flashy, expensive cars and you *did* just get that new sports car. So I guess excessive masturbation *does* shrink your dick, huh?"

Rich just stood there for a moment as though he had been shot and was waiting to fall. A few laughs erupted around the room. He gritted his teeth then his eyes raked the room with indignation. He bellowed ferociously, "Heifer, you must be about five pounds from a surprise visit from Richard Simmons."

"Listen Pencil Dick," Effie barked. "I've taken well more than my fair share of your crap. Back off and leave me alone."

"Looks like you've also taken more than your fair share of lunch, Heifer," Rich thundered.

Her eyes narrowed with contempt. As she opened her mouth to speak, their boss, Raymond Ludgreen came flying into the office, eyes wide with surprise. "Hale—St. Martin—In my office—NOW!" he shouted. "Everyone else wasting this paper's time, either get back to work or you are all fired!"

Effie shot up out of her chair, sending it rolling backward. Her heart was hammering and she was shaking, she was so angry. It didn't matter how much trouble she was in, it felt good to finally stand up for herself. Rich Hale deserved to hear every word of it! She had put up with him for much too long. Sandra was right. Effie had no one to blame but herself for letting him treat her that way for so long.

All eyes were on Effie as she stormed toward the door. Rich was standing in the middle of the room with a smirk on his face like a little boy who had gotten away with stealing cookies from the cookie jar. When she passed him, she wanted nothing more than to claw his eyes out and get rid of that smug expression. Instead, she shot daggers with her eyes then headed out of the room.

Inside Mr. Ludgreen's office, Effie took a seat in one of the two uncomfortable chairs across the desk from her boss. The cushions were too firm and the supports on the armrests pressed into her thighs too hard. She winced in pain for a moment then tried to hide the level of her discomfort. Rich had not followed her in.

"Sir," Effie began.

Mr. Ludgreen held up his hand to silence her. "I don't want to hear any of it until both of you are here because what I have to say is only going to be said once."

A few moments later, Rich sauntered into the office and closed the door behind him like he was getting ready for a friendly afternoon chat. He looked at Effie as someone would a cockroach needing to be stepped on. He grabbed hold of the empty chair and pulled it as far as he could from Effie then sat down.

"Sir," Effie began again.

"I can't believe the two of you," said Mr. Ludgreen, ignoring her. "Your schoolyard behavior will not be tolerated in my newsroom. I'm not running a daycare in here and I won't have my staff acting like children. I could have both your jobs for the display in there today."

Rich flashed a superior grin at Effie then turned toward Mr. Ludgreen with a look of seriousness. "Let me explain everything, Raymond. That way I can get back to my big article for the Sunday edition," he said. "To tell you the truth, I should have brought this situation to your attention a long time ago. I just didn't want to bother you with petty office problems."

Effie blinked in surprise.

He continued, "You see Ray, Effie has been after me to go out on a date for months and months." Effie's jaw dropped and she let out a startled gasp. "I've told her *no* time and time again but she just won't accept it. She's nice enough but she just isn't my type. Besides, I don't believe in dating people from the workplace."

"Sir, I never—" she blurted.

Rich waved her off then kept right on talking. "Like I said, she's a nice girl and everything, Ray. I didn't want to get her in trouble. That's why I never said anything about it before. She just has to learn that no means no. I mean she asked me a couple of times today and I told her I just wasn't interested both times. I guess she's just upset by my rejection."

Mr. Ludgreen sat back in his chair. Effie did not know what to say. She just sat there stupefied. She knew that Rich was a snake but never, in her wildest dreams, had she thought he would pull something like this. She looked from Mr. Ludgreen to Rich and back again. Her mouth opened to talk but no words came out.

"Well, Rich," said Mr. Ludgreen, "I guess that about sums it up then. I know you have an important article that you are working on. Why don't you go ahead and go back to work. I think Ms St. Martin and I can finish up here by ourselves."

Rich got up to leave. "Should I close the door on my way out, Ray?"

"Please."

"Sir," Effie said as the door closed behind Rich. "I can assure you—"

Mr. Ludgreen looked at Effie for a moment and as he did, his eyes narrowed with disgust. "Ms St. Martin, you have the makings of a great journalist. You've written some darn good pieces considering the topics you've been given. I think you have enough talent to make a very healthy career here." He paused for a moment. "But you can't pursue co-workers like you did Hale.

She tried to break in. "—But, sir—"

"The way you've harassed Hale is grounds for dismissal. I could have your job for this, St. Martin. Do you understand how serious this is?"

"I never did what he said, sir," Effie whispered almost too quiet for herself to hear.

Mr. Ludgreen went on, not having heard her. "I understand how lonely it can be when you get turned down after asking someone out. He said no though, Effie. That means drop it and leave him alone." He leaned toward her and tapped his finger on the desk. "Ms St. Martin, you are too good a reporter to lose over an incident like this. Maybe you need a break from this place."

Effie shook her head. "No, sir. Please, no."

"I don't think I've seen you take a single day of vacation, call in sick or even come in late since you started here. That's a long time to go without a break." He got up and walked around the desk, perching on the edge next to her. Effie shook her head in disagreement. "You need some time away," Mr. Ludgreen said as he reached out to pat her arm. "You need to let things cool down."

She gave him a pleading look. "I don't need a vacation, Mr. Ludgreen," she cried. "I haven't done anything wrong. I just want to keep writing."

"It wasn't a suggestion, St. Martin. It was an order. You have much more vacation time coming than you could possible use. I want you to take—" he thought for a moment. "I want you to take a week or two—"

"A week or two!" Effie broke in. "Please, sir, no. I don't need to take any time—"

"Yes, you do. Everyone needs time away from here once in a while. That includes you. You need time to get your mind off—uh—Hale."

"But, sir—"

"Ms St. Martin," said Mr. Ludgreen. "You will go out to your desk and finish up the articles you have going for tomorrow's paper then you will leave for two weeks of vacation or I will fire you right now."

"One, sir. One week. Please." She gave him a pleading look.

"No, St. Martin. Two weeks."

"But just a minute ago, you said a week or two. If I have to take time off, I prefer that it be only one week."

Mr. Ludgreen sighed and pressed his fingers to his eyes in exasperation. "I know what I said a minute ago and if you don't get out to your desk and finish up the articles for tomorrow's paper, I am going to make it a permanent vacation."

"But what about the stories I have scheduled to cover over the next two weeks? I can't just cancel them or ask the community to reschedule their events around my schedule."

He answered, "We have plenty of part-timers who can fill in while you're gone. Just leave a list of your scheduled appointments and I'll assign someone to take your place."

Effie looked at him, her face etched with sorrow. "I could write from home, sir. I could e-mail the stories in."

"St. Martin! You just aren't getting it," Mr. Ludgreen said. "You are taking two weeks of vacation, effective at the end of the day or you are no longer an employee of the *Lansing Sun Press*. End of story!"

"Yes, sir," muttered Effie as she rose to leave. She cast one last look of sadness his way.

Mr. Ludgreen's shoulders drooped. "I'm sorry, St. Martin. My decision is final."

Effie trudged out of Mr. Ludgreen's office. She wanted to disappear. Rich Hale's teasing had nearly made her lose her job. She couldn't argue her side of the story with him in the room and she couldn't even do it without him there.

As she rounded the corner on the way back to her desk, she ran directly into Rich. He was leaning against the wall, peering down his nose at her. A sneer spread across his lips. "Don't ever mess with me again, Heifer. I have way more clout around here than you do. You will lose every time."

Effie tried to go around him but he put his arm against the other wall, blocking her way. She looked up into his eyes. "I was just wondering something, Heifer," he whispered, leaning so close she swore she could feel his lips brush her ear. "When you wear high-heels, do you strike oil?"

Rich broke out in a fit of laughter, and as he did so, he wrapped his arm around her holding her in place. Effie pushed and struggled to get free from his embrace then ran toward her desk. When she turned and looked back, Rich was still standing in the same spot, laughing.

Why did life have to be like this for her? Was it really that much of a crime to be overweight? It was just like nothing had changed since her childhood. The bully who was teasing her was still getting away with murder.

Effie grabbed her chair and pulled it back to her desk. No one had bothered to touch it while she was with Mr. Ludgreen. In fact, no one even bothered to look up when she returned. Sandra and a few of the others had disappeared during her absence and those who were still there seemed to have their nose to the grindstone.

Effie flopped down in her chair. Screw them all! She had work to do.

As she sat looking at the articles she had to finish, she began to wonder if maybe she did need a vacation. On one hand, if she went away, she could miss the article that would put her on the front page of the paper. On the other hand, Mr. Ludgreen had said he was not willing to allow her to write from home. It would be even worse to actually see the opportunity and not be able to grab it than it would be to miss it altogether. Mr. Ludgreen was right when he said that she had more than enough vacation time coming to her. Money really wasn't a problem either. She lived a very simple life without many bills so most of her paychecks went directly into savings.

Effie sighed. There was no sense in wasting any more time thinking about vacation. She pulled her keyboard in front of her and positioned her notes so she could begin writing. By 4:30 that afternoon, she had not seen nor heard from Rich even once and she had finished more articles than could possibly fit in the next three editions of the *Community* section.

After cleaning up her desk, Effie picked up her purse and the stack of articles and slipped out of the office. When she stopped into Mr. Ludgreen's office, she dropped the stack of articles in the middle of his desk. Her voice cracking, she said, "I'll be back in two weeks sir," then turned to leave.

Mr. Ludgreen looked at the number of articles in front of him then up at Effie. He cleared his throat. "Uh, St. Martin," he said. She stopped and turned to look at him. "Any plans for your vacation time?"

Oh sure. Now he was playing the sympathetic boss. Raymond Ludgreen wasn't the tiniest bit better than Rich Hale. They could both take a long walk off a short pier as far as she was concerned!

"I'm not sure right now, sir," she said in a cool voice. "I can't imagine a very exciting vacation by myself."

"You're a top notch writer, St. Martin. I can see you going places with this paper one day." He looked into her sad eyes for a moment. "You just need a break. You just need a break."

Effie rolled her eyes and shook her head. "With all due respect, sir, I want to go on record saying that I am not the one who started that argument today and it wasn't about what you think it was—Whether you believe it or not." She turned to leave again.

"I know," Mr. Ludgreen mumbled, causing Effie to spin around on her heel.

"You know?" Mr. Ludgreen nodded his head. Effie stammered, "You know what that argument was about?"

"Ms St. Martin, I was a journalist long before you were even walking. I might not be out chasing down the stories like you kids but that doesn't mean I've lost my touch." He stopped as if to reflect and chuckled a bit. "There isn't much this old goat misses around this place."

She cast Mr. Ludgreen a scorching glare. "If you knew what was going on all along, why am I the one being disciplined?"

"Shut the door and sit down a moment please, Ms St. Martin," he said.

Effie grabbed the handle and swung the door shut so hard, the bang echoed through the building. She paced back and forth in front of the door for a moment but did not take a seat. She stopped and looked at Mr. Ludgreen. "I have put up with that for five years. If you knew about it the entire time, why isn't something being done about him?"

"It's not that easy, Ms St. Martin."

"It should be that easy. There are laws—"

Mr. Ludgreen sucked in a deep breath. "Why is it you never said anything about it?" His question knocked Effie off balance. She had mentioned laws. He was supposed to be the one shaken.

"I—Because—" She sat down on the front edge of the same chair she had sat in earlier, trying not to pinch her thighs with the armrest supports.

"Ms St. Martin," Mr. Ludgreen began in a quiet, even voice, "I cannot just fire Richard Hale or send him away on vacation. He is a very important journalist for this paper. Thousands of people around the state buy this paper just because of his articles. The truth of the matter is, I wish I knew a better way to handle this situation. Rich Hale's articles sell papers, though, and that is the bottom line."

"I'll—I'll get a lawyer," she stammered.

Mr. Ludgreen cut in. "You'll get a lawyer and what, Ms St. Martin?" She didn't answer. "You'll get a lawyer and make yourself look like a fool because right now, I *have* to stand behind Rich. If anything regarding this went to court, I would *have* to say that you were the one harassing him. When everything is over with, no paper in the state of Michigan will ever touch you again. You would put yourself out of a job."

Effie's eyes took on a hunted look. "It's not fair, sir," she said, her bottom lip curling.

"St. Martin, you're a journalist," said Mr. Ludgreen. "I think you know that life isn't fair." He paused, studying Effie's face. "Take the vacation, kid. I promise that when you come back I'll work something out to make up for it."

A spark ignited in her expression. "If I go along with this, I want a cover story, Mr. Ludgreen."

"I can't promise you that. What I can promise is a bigger story than you are used to."

"That's not good enough, *Ray.*" Effie drawled his name sarcastically. "I'm sick of people walking all over me. Rich isn't going to do it anymore and *you* aren't either."

"Excuse me, St. Martin?" questioned Mr. Ludgreen.

"You heard me," said Effie. "I'm not going to take this anymore." She tapped on a bulge in her purse, a smile spreading across her lips. "I'm recording this entire conversation. I have proof that you knowingly allowed Rich to harass me. That makes you just as guilty as him, doesn't it?"

Mr. Ludgreen shot up out of his chair. His knuckles turned white as he pressed on them on the desk while leaning across to look directly into Effie's eyes. "We need to work this out here and now," he hissed.

"I think we pretty much have it worked out, Ray. I'm going to go ahead and take that vacation and I want your word that you will give me a cover story when I come back."

Silence.

He sat down and studied Effie's face as if he could see into her mind and tell what she was thinking. Finally, he sucked in a deep breath and smacked his lips. "Fine, St. Martin but I want the tape."

"I don't think so." She shook her head. "I'm no idiot, sir. If I give you the tape, you will have my proof of all this as well as my job. I think I'll hold onto the tape until after my cover story runs. Well, that and we'll have to have a little talk about what to do about Hale too. Then, and only then, can you have it."

Mr. Ludgreen squirmed for a moment. If something like this got out, it would cost him his entire career. He'd worked too long and hard to get where he was and he was too close to retirement to screw things up. "Fine," he said and stuck out his hand to shake on it.

Effie ignored his hand and rose to leave. "I'll be back in two weeks, Mr. Ludgreen," she said, then turned and walked out, her hand on the bulge in her purse. Perhaps Raymond Ludgreen was not as keen as he thought he was. Effie wasn't sure what combination of items was making the bulge in her purse but she knew it wasn't a tape recorder.

Maybe a road trip would be the ticket after all. If she stayed home during her vacation, she ran the risk of Mr. Ludgreen stopping by or calling her about the tape. If she had any kind of contact with him at all, she knew there was a chance she would slip up and let on that there really was no tape at all. If she did that, her job was as good as gone.

Chapter 2

By the time Effie reached home that evening, her conscience was working overtime. What had she been thinking? What kind of idiot acted that way in a professional setting? And then there was the whole scene with Mr. Ludgreen. Who was she kidding there? He was sure to figure out that there was no tape and fire her right away.

Effie slumped in her favorite chair without opening the shades or turning on a lamp. If she had just kept her mouth shut like always, she wouldn't be in this mess. She pinched her eyes shut and gritted her teeth. "How could I have been so stupid?" she thought out loud.

She got up and stomped around her apartment, trying to locate her atlas. Effie had to figure out someplace to go. She couldn't just leave without some kind of plan. No one in the world did that. Well, criminals did that. Low-life scum did that too. And people who had something to hide did that. People like Effie.

She flipped through the maps. Staying in Lansing was too much of a risk. Effie needed to find someplace to go where she wouldn't have to worry about running into Mr. Ludgreen. If he thought for a second that she didn't have a recording of their conversation, she could kiss her beloved writing career goodbye.

She could not let that happen. She just couldn't. Once she had a chance to write a great cover story, everyone would see that she had just as much talent as Rich. Then the fact that there really was no tape would be water under the bridge.

But what if Effie's big story came along while she was out cruising across the countryside? The thought of missing the perfect story made Effie's face grow hot. She knew it was going to happen while she was gone.

Damn those men! If it wasn't for Rich Hale and Raymond Ludgreen, Effie would be able to get her story the way a real journalist does. She would be free to sniff it out on her own instead of blackmailing Ludgreen.

Then again, this could be a sign that it was time for her to move on. Maybe she had outgrown the *Lansing Sun Press*. She could always check with a few other newspapers along the way. With her talent and experience, any of them would be lucky to add her to their staff.

On the other hand, leaving the paper might be exactly what Ludgreen wanted her to do. It would be an easy way for him to erase a tense situation. And it certainly wouldn't hurt Rich's feelings to think that he had played a role in driving her out of the place.

Effie was practically foaming at the mouth with rage. Screaming, she picked up a pillow and chucked it across the room as hard as she could. It didn't really make her feel better but it alleviated enough tension for her to find a suitcase and start tossing in clothes. Those men could force her into a vacation but there was no way they were going to force her out of her job!

Chapter 3

Effie's attention snapped back to the road and for one panicked moment, she didn't know where she was. Then she passed a Highway 70 sign, followed by a small, green, *Welcome to Oklahoma* sign. Relieved, she sighed. She was on the right track.

She realized that thinking about Rich Hale and Raymond Ludgreen was doing her no good. Rich had made the past five years at the paper miserable and now there was no way he was going to ruin her vacation too—mandatory or not.

Effie looked down the road and thought about the possibilities that lay ahead. She smiled at herself. The entire country was in front of her, just waiting for her to come along. Maybe life wasn't so bad after all. For the first time in a long time, Effie felt good enough to sing along with the quirky song drifting out of the radio.

The sinking sun in the western sky told Effie that it was time to think about stopping for the night. Knowing that it wasn't likely she would find a four-star resort in that neck of the woods, she pulled into the Sleepy-Z Motel in Gibbs Hill Oklahoma. The sign out front declared that it was clean, friendly and had the cheapest rates around. Effie retsrained a chuckle. Even if the owner charged $300 a night, it would still be the cheapest rates around since there didn't appear to be another motel for miles.

The dusty brown paint seemed to make the long, low building blend in with the landscape surrounding it. Effie looked down the row of matching doors to a flickering neon sign that read, "Office," with a bright red arrow pointing to the door beneath it. She pulled up near the door and went in to register for the night.

Behind the counter, an older woman with greying hair sat working on a crossword puzzle. As soon as the door closed behind Effie, the woman popped up from her chair and she stood waiting with a wide smile on her face.

"Evenin', stranger," she drawled. "What kin I do fer ya?"

Effie smiled warmly. "I'd like a room for tonight, please."

"Oh my!" The old woman's eyes lit up like the Fourth of July and she clapped her hands together. "What a beautiful voice! You really are a stranger ta these parts, aren't ya?"

"Yes," Effie said, giggling. "I'm from Michigan."

"Michigan," the old woman repeated. "Well I'll be! You sure are a long ways from home. You travelin' all by yerself or is yer gentleman out in the car?"

Effie shook her head and said, "All by myself, ma'am."

The old woman leaned over and looked out the window at Effie's car then grabbed a form from a stack on the counter. She placed it on a small clipboard with a pen chained to it and pushed it across the counter toward Effie. "I'm jus' gonna need ya to fill out this here form and it'll be $32.50 for the night."

After filling out the form, Effie dug into her purse and laid exactly $32.50 on the counter then waited for the old woman to get a key from the rack on the back wall. She grabbed one key then turned around and looked at Effie, one eyebrow raised in a questioning slant. Instead of giving Effie the key in her hand, the old woman put it back on the wall and grabbed another. With a cheerful expression on her face, she handed it to Effie.

"Yer gonna be in room 12," the old woman said, smiling.

Effie smiled back. "Thank you, ma'am."

As Effie turned to leave, the old woman interrupted her. "If yer lookin' for a good meal, I kin suggest a place…If ya want, that is."

"Please," said Effie. "I would like that."

The old lady leaned across the counter and pointed down the road. Effie looked in the direction she was pointing. "If ya go down the road a ways, you'll come right into town. Right downtown, you'lll see the Posty's Office and a few other buildin's and the grain elevator down on the right. On the left, yer gonna see a couple a blocks with a whole row of buildin's all connected with parkin' out front. Part way down that first block is the Coon Pit Bar. Now it don't sound like much and it sure as shootin' don't look like much—inside or out—but I'll tell ya what—Ya go in there and order yerself the chicken dinner. They got the best damn chicken dinner in there that money kin buy. If they ask, ya jus' tell 'em Ruthie sent ya down from the motel."

"Thanks," said Effie, turning the room key over in her hand. "I'll be sure to order the chicken dinner."

She scooted out the door, moved her car to the space outside room 12 and climbed up the step to the walkway in front of the rooms, overnight bag in hand. By every other door, a light was attached to the wall. A few of the rooms had lawn chairs and flowerpots or boxes out front. One even had an old charcoal grill near the door. It looked almost as if people lived there. A sudden feeling of pity came over her. While staying at places like the Sleepy-Z Motel for the night was OK, Effie wouldn't want to live there. She couldn't help but think about how horrible it must be to have to live in a place like that.

Effie walked up to room 12 and slid the key into the lock. She jiggled it around a few times before she heard the lock click. As the door swung open, she stepped into the darkened room and felt the wall for a light switch. As soon as the lights flicked on, Effie flopped her bag down on the bed and looked around for a remote control for the television.

"Great," she mumbled, "someone lost the remote. That's probably why that woman put me in here." Then Effie took a second look at the television. Her heart sank. Sitting right there was an old television set with a dial to change the channels. She strode to the door and yanked it open so she could look at the sign. It advertised color T.V. but it did not say anything about cable television. Effie slammed the door then spun around to look at the television again. No cable box on top of it or anywhere near it.

No cable television! That meant staying up late enough to watch the evening news or actually trying that bar the old woman had mentioned. She was tired from a long day on the road and neither option sounded very good as far as she was concerned. Effie let out a little huff as she peeked out the window in the direction of the bar. Maybe she could catch a little Weather Channel down there—If they had a television—And cable.

Chapter 4

Effie sat alone at a table in the front corner of the Coon Pit Bar, taking in the room. A smoky, blue haze hung in the air and the weak lighting that shone through it only served to make it appear murkier. The tired carpet was as grey as a dead fish and fraying along every seam. Just as Ruthie from the *mo-tel* had said, it wasn't much to look at.

There was a television mounted on the wall behind the bar and unless Effie was mistaken, it looked like there was cable. Unfortunately, a group of men sat with beer in hand and eyes fixed on some sort of hunting program. Effie cringed. She knew there was no way she could come between the throng and their television. Not that it mattered anyway. The juke box in the opposite corner was blasting old country western tunes so loud, it would have drown out the noise from a five alarm fire.

Giving up on a weather forecast, Effie turned her attention toward the row of people seated at the bar. The majority of them were men. She supposed that they weren't unlike the type of people you would find in a bar in any town that size. They bore the deep creases of weathered faces and calloused hands. They were farmers or ranchers or whatever it was that people did in Gibs Hill, Oklahoma. Just like the people in any other small town, they worked in the dust, heat and sun all day then gathered at the local watering hole in the evening. Cool drinks and ever present familiar faces brought them together.

Effie's gaze traveled from one individual to the next until her eyes fell on a skinny woman seated alone at the far end of the bar. In her own town, Effie would have taken her for a two dollar hooker with her hiked up miniskirt and her two sizes too small leopard print tank-top. Even the pale ringlets that hung down her back did nothing to enhance her appearance.

Before she could finish her assessment of the blonde, Effie realized that the waitress was headed her way with a steaming plate of food. She stopped half-way to the table to listen in on a joke and as she erupted in a fit of laughter, she playfully swatted at the man who had been telling the joke. She seemed so happy. "Why can't I find that kind of joy in life?" Effie wondered aloud.

The waitress sat a chipped plate piled high with chicken, mashed potatoes and a warm buttermilk biscuit in front of Effie with a smile. "Here ya go, ma'am," she said. "Anything else I can get for ya before I go check on the wild bunch at the bar?"

"I think I'm fine with the chicken dinner, thank you." Effie smiled up at the waitress and hesitated momentarily before opening her mouth to speak. "You wouldn't happen to know—Never mind."

"You and everyone else here was wonderin' somethin' or other tonight. I either don't want to or can't answer most of their questions," she said, nodding toward the bar. "No matter what your question is, I'm sure it's a lot safer than theirs. Maybe I can answer it for ya.

Effie looked down at the food then back up at the waitress and chuckled lightly. "The hotel I'm staying at doesn't have cable and I really don't want to stay up for the late news tonight. I was just wondering if you've heard the forecast for tomorrow. It was so hot today," Effie said, fanning her face with her hand. "It had to be triple digits. I don't think I've ever experienced heat like that. It was like I'd been thrown on a giant grill."

The waitress allowed a wide grin to escape. "You must be stayin' down at ol' Ruthie's place," she said, nodding. "It was 107 degrees here today and we're supposed to get more of the same for the next three days. Of course, you know how them weather forecaster people are. There ain't many times they get that forecast quite right."

"I can't figure out how people live in this kind of heat," said Effie. "I don't think I could handle much of it. I had my car window down most of the day today and even the wind was hot."

The waitress winked. "With the forecasters we got around here, it could only get up to 65 degrees tomorrow and they wouldn't be able to tell ya to expect it."

A bell rang at the other end of the bar and the waitress looked over her shoulder at the window to the kitchen. More food sat waiting to be delivered to a table. She tapped Effie's table several times. "You enjoy your meal and I hope the weather ain't too hot for ya tomorrow," the waitress said as she turned and walked away.

"Thank you," Effie said, inhaling the delicious scent of the chicken in front of her. Even if it was only half as good as it smelled, it would still taste like a little piece of heaven.

Effie picked up a crisp chicken leg and sank her teeth into the tender, juicy meat. The flavor filled her mouth and seemed to consume her mind. It wasn't just food, it was an experience and compared to the fast food that had become her steady diet, it was pure ambrosia.

While she was eating, Effie slipped into a daydream. A gentle smile spread across her face as she imagined a handsome man at the bar catching her eye from across the room. He would send her a drink and, tipping his hat, he would ask if her could join her. After hours of flirting and trading stories, he would ask her back to his ranch where he lived in a huge old farmhouse, all alone. They would make passionate love all night long and in the morning, he would beg her not to go. Then they would get married and Effie would never return to her miserable life in Michigan.

A burst of laughter from a group of men at the bar, snapped Effie back to reality. They sat, some of them looking directly at her, obviously making jokes about her weight. She tried to reason with herself that it wasn't her they were laughing at but it was no use. The men were complete strangers and seemed to only see the outside package—a single fat woman eating fattening food, probably gaining more weight as she sat there. As far as they were concerned, they didn't know her and it didn't matter if they stepped on her feelings or not. She was just another outsider and by the next morning, she would be gone.

Even after years of seeing people (men in particular) act that way toward her, it still hurt Effie just as much. Why did people have to be that way? She tried to look at everyone as *a person with feelings*. She never said mean things out loud even if she didn't like the way a person looked or acted. Why couldn't other people be that way toward her? Why couldn't they see that she was more than just fat?

She looked down at the piece of chicken in her hand and the half eaten biscuit on her plate. It suddenly didn't taste as good as it once had. Effie put the chicken down and pushed the plate away from her. She scolded herself for enjoying the chicken so much *and* for even entertaining the thought of falling in love. *Men don't fall in love with fat girls, stupid. You'll be single forever.* The thought echoed in her head.

Effie retrieved a little blue journal from the bag in the seat beside her and wrote in the date. At least she could enjoy the rest of her iced tea while she jotted the high points of the day. Anyway, who knew? Maybe one day she would get inspired and use the notes to write an article or a book.

Before she began writing, she closed her eyes for a moment then opened them and scanned the room to see if anyone was looking. No one was. The men who had been laughing at her had turned their attention elsewhere.

The blonde at the far end of the bar had a fresh drink in front of her and she had been joined by three men. One was seated on either side of her and another was standing close behind. They looked like a natural fixture in the bar but for some reason, Effie couldn't seem to take her eyes off them.

None of the men around the blonde were very handsome. The man in the back had a scruffy goatee and shaggy brown hair that was topped with a dirty grey cowboy hat. He wore dirty jeans that looked so worn that they might fall apart at any moment. At the corner of his back pocket closest to her, Effie could see a large hole that showed off the greying underwear he had on underneath. The plaid shirt he had on looked more scraggly than the carpet on which he was standing. Even from a distance, hanging strings were visible and the cuffs looked as though they had been worn right off the shirt.

The man kept whispering something into the blonde's ear. She looked as though she was objecting to what he had to say. Her head hung low over her drink and she kept shaking it.

The man on the blonde's right was about the same height as the man with the goatee. He had the same rounded nose and facial features as the other man except that his face translated the extra weight he carried into a fleshy wattle under his chin and his hair curled up around the edge of his green and white cap. Effie decided that the two men looked enough alike through the face that they had to be related. He was quite a bit rounder than the man with the goatee and probably weighed as much as the man and the blonde combined. Though his clothes did not look as worn as the other man's, they looked just as grimy.

The man with the goatee must have felt Effie watching them because he suddenly turned his head and looked directly at her. His eyes were so dark, they were nearly black. It was almost painful for Effie to rip her gaze from his and pretend to look for a clock. After she spotted it, she pretended to compare the time on it to the time on her watch. She dropped her eyes to the paper in front of her, flipping through the pages, attempting to make it look like she was searching for something. When she glanced back at the group, the man was still looking at her. Only half-hoping that he would turn his attention away from her, Effie flipped back to the page with the day's date on it and began writing.

It worked. When she looked up again, Effie saw that the man had turned his attention back to the blonde. As she studied the third man, she made an effort to make it less obvious that she was watching.

The third man was silently standing on the blonde's left. He was thinner than the man with the goatee. His jeans and t-shirt looked both cleaner and newer than either of the other men's clothing. His sandy brown hair was trimmed and he wore no hat. He was clean shaven except for a neatly trimmed moustache. This man was the only one of the three to wear glasses and even from a distance, they looked out-dated.

Effie turned her attention back to the blonde. She smiled at herself and noted how ugly the blonde looked sitting there. Her nose was long with huge nostrils and her face was pitted—probably from acne when she was young. When she opened her mouth, her teeth were crowded and crooked. She had on gobs of make-up and Effie couldn't help but think that it didn't matter how much the woman wore, she would never be attractive.

Pretty or not, it seemed that being skinny was enough to get three men to cozy right up to the blonde. Effie had seen plenty of rubenesque women whom she believed were very beautiful. They had beautiful faces and wonderful personalities but being plump seemed to make them ugly to the average male. She could not understand how the ugly blonde became beautiful just by being skinny and the beautiful women became ugly just by being larger.

She looked down at the date written in the journal in front of her and tapped her pen on the page a few times then continued writing about her day. She could not keep her mind on the journal entry though. Effie's eyes kept flipping back to the little group at the far end of the bar. When she looked closer, the skinny blonde looked angrier and the only one of the three men talking with her was the still one standing behind her.

"Will there be anything else?"

"What?" Effie asked with a start, her attention snapping to the waitress in front of her. She hadn't even seen her walk up. The waitress looked at her like she was nuts. "Oh. There won't be anything else, thank you."

The waitress gave a little grunt then laid a bill on the table and said, "I'll be back to pick this up."

As the waitress walked away, Effie looked back down the bar to watch the group for a little while longer. She sucked her breath in. They were gone! She quickly scanned the rest of the bar just in time to see the group walk out the back door. A prickly feeling ran up the back of her neck. She was not sure but it looked like the two guys who were seated on either side of the blonde were holding her arms and she was struggling. The guy walking behind the group had one hand between the two almost like he was holding something into her back.

Effie looked around the room to see if anyone else had witnessed the group or appeared to think their behavior was odd. No one was even paying attention. A few men were loudly talking about trucks and the rest appeared to either be watching television or were absorbed in their own little worlds. Effie was curious about what she had seen and quickly decided that she was going to slip out the back door to see if the group was still out there.

She grabbed her book and journal and jammed them into her little shoulder bag, then looked down at the bill. $5.97 was written in red at the bottom with a circle around it. Effie frantically fished through her wallet and pulled out a $20 bill. She walked toward the backdoor and stopped in the middle of the bar near the cash register. She held up her hand with the bill and the money, waving it at the waitress then laid it down on the bar and continued toward the back.

"You forgot your change, ma'am," shouted the waitress when she saw the $20 bill.

"Keep it," replied Effie as she reached the back door. She twisted the handle and pushed hard against the door but it would not move. She turned the handle the other way and pushed a little harder but the door still would not budge. Her mind was racing and she was sure that the group would be gone before she could get out there. She turned and quickly walked toward the front.

"Nothin' out there but some old pallets and a trash dumpster," said the waitress as Effie walked by.

"Oh. Thanks," said Effie. Not wanting to draw more attention to herself, she added, "I forgot which door I came in. I'm just looking forward to getting back to my motel for the night."

Chapter 5

Effie stood out front the Coon Pit Bar, staring down the street. If something really was going on with the blonde and the three men, this could be the opportunity she'd been waiting for. This could be her big story.

She raced down the block and headed around the building, toward the back. As she reached the corner of the alley, she stopped. Chances were, they would be long gone by then. But if they were still down there, she did not want them to see her. She sucked in a deep breath, closed her eyes and pressed her body to the building. Very slowly, she leaned to the side just enough to peer around the corner.

It took a moment for Effie to search the darkness. Unfortunately, the dumpster the waitress had mentioned was blocking a large area from view. What she could see, though, was a single light over a door that had to belong to the bar. Jammed under the handle was a pallet and right next to that was a small group of people.

"Damn that dumpster," whispered Effie, leaning back from the corner. It sat a few feet away from the building, affording her only a partial view.

Suddenly she heard breaking glass and a quick pop. She poked her head around the corner again only to be greeted by darkness. They had broken the light! Something had to be going on—Something terrible. Why else would they break the light? If she wanted to know what was going on down there, she was going to have to get closer.

Effie stepped back from the corner and tried to calm her nerves. She couldn't just go tromping down there, she had to do it right. She swung her bag onto her shoulder and adjusted it so it would stay in place comfortably then looked around the corner again. All she had to do was make it down to the dumpster. As long as she was quiet, she could probably hide behind it and they would never know that she was there. From that point, she would be able to listen in on their conversation.

Craning her neck, Effie took one last look up and down the street to make sure that no one was coming. If she was going down there, it was the perfect time. She closed her eyes for a moment then slipped into the shadows.

Tip-toeing down the alley in silence was easier said than done. The building was old and deteriorating. Pieces of brick had broken off and lay like giant crumbs on the ground. Like a cat stalking its prey, she had to keep one eye on the ground and the other on the small group. There was no telling what they were up to or what they would do if they saw her sneaking up on them.

Finally, she reached the dumpster and when she did, she sucked in the stench through her nose. Effie wasn't sure if she'd held her breath all the way from the corner or not. She had made it that far though, and at least the hard part was done. All she had to do now was crouch down and maintain her silence.

"You screwed Hank, didn't you, Angie," a rough voice barked.

"I already tol' you I didn't Jimmy," the woman said.

"You're a liar and a whore, Angie," the guy said. "I heard it all over town. The guys ain't gonna lie to me. They ain't got no reason to. They told me you been runnin' out and doin' Hank every time I leave on a run."

"It ain't true. I ain't doin' no one behin' your back, Jimmy."

"Shut up you whore!"

Effie peeked around the corner of the dumpster in time to see the guy with the goatee slap the blonde across the face. The two guys who had been beside her were holding her arms so she was forced to face the man who had to be Jimmy.

"I know all you can think about is gettin' a man between your legs."

"That ain't true!"

"If you say another word, I'm gonna smack you up again, whore." She opened her mouth to speak again and he raised his hand to slap her. She quickly closed her mouth. "That's more like it," he said. "Now I been in your place, Angie. I been through your dresser. I know you have a whole drawer full of sexy underwear thingies and I ain't never once seen you wear one of those thong thingies for me. It just makes me think you're that much more of a whore."

"No!"

Effie cringed as soon as she saw Angie open her mouth to say it. Before the word was even all of the way out of her mouth, Jimmy smacked her so hard, she head snapped back.

Effie thought about going to find the police. She couldn't sit there and watch a woman get beaten by three men. But before she could stand up to sneak off, she was stopped dead in her tracks.

"Come on, Jimmy," said the guy with glasses as he let go of Angie's arm. The big guy immediately snatched it and pulled both arms behind her.

"What's wrong, Destry? You gettin' yellow on me?" asked Jimmy.

Destry shrugged. "I thought you said we were just going to scare her a little. You didn't say nothing about smacking her around. It ain't right."

Jimmy stepped toward Destry and poked his finger into his chest. "And it ain't right for her to go sleeping around behind my back, is it?" He glared at his friend. "Let me just remind you that you wouldn't be standing here today if it wasn't for me so you damn well better show me a little respect and do as I say."

"Come on Jimmy."

"Ya know what, ya little sissy?" barked Jimmy. "You don't gotta watch. Just go over by the dumpster and watch down the alley for all I care!"

"Fine," said Destry as he stomped off toward the dumpster.

Effie's breath caught in her throat. She looked over her shoulder in a panic, trying to figure whether or not she could make it to the street before any of the men could get to her. She knew she couldn't and with each step Destry took toward the dumpster, her heart beat harder. She was trapped.

"Freaking idiot," Destry muttered, stopping on the other side of the dumpster.

"You stupid whore," Jimmy growled, smacking Angie again. Tears were running down her cheeks as she pulled her arms, desperately trying to get away.

"Yeah. You cry about it ya whore. I know you been out screwin' Hank every time I leave town and when you can't get him to do you, you run around dressed all slutty, tryin' to find some other guy who'll do ya."

The big guy laughed at Jimmy's comment. Jimmy glanced at him and let a wide smile dance across his face. "I got an idea Angie. Seein' as you like to spread your legs when I'm not around, I think you should put on a little show for me and my brother." He paused for a moment and looked around behind him.

"You see, Harry here ain't been gettin' any and instead of goin' home and watchin' a porno or readin' a magazine, I think he would like to watch you spread yer legs just like you do for Hank when I'm gone."

"Please, Jimmy—No!"

"I told ya to shut up, whore! Yer going to put a little show on for us right now or yer gonna be sorry for it." His face was inches from Angie's. Jimmy sucked in a deep breath then bent down and licked her neck. He stepped back and laughed a little. "You even taste like a dirty little whore."

Jimmy pulled a knife out of a pouch on his belt and sliced down the front of Angie's shirt. He pulled the two pieces of fabric wide, exposing Angie's lacy, black bra.

"Stop, Jimmy, please," she cried. "Please don't do this to me. I ain't done nothin' wrong." Angie made another attempt to jerk her arms free but Harry was more than twice her size and only laughed at her efforts. "We can go home and make love like we always do!"

Jimmy's face contorted in anger. He nearly growled as he said, "That wasn't makin' love you whore! That was just you usin' me to fill that hole between your legs!" He raised his arm high and swung the back of his hand across her mouth, splitting her lip. A trickle of blood ran down her chin and dripped onto her right breast. She whimpered.

He slipped a finger under the front of her bra and pulled it away from her body. With one quick flick, he sliced through the thin piece of fabric and peeled both cups away, leaving her breasts to hang free.

"Oh Angie," he whispered. "Mmm baby. You might be a whore now but those are the tits I fell in love with." He viciously pinched her right nipple and laughed as he dropped his head down to take it into his mouth. He bit down on it, tearing through the flesh and causing it to bleed. She winced and let out a strangled cry of pain.

"Jimmy, please…" He smacked her across the face. "I promise I'll never do anyone else again." He smacked her again. "Please, Jimmy. Please. I love you." Another smack.

"Shut up!" thought Effie.

"If I have to tell you to shut up again, whore, I swear you won't know what hit you!"

Jimmy grabbed Angie's skirt and hacked at it until it fell to the ground. His eyes got big. "Well, well, well," he said, laughing. "Looky what we have here! The whore ain't wearing no underwear at all. She really was looking to get a man between her legs tonight. I'll bet you wasn't even expectin' me back in town."

He spoke directly to his brother. "She looks good enough to eat, don't she Harry?"

"She sure does, Jimmy," he replied. "It ain't no wonder why Hank's been screwin' her. Heck, I'd probably do her too if I had the chance."

"I'll tell you what, Harry," smirked Jimmy. "Since yer my only brother in this here world, I'll let you have a little taste of her."

"Really, Jimmy?"

"Sure thing, bro. Ain't brothers supposed to share?" Angie looked mortified. She opened her mouth like she was going to scream. As Jimmy stepped forward and roughly grabbed Angie's throat with one hand, Harry laughed. "Don't you dare scream you dirty whore or I'll cut out your tongue and make it so you can't scream! Yer getting far better than you deserve."

Jimmy kept his hand on Angie's throat. He nodded his head slightly and said, "Take her shirt and her bra the rest of the way off and give me her bra. I'll tie it around her mouth and use it as a gag so she can't scream." Harry did exactly as he was told and handed Jimmy Angie's bra. Angie started to say something but when she did, Jimmy tightened his grip around her throat. He quickly forced the back part of her bra into her mouth then wrapped it around her head and tied it tightly in the back.

Effie's hand went to her own throat. Never in her wildest dreams had she imagined that she would witness something like this. It was sick and she wanted nothing more than to run off and find the police so she could make it end. It was too risky. There was no telling what they would do if they got their hands on her. She was going to have to stay there until she was sure that she could make a break for it undetected. She leaned back a little bit incase Destry decided to walk around the end of the dumpster and as she did so, she realized that her right foot was starting to tingle like it was falling asleep.

As quietly as she could, Effie crept to the other end of the dumpster. When she looked around the corner, her mouth dropped open. They had forced Angie to the ground and Jimmy had her shoulders pinned to the ground while Harry kneeled in front of her.

"She sure looks tasty," he said as he unbuckled his jeans and leaned onto her, forcing her legs apart.

Angie wriggled around, trying to pull her hips away from Harry. Effie could hear her trying to scream through the gag and she wanted to run to her side to help but fear froze her in place. Jimmy leaned over and laughed in Angie's face, knowing full well that she was wasting her energy.

As Harry laid the full weight of his body on top of Angie, he forced himself into her. Jimmy let go of her arms and stood over them with a wicked grin on his face. His eyes glinted with glee.

Effie squeezed her eyes shut but the scene played on in her head. She tried to think of a way to get out of the alley. Her mind was blank, though, except for the image of Harry raping Angie. What a fool she'd been to sneak down the alley in the first place.

Harry worked his body into a terrible rhythm, breathing hard and loud. "Oh Angie," he moaned. "You whore! You feel so damn good!" His breaths came shorter and faster until his hips froze in place. He made a few little, sharp thrusts, "Mmmmm."

He laid on top of Angie for a moment. When he caught his breath he rolled off her, stood up and pulled up his pants. "Dang, Jimmy!" he said. "That was a fine piece of woman!"

Angie didn't make an attempt to move. She just laid there, limp, blood smeared on her face, tears streaming down her cheeks. She reminded Effie of a flimsy, old rag the way she laid there.

Jimmy crouched down beside Angie as he pulled out his knife and lightly ran the tip over he belly. "What're you crying for ya whore?" he asked. "You didn't get nothing tonight that you didn't deserve."

Angie rolled her head away from him.

"What? Yer Mad? Didn't you get enough dick tonight yet?" He paused. "Must be Hank give you more than Harry could. I'll tell you what, kitten," he growled. "I'll fix that for ya!

Jimmy lifted his hand then drove the knife into the crest between Angie's legs. Her entire body jerked in pain and she let loose a scream even Effie could hear loud and clear.

"Oh God!" cried Destry as he realized what Jimmy had just done and what he was about to do. "Don't!"

But it was too late. Jimmy never even hesitated. He jerked the knife up then slashed across Angie's throat again and again, blood splashing onto his face and hands. Only a gurgling sound came from her throat. She fought as best she could but within seconds, she lat motionless. Dead.

Effie had to get out of there! Jimmy had murdered Angie! And Effie had seen it. She had seen all of it! She had to try to run around to her car. She pushed up from the ground and tried to stand but as she did, she fell backward and banged against the dumpster. Her foot was asleep and felt like a little stump on the bottom of her leg.

The noise drew Jimmy's attention toward Effie. "Get 'em," he shouted when he realized that they weren't alone. He leapt to his feet and shot toward Effie like a bullet out of a gun. Effie had never been able to run fast but she scrambled to her feet as quick as she could and began making for the end of the alley.

Harry stood watching everything with a look of amazement on his face. Destry, however, did not. He realized what Jimmy had seen and began sprinting down the alley, too. In the blink of an eye, he was past Jimmy. Effie looked over her shoulder and everything seemed to go into slow motion. She hadn't made it to the corner when Destry leapt forward. He grabbed hold of her, dragging her down with him. As she went down, she covered her face with her arms. The ground ripped at her skin and there was a deep, stabbing pain in her side. It was suddenly like time had caught up with Effie and hit her with full force. Destry's arms were wrapped tight around her legs but even if they hadn't been, she would not have tried to get up and run. When she drew in a deep breath, it was like a thousand tiny knives jabbing into her chest.

Destry rolled her over. She could not fight. There was another sharp pain as a piece of broken brick tore into her back. She tried to ignore it and concentrate on breathing. The more air she drew in, the less it hurt to breathe.

She looked up at Jimmy towering over her then at Destry as he climbed up her body and lay on top of her, pinning her to the ground. For a moment, no one said anything. They just looked at one another. It was Effie who broke the silence. She had to try to get someone's attention, somewhere. She opened her mouth and let out the loudest scream she could.

Immediately, Destry's giant hand clamped over her mouth. Effie bit in with all of her might and the flavor of blood spilled over her tongue. The hand was snapped away. Destry yelled something at her but her ears were ringing and she could not make sense of what he was saying. Another sharp pain shot through her side. It was Jimmy, or rather, his foot. He was kicking her over and over. His foot connected with the side of her head and suddenly, everything went black.

Chapter 6

When Effie came to, her head was pounding as hard as a midnight freight train. But even that was minor compared to her arm and her back. As much as she wanted to, she didn't dare move so she could assess any of her injuries for fear that she would draw attention to herself. All three of the men were standing in a close circle next to her.

"What we gonna do, Jimmy? She seen us. She knows what we did!" cried Harry

"I knew this was all a bad idea tonight," said Destry.

"Would you two sissies just shut up?" snarled Jimmy. "Ain't nothing for neither of you to worry about. I'm gonna fix everything just like I always do."

"You do realize that you murdered Angie and now we've assaulted this woman?" said Destry. "This isn't some harmless prank that you can smooth over. This is serious."

"Well I suppose we can't have no witnesses then, can we?"

No witnesses? That was all Effie needed to hear. Jimmy intended to kill her. There was no sense in laying there, waiting for him to end her life too.

Effie tried to slowly roll onto her side and as she did, the broken brick she was laying on tore into her back a little more. It felt as though it was ripping her open. She tried to ignore the pain but it was too much and a low gasp escaped her lips.

Jimmy was on his knees in a split second, his hand on her throat and his face inches from hers. The stench of stale beer hung in the air as Effie stared into his eyes wondering if she was looking at the last person who would ever see her alive. Jimmy whispered, "I seen you watchin' us inside the bar. I shoulda known you'd be trouble then."

His eyes narrowed as they raked over her face. "I don't recognize you so you must not be from around these parts." He paused, his eyes locked on hers. "I'm gonna ask you some questions and that means I need some answers ya fat cow. I'm gonna let up on my grip on your throat. When I do that, I'm gonna ask you some stuff and yer going to answer me perfectly. If you don't, I will kill you. If you try to scream, I will kill you. Fact is, I don't know you from Adam and I know you seen more than you shoulda. If you don't do exactly as I say, you're gonna end up exactly like that other whore over there. Are we clear?"

Effie blinked and nodded her head the best she could with his hand around her throat, her eyes wide with terror. She knew she was in serious trouble and it wasn't the time to panic. These guys meant business. She knew she did not want to end up like Angie.

Jimmy clenched his jaw. "OK then. I'm gonna let go now and we're gonna get some answers jus' like I said, right?"

Effie nodded again. Jimmy let up his grip and let his hand trace a line down between her breasts. She shuddered.

"How much did you see," asked Jimmy in a low, even voice.

Effie thought for a minute, unsure of how to answer. When she could think of nothing else, she decided on the truth. "Everything," she whispered. "I saw the group of you inside the bar. I saw you go out the back door and I snuck around the front of the building."

"So you was down there the entire time?"

She shook her head but did not utter a word.

"We can't very well just let you go then, can we?" Effie froze in place and held her breath. "That only leaves two options in my book."

Effie closed her eyes then opened them again to look into his face. She knew he was going to kill her. What would they do with her body? Would they dump it in the woods? How long until anyone she knew came looking for her? Would anyone come looking for her? A big tear rolled out of the corner of her eye.

"I can either kill ya right here or we can take ya with us until I decide on something else to do with you." Jimmy let loose a low chuckle. "Now I didn't plan on killin' Angie tonight and fact is, I just wasn't my style." He paused and just stared at her face. "You got a car around here?" Effie nodded her head.

Harry was getting antsy. "What are we gonna do, Jimmy?"

"Shut up 'til I tell you to say something, Harry." He shot Harry an unhappy glance then returned his attention to Effie. "Where are your keys, doll?"

Her lip started to tremble. "They're in my b—They're in my bag."

"Where is it?"

"I don't know. I—I think I dropped it. It might be over by the dump—over by the dumpster."

Jimmy nodded toward the dumpster. "Go have a look, Harry." Harry made his way toward the dumpster and found the bag right away.

"I found it, Jimmy," he shouted then waddled back toward them, digging around in the bag until her pulled out a set of keys. "Keys are in here jus' like she said." His eyes danced with delight as he held up a set of keys on a ring with a blue crescent moon attached. He dropped the keys on the ground next to Jimmy and backed away.

"Ok," Jimmy said as he looked the keys. "Now, we can't very well let you go because you'll go runnin' to the police and we can't have that. We also need to do something with that whore, Angie." He traced around Effie's throat with the tip of his finger then looked down at the top of her breasts. His mouth spread into an awful smile with stained, crooked teeth and stale beer breath. "Lucky for you, I like red hair and I like a big soft woman with nice big tits."

Effie shuddered at the thought of what he was going to do to her.

"Yer gonna tell me where your car is and Harry is gonna go pull it around. We're gonna put that whore in the trunk because we can't leave her body or someone will find it before long. If that happens, them coppers will most likely come sniffin' around cause everyone knows me and her was together. They might send me to jail again and I sure don't wanna go back there. Everything is gonna be nice and smooth and you ain't gonna try anything stupid. Are we clear?"

Effie nodded.

"Now talk to me about your car, doll."

Effie struggled to suck in a deep breath. "It's silver Saturn and it has Michigan plates on it."

"Where is it parked?"

"Around front. It's near the door to the tavern—"

"Tavern," he laughed. "What ya tryin' to do? Make it sound all fancy or something? Around these parts, it's a bar, plain and simple."

"Fine. Whatever you prefer to call it. It's near the door to the bar—Same side of the street."

"Now don't get smart with me, doll. I'm not someone you want to piss off."

She just stared into his eyes. Jimmy traced her lips with his finger and laughed when Effie clenched her teeth in reaction.

"You got a lot of fire in you, girl. I like that in a woman. I think I'm gonna keep you around for a while." He laughed in her face. "It's gonna be fun playin' with you."

Jimmy picked up the keys and tossed them to Harry. "Ok. You heard what kind of car she has and where ya can find it. Go around and get it. Bring it back here and you and Destry can load the whore into the trunk. I'll hold the fat chick here until you two are all set. And think for once, Harry. Don't go jumpin' in her car if someone who knows it ain't yours is out there."

He turned his attention back to Effie. He slid a hand into her shirt, roughly handling her breast. "You scared, baby doll?"

Effie did not move.

"Well don't worry, honey. You're bein' a real good girl. You just keep bein' good and we'll get on just fine." Jimmy's fingers found a nipple and he roughly pinched it. He laughed again.

"You got a plan for after that, Jimmy?" asked Destry

"Yep."

Destry looked at Jimmy with a puzzled look on his face but didn't say anything.

"You and me are gonna get in baby doll's car and Harry is gonna get in our truck. We're gonna drive up to the cabin. We'll haul Angie's body out into the woods and bury her. No one'll bother us there and it's far enough away from anything, the fat chick here could holler all day long and no one would ever hear her." Jimmy paused for a moment. "Ain't no one would come lookin' for her out there."

"You sure that's what we should do?"

"Don't question me, Destry. I always take care of things, don't I? You jus' do what I say and you ain't got nothin' to worry about."

Jimmy climbed on top of Effie, straddling her hips. She struggled against his weight but he was too heavy for her to move and the more she fought, the more the brick dug in. She was completely at their mercy and decided to temporarily give up her fight. An opportunity would present itself and when it did, she would be ready to run.

Jimmy leaned forward, pinning Effie's arms to the ground. His eyes sparkled with delight as he pressed his hips into hers.

"Please," whispered Effie.

"Please what, baby doll? Please do it more? Please press harder?"

Tears ran out of the corners of her eyes and dripped onto the pavement. "Please, don't."

Jimmy let loose a snickering laugh at her request then lowered his head so it was just above hers. She could feel his warm breath on her lips and it made her stomach churn.

"I think you would like it if I was inside ya, baby doll. I'll bet you ain't never had a man half as good as me. Probably a fat chick like you ain't never had any good sex at all. You probably jus' had guys with little peckers and no talent." Effie closed her eyes and tried to hide her face on her shoulder. "Don't worry, baby doll. I think yer kinda pretty for a big fat girl. Yer a lucky one too. If I decide to do ya, I know it'll be the first time a chick like you would be screwin' someone as good as me. I know ya'd never have a chance to screw someone as great as me otherwise." He stuck out his tongue, lapping at her lips.

"No," she whispered.

Jimmy covered Effie's mouth with his own before she could utter another word. She tried to move her head away—to free her lips from his. No matter what she did, he was able to keep his lips on hers. In the end, she just closed her eyes and silently wished she had never snuck into the alley.

As Jimmy pulled back from the kiss, he let a low laugh escape.

"You know baby doll—Dammit!" A pair of bright headlights suddenly shown into the alley. For a moment Effie allowed herself to feel relief, thinking the headlights might be the police or someone else who might help her. When she felt Jimmy relax a little, her relief was washed away by a feeling of doom. As the car drove past, she saw that it was her own. Harry had done exactly as he was told.

Chapter 7

"We got Angie in the trunk," Harry said as he and Destry walked over to stand beside Jimmy. "What next?"

Jimmy stared at Effie with a wicked grin. "We're goin' to the cabin, Harry," he said. "Yer gonna go 'round and get the truck and drive it there. Destry is gonna drive the fat chick's car and me and her are gonna ride in the back seat together so she don't try no funny business."

"You have a motel room around here?" Destry asked Effie. She just stared back at him.

"What the heck do ya care about that for?" questioned Jimmy. "It ain't like we got time to go there. We gotta get on the road."

"I know, Jimmy. I was just thinking—"

"Well that's your problem. Don't think no more unless I tell you to.

"——I was just thinking," continued Destry, ignoring Jimmy, "if she has a motel room, she probably has stuff in there."

"So."

"So if she has stuff sitting in there and she doesn't check out when she is supposed to, they're gonna go in there and find her stuff—"

"You think she has some valuable stuff in there?"

"——No. I think they'll think something's up when they find a bunch of her stuff and no sign of her and they'll call the cops."

Jimmy thought for a moment then said, "Yer onto somethin' here. You got a motel, baby doll?"

Effie did not make a sound or move a muscle. She just stared into Jimmy's eyes. He slapped her across her right cheek. She flinched as he did so then continued to stare at him in cold silence.

"Jimmy..." Harry began. Jimmy held up his hand to quiet him.

"Listen here, woman," he growled. "If you think I was lyin' about killin' you for not answerin' me straight, yer wrong—dead wrong. Now either you tell me if you got a motel room or yer gonna end up in the trunk of yer car like that little whore.—And bein' as yer so damn fat, it'd be hard to just shove ya in there with her so we'd have to cut ya up in little pieces first."

The look in Jimmy's eyes told Effie that he was serious.

"Yes," she whispered.

"The one right here in town or is it up the road a bit?"

Effie closed her eyes and sucked in a deep breath. A sharp pain shot through her chest. She knew she had to be calm. As long as she was calm and did as she was told, she had a chance at making it out of this alive.

"The motel just down the way," she said. "I'm in room 12 but I didn't take anything into the room yet," she lied. "The key is in the left, front pocket of my jeans. You can check the room if you want."

"Don't go tellin' me what I can and can't do!" He reached into her pocket, pulled out the key and held it out for Destry to take.

"It's possible that she's telling the truth, Jimmy," said Destry as he grabbed the key and spun it around his finger.

"And why do you think that?"

"She had a lot of bags and stuff in her trunk." Destry thought for a minute then added, "I'm sure you're thinkin' that we should go check her room anyway though. I completely agree with you, Jimmy."

Jimmy smiled. "You know I wouldn't overlook checkin' her room no matter what. I'm just glad yer smart enough to agree with me." He looked down at Effie, winked and ground his pelvis into hers. "Just a preview baby," he whispered. Her face twisted in pain. The added pressure forced the brick to tear into her back a little more.

Jimmy sent Harry around to get the truck and told him to meet them at the motel then barked a command at Destry. "Hold the fat chick while I get up."

Destry bent and grabbed Effie's hands while Jimmy got to his feet. Effie made no attempt to struggle free. The pain was too much. Even the tiniest movement felt as though her back was being shredded by the brick.

"Get up," Jimmy spat at Effie.

Effie tried to move but immediately closed her eyes and ground her teeth together, preventing a cry of pain from escaping her lips. She sucked in a deep breath.

"I can't," she said. "My back—pain."

A stern look settled on Jimmy's brow. "We don't have the time for this," he said, reaching out and roughly grabbing one of her hands from Destry. "Help me get her up and into the car."

The two men pulled her up together. As Effie rose toward a standing position, Destry placed his hand on her back to help support her. He jerked his hand back and looked at it as soon as she was firmly on her feet. He looked from his hand to Effie. Destry's hand was covered with blood and the back of Effie's shirt was soaked a deep crimson color.

"Oh my God, Jimmy," sputtered Destry, holding up his hand. "She's hurt pretty bad. We need to do something."

"We'll take care of it when we get to the cabin," said Jimmy.

Destry shook his head. "I think we need to do something before that."

"Stop thinkin' then, Destry! I said we'd take care of it when we get to the cabin. Now I don't want to hear nothin' about it again." He jerked Effie around and shoved her into the backseat of the car then climbed in behind her. Destry was still standing there looking at his hand.

"Get in the car and drive to the motel, Destry. The longer ya stand there lookin' at yer hand like a fool, the bigger yer chances of gettin' us caught. I don't want to have to tell ya again. Get in the car and drive."

Destry looked from his hand to Effie one more time before wiping it on the back of his jeans. He wetted his lips and swallowed a lump in his throat. Jimmy glared at him. Before he could say another thing, Destry slid behind the wheel and started the car. As he flipped on the headlights, the dashboard lit up. He looked at the gages, his eyes falling on the fuel.

"Umm, Jimmy." His voice was barely a whisper.

"What is it, Destry?"

"We're gonna need gas soon. It's pretty low. There's no way we'll make it even a fraction of the way to the cabin from here on it."

"Well in case ya didn't notice, we only got one fillin' station in town. Don will be workin' tonight and even if he is slow as a retard, he knows this ain't our car. There ain't no way we're goin' there. There's probably enough gas in here to make it down the road a ways to a station where we ain't so likely to be known so well. I ain't about to risk gettin' caught on account of us gettin' gas right here. The sooner we get to the motel, the sooner we can get down the road and get us some gas. Now get!"

46

As Destry shifted the car into drive and began to make his way from the alley to the motel, Effie closed her eyes and silently tried to fight back more tears. There was a growing lump in her throat that made it harder and harder to swallow back the tears. In the back of her mind, she knew Jimmy would never let her go alive. She knew too much. It wasn't a question of *if* Effie was going to die, it was a question of *when* she was going to die.

Chapter 8

Destry pulled Effie's car past Harry and into an empty parking space outside room 12 of the Sleepy-Z Motel. Jimmy reached out and tapped Destry's shoulder.

"Get in there and have a look, boy."

Destry just turned around and looked from Jimmy to Effie. "You sure this is the way we should do this, Jimmy? I mean I don't wanna get in trouble or nothing—"

"Don't get yellow on me, Destry. This is the way we're gonna do it. There ain't no other way that'll keep us outta trouble. Now get in there before I have to send Harry in and if I have to send him in, you know he'll probably screw somethin' up."

Destry opened the door and climbed out, looking back at Effie as he started toward the room. An older gentleman was sitting outside the door a few rooms down and he curiously looked at Destry as he slid the key into the lock. The man mumbled something to him but rather than say anything back, Destry just walked into the room and closed the door behind him. He stood with his back against the door and his eyes closed for a moment then found the light switch and flipped it on.

His stomach contracted into a tight ball. Right on the foot of the bed sat an overnight bag. Effie had lied to Jimmy and Destry knew that meant more trouble for her. He grabbed the bag then walked over and looked between the bed and the far wall. Nothing. He pulled open the drawers under the television. Nothing. Except for the one overnight bag, the room was completely empty. He dropped the key on the table next to the television then walked over and pulled the door open, testing the handle to see that it was locked. Destry looked over his shoulder.

He could not let Effie sit there bleeding all of the way up to the cabin. If he wet a towel, she could at least wash the wound out a little. Destry swung the door closed and walked into the small bathroom. A washcloth and two towels hung on a rack next to the sink. Someone started pounding on the door. He quickly grabbed a towel from the rack and soaked it under the faucet. Whoever it was kept pounding on the door. He grabbed a dry towel, ran out and pulled open the door. Standing right in front of Destry was Harry.

"Jimmy sent me to see what was takin' you so darn long."

"Shut up ad' let's go." Destry pushed his way past Harry and pulled the door closed behind him.

"Don't talk to me like that."

Destry spun around and poked his finger into Harry's chest. He spoke in a whisper. "Don't start with me right now. I got things on my mind. Don't you realize what we did tonight?"

"So?"

"So we've been friends for a long time. I've pulled a lot of crap with you and Jimmy over the years."

Harry got a goofy grin on his face and laughed. "Yeah. We had a lot of fun over the years, ain't we?"

"No. I got in a lot of trouble for the stuff your brother got us into and now this."

"Jimmy'll set everything right so we don't get in no trouble." The smile faded from his face.

"Harry, we helped Jimmy kill Angie. We helped *kill* her and you raped her. No matter what he does, no matter how you put it, that's wrong and there's nothing Jimmy can do that'll make it right. Nothing."

"It's gonna be OK." Harry shook his head at Destry.

Destry rolled his eyes. "Just get in the truck and drive, Harry. Your brother says we gotta head up to the cabin and right now I can't think of anything else to do."

When Destry opened the car door and climbed in, the first thing he heard was Jimmy's angry voice. "What the heck took you so long? I almost think yer tryin' to get us caught."

"Sorry, Jimmy. I was just checkin' the room real good. I wanted to make sure nothin' was in there."

"What the heck you got there," asked Jimmy, nodding at the overnight bag and towels in Destry's hand. "Was that bag in her room?"

Destry looked into Effie's eyes. They were all puffy and red from crying. "She probably forgot that she took it in earlier."

Jimmy looked at Effie, his eyes burning with anger. The veins in his neck stood out in livid ridges. He began, almost in a whisper, "You lied to me you fat whore! You said you didn't leave no bags in yer room! Ya ain't nothin' but a big, fat whore! If we weren't someplace where people can see, I'd beat ya to death for tryin' to pull that stunt on me."

Destry hesitated for a moment then held out the towels for Effie to take. She reached out and took the towels from him. As she did so, Jimmy cranked the window down as far as it would go and he grabbed at the towels, pulling the wet one from her hands. He wiped the blood from his face and hands then tossed it out the window. Destry shot a dirty look at him. Jimmy scowled back.

"We don't need nothin' like that."

"I got them so she could clean up that gouge on her back some."

"There ain't no way I'm ridin' all the way up to the cabin next to a wet towel. She don't need that. She don't really need the other one neither." Effie tightened the grip on the other towel but Jimmy didn't even try to take it away from her.

Destry started the car and pulled out of the parking space. "I guess we better get down the road so we can fuel-up the car and get up to the cabin then, huh?" He was angry and it showed when he pulled out onto Highway 70 and pressed the gas to the floor.

Effie pulled the back of her shirt up a bit and peeled it away from the wound. She did her best to place the towel so it would press against it when she sat back against the seat. Jimmy just sat back, a lurid grin curling onto his lips. She could see in his eyes that he was mentally undressing her and she was sure that he was thinking up sick things to do to her. She turned her face away from him and gazed out the window at the dark landscape as it whizzed by.

"What's yer name?" asked Jimmy.

Effie did not answer. She just continued to stare out the window. She felt Jimmy brushing her hair off her shoulder.

"Come on, baby. It ain't gonna hurt nothin' to tell me yer name now. That is unless you want me to keep calling you fat chick or fat whore. You might as well tell me."

She turned and stared into his eyes with a piercing glare. "Effie," she said. "My name is Effie St. Martin." Destry glanced back at her.

"Effie, huh," Jimmy laughed. "Well I suppose that sure is fittin' name for a fat chick. Makes ya sound like a cow. I don't think I like it though. Ya look like you been eatin' lots of cookies so I think I'll call you Cookie after the sweet tastin' thing that ya are."

She gritted her teeth. "My name is Effie."

"Not anymore it ain't. Now yer name is Cookie. I always did like sweets."

Effie turned back toward the window and closed her eyes. Jimmy had given her a pet name and that meant that he would probably keep her alive for a while. With that little bit of comfort, and the monotonous thumping of the road, she allowed herself to be lulled into a state somewhere between sleep and wake.

Chapter 9

When Effie opened her eyes again, they were pulling into a gas station and Jimmy was pulling a wad of cash out of her bag. She wanted to jump out of the car and run. Even if she only made it to the cashier in the station, she thought she would be safe. When Effie leaned forward just a little bit, pain shot from the gouge on her back. It forced her to suck in a deep breath and tears welled up in her eyes.

"Don't try no funny business, Cookie," said Jimmy, looking at her. "We ain't very far yet. We got quite a ways 'til we get to where we're goin' in Colorado. I'd hate for some kind of accident to happen that would make ya end up dead."

Harry was already out of the truck and filling it with fuel when Destry pulled in behind him. Jimmy grabbed Effie by the chin and forced her to look into his eyes. "If you scream or do somethin' else to draw attention to us, I will slice you open from that big fat belly all the way to yer neck. Just stay quiet and act like nothin's outta the ordinary."

He rolled down the window and called Destry over. "Cookie has a lot of cash here so get some beer and smokes and some food-type stuff when ya go in to pay. Get me a couple cans of my chew too."

"What about stuff for her," questioned Destry.

"What the heck do you mean what about for her?" Jimmy reached over and grabbed her chin again, forcing her to lean forward. A loud gasp escaped her lips and her face contorted in pain. "You think this hunk of blubber needs somethin' other than what we need?" Destry glanced over his shoulder then let his gaze settle on Effie's face. Tears streamed down her cheeks as she silently cried. "You think she's better than you and me and Harry? Is that it?" A wicked sneer danced across Jimmy's face. "She might think she's better but I'll tell ya one thing right here and now! I don't know about you anymore but *I* am worth ten of her. It don't matter what time it is and it don't matter what day it is. I am worth ten of her." He pushed Effie away and as he did, she reached up to brush the tears off her face.

"I get your drift, Jimmy," said Destry then he turned to finish with the fuel.

A burst of laughter shot from Jimmy. Destry spun around and gave him a questioning look. "I changed my mind," giggled Jimmy. "Lets get something special for Cookie." Destry continued to look at him. "Get some—" Jimmy could not keep from laughing. "Get some cookies for Ms Cookie. He continued laughing at his own joke and Destry just reached in the window and took the wad of bills from Jimmy's hand.

Harry joined Destry by the car. He looked in at Jimmy who was still laughing and asked, "What's so funny?" Destry shook his head and started walking toward the building.

"Cookies for Ms Cookie—" laughed Jimmy, calming down a little. Not understanding Jimmy's joke, Harry laughed a little then turned to waddle off behind Destry.

Just then a police car pulled in at the pump across from them. Effie's heart skipped a beat and her breath caught in her throat. She tried desperately to catch the officer's eye when he got out to pump his fuel. The officer looked over at her and nodded. As he did so, Jimmy scooted over close to her and put an arm around her shoulders. He stroked her cheek then leaned toward her and kissed it.

He whispered into her ear. "Act all lovey-dovey right now or yer dead before that cop can even walk over here. And when I'm done with you, I'll kill him too."

Effie forced a smile and dropped her eyes to her lap. She knew Jimmy would not hesitate to do exactly what he said. The officer turned back to watch his pump. He finished up, paid and was on his way before Destry and Harry could return. A large tear rolled down her cheek.

"Good job, Cookie."

Harry and Destry hauled out several paper bags of food and placed them in the bed of the truck. Harry took a moment to open a 24 pack of beer then took a few cans for himself and put them in the cab of the truck. He held out the carton for Destry to take and when he did not take it right away, Harry just piled it on top of the bags still in Destry's arms. When Destry reached the car, his hands were too full to open the door so he just shoved the beer through the open window next to Jimmy.

"Watch it, ya tard," barked Jimmy.

With one hand free, Destry was able to open the car door and after doing so, he tossed the rest of the bags into the passenger seat and climbed in behind them. The evening events had worn on him and he sat just gripping the steering wheel for a moment. Jimmy reached over the seat and rooted through the bags until he came up with a bag of corn chips. He looked at it as if it was a prized trophy. He ripped open the bag and shoved a handful into his mouth before cracking open a cold can of beer. He brought the it to his lips and guzzled half the can down then let loose a loud burp.

"Now that's what I call good!"

Destry finally released the wheel and turned toward the bags next to him. As he dug through them, he kept glancing at Jimmy and Effie. He finally held up a bottle of water.

"Don't tell me you've turned into a granola-eatin', water drinkin', tree hugger on me." Jimmy laughed then took a slug of beer, a trickle of it soaking into his goatee.

"It's not for me, Jimmy," said Destry. "It's for Effie."

"You mean it's for Cookie"

"Fine. Whatever, Jimmy. It's for Cookie." He twisted the top off and handed it back to her. She tried to smile as she reached out to take it from his hand but a sharp pain shot through her back. She forced herself to grab the bottle.

"Jimmy," Destry pleaded. "Shouldn't we at least have a look at her back? She's in a lot of pain."

"Christ, Destry! If I told ya one time, I told ya a thousand times, ain't no one gonna bother with Cookie's back 'til we get up to the cabin."

"But—"

"No buts, ya sissy boy. I ain't gonna tell ya again!" Jimmy shook his head then mumbled to himself, "Jesus! If I thought he was gonna be such a girl about this, I woulda had him drive the truck and had Harry drive this P.O.S. At least Harry don't never get no stupid ideas like him and he don't ask no questions. Somebody musta hit Destry with a stupid stick while I was on my last run cause he's dumber than he ever was. Harry must have twice the brains that jerk-off Destry has." He shook his head again as if he was agreeing with himself.

Defeated, Destry gave Effie an apologetic look then turned around and started the car. He knew she was hurt bad and was in a lot of pain and it was his fault. He also knew that there was no way Jimmy would let a professional look at the wound. As he pulled out of the gas station onto the road behind Harry, Destry looked down at the bag next to him. He had purchased a little first-aid kit. He knew Jimmy would never bother checking her back and Harry did not have the brains for it so he would check out Effie or Cookie or whoever the heck she was now. He would do what he could for her while Jimmy took the time to figure out what he wanted to do with her next.

Chapter 10

Effie woke with a start. Warm breath on her ear jerked her out of sleep. When her mind cleared, she realized that they had stopped. They were pulled off on a dark stretch of road and Destry was no longer in the car. Jimmy had moved over right next to Effie and was making a drunken attempt to act romantic.

Effie stared out into the moonless night. "Where is the guy who was driving?"

"It don' matter where Deshtry ish," slurred Jimmy. "We're aaalll alone, Cookie...We finally got ush shome privashy." He ran a finger down her throat and she tried to push it away before he slipped it into her shirt. Jimmy grabbed her wrist, squeezing it as tight as he could. "I tol' you notta try nushin, ya fat cow," he growled.

Effie was determined not to let him see her cry again, no matter what he said or how much he hurt her. She just clenched her teeth together. "Where is he," she whispered. "Why have we stopped? Where are we?"

"One," said Jimmy, pointing a finger at the roof, "It don' matter where he ish. B, We're takin' a pishhh break. And four, you ain' got no reashon ta know where we are."

She turned her head away from Jimmy and tried to make out the lay of the land. It looked like they were in some big hills, maybe even low mountains. Tall pines lined the road and other than the stars, there wasn't a light as far as she could see. Before she knew what was happening, Jimmy pulled out a knife and pressed it against Effie's throat. She breathed as shallow as she could and did not dare to swallow for fear that Jimmy would slip in his drunken state and slice into her throat.

"Open yer bloushe and shhhow what yer got under there." When Effie didn't move to do as she was told, he repeated himself and added, "DO IT NOW OR I'LL SHLIT YER THROAT JUSH' LIKE THAT OTHER SHLUT!"

Effie's hands were trembling but she raised them and started fumbling with the buttons on the front of her shirt. She already knew Jimmy was capable of rape and murder. Nothing could be worse.

"That'sh my good Cookie," he said as she worked on the buttons.

When she reached the bottom, she silently folded her hands in her lap but did not pull the two sides of her shirt open. Jimmy didn't need her to do that. He tossed the knife in the back window and quickly grabbed the back of Effie's neck with his left hand. He slid his right hand over her breast and forced his lips onto hers. She was overcome by the scent and flavor of beer. It made her choke but even that did not stop Jimmy's kiss. She pressed her lips together and tried to pull away but he was much stronger than her. The harder she tried to pull away, the more she realized how powerful he was.

The dome light suddenly blazed. "Christ, Jimmy! Can't you wait 'til we get to the cabin?" Destry reached over the seat and pulled Jimmy off Effie.

"Why shhhould I wait? She'sh jush a dirty whore like every other woman. Not one of them meant for anyshing more then pleashin' a man." Jimmy sat back with a half-cocked smile on his lips, his eyelids floating halfway between open and closed.

Destry scowled. "She's hurt. If we can't take the time to look at her back, there ain't time to mess around with her either!."

"Aw hell, Deshtry! I wash jush playin' with Mish Cookie a little bit while you wash out takin' a pish break. I wash jush shamplin' the shweet treatsh." He chuckled a little then added, "Who the hell d' you think you are anyway? You shink yer a docter or shomeshin?" Destry did not answer. He just climbed in the car and started it up. "Ya shink yer shmart ash me sho ya can make the deshishions?"

"I'm not like you, Jimmy," snarled Destry as he turned around and pointed a finger in Jimmy's face. "I sure as hell ain't as stupid as you. I can tell you that much."

Jimmy leaned forward. "Sho you shink yer shmarter then me. Ish that it?"

"Damn straight, I am."

"Well if yer sho much shmarter then me," began Jimmy, "Why don' you tell me what you would do right now if you wushme?"

"If I was you, we wouldn't be in this situation to begin with."

"Well…Well you are in thish shituashion to begin wishhh, Deshtry, sho what would you do?"

"I'd start by having a look at Effie's—"

"Cookie!"

"—Fine! I'd have a look at Cookie's wounds—especially the one on her back. I'd clean it up and see what I could do to fix it up."

Jimmy let loose a loud, boysterous laugh. "That'sh whyy I'm makin' the deshishionsh. You would make a wushy deshishion like that you might ash well wear pink pantiesh yer shuch a girl."

Destry just spun around and gripped the steering wheel. "Screw you, Jimmy! You got me in trouble for the last time!" He slammed the car into drive and stomped on the gas. The car tore off the shoulder and onto the road, throwing loose gravel behind it.

"Ohhhh watch out now the wushy boy gotsh shome gutsh now," laughed Jimmy. He shook his head wildly and waved his hands in the air. The faster Destry drove, the more excited he became. He rolled down the window, stuck his head out. "Watchsh out here comesh wushy boy wifth gutsh! Wooooooo-weeeeeeee!"

Effie pressed her fingers to the seat beside her. Never in her life had she been in a vehicle traveling so fast. More than anything, at that moment, she wanted to slip the seatbelt across her body and click it into place. She dared not move, though, for fear that it would excite Jimmy even more to see her afraid.

A distant set of tail lights ahead appeared to get closer and closer. As they rocketed past an old truck by the side of the road, Effie thought she recognized it as Harry's. For a second, Jimmy looked at the back of Destry's head like he was crazy. It was like his brain was working overtime and he couldn't form words. And then he did. At first the words came out garbled. When Destry did not respond, Jimmy repeated himself.

"Hey ya idiot," he said. "Did yer momma bang ya so hard that ya can't ever sthee no more? That wasth Harry back there and now we nome pathed 'im by. Ya mutht-thbe the dumbetht-th fuckin' idioth on the road. Don't ya go pathin' by my brother like that without theein' whath a matter! Sthop thith car right now, ya thard!"

Destry suddenly slammed on the breaks and, not expecting it, Effie and

Jimmy rocked forward. Smashing against the front seat. The tires squealed as the car skidded down the road. Effie closed her eyes tight and mouthed a silent prayer. "Please God, don't let me die like this—not with these people. Don't let the us lose control." When the car finally stopped, Effie thumped back against the seat.

Destry was angry. He leapt out of the car and nearly pulled the back door off its hinges as he opened it and grabbed hold of Jimmy's shirt. He leaned in and looked Effie directly in the eye. "You stay here and don't move an inch. If ya do that, I'll see to it that yer taken care of. If ya don't, I will make every second of the rest of yer life a living Hell. I mean it! If ya try to run, I will hunt you down myself." Then he turned his attention to Jimmy. He pulled him out of the car.

"You and me are gonna have it out right here and right now. I've known you and Harry a long time and I've been through a lot of stuff with you. You've been like a brother to me. Right now, though, we are in big trouble and you gotta learn that you don't have the answer for everything. You gotta listen to me and Harry. If you can't listen like a normal person, I'll talk to you the only way you know how."

By that time, the truck they had blown past was pulling up behind them. After coming to a stop, Harry climbed out from behind the wheel. Jimmy just stood looking at Destry. The combination of the fresh air, Destry's driving and his words served to sober Jimmy up a little.

Harry lumbered up beside them. "What ya up to?" he questioned.

"Shut up, Harry," both Destry and Jimmy said at the same time. Destry continued to speak. "You just stay outta this, Harry. Me and Jimmy are just gonna have it out."

Destry and Jimmy stood nose to nose, staring into one another's eyes. Both of them had their hands curled into fists, knuckles turning white. Effie sat watching the two, unsure of what to do. They were so intent on staring one another down, they probably would not have noticed if she slipped out of the car and made a run for it into the woods.

Did she dare do that? She had no idea where she was or how far from a town they were. If she did escape, they would probably hunt her down and kill her on the spot. If she did get away and they didn't catch her, how long could she survive out there on her own? It had been a long time since her years in scouting and she had spent a lot of years as a city girl. She didn't know if she could even remember any of the survival skills she had learned along the way.

Effie decided that it was probably better to play to *her* skills. She had always been able to persuade people by talking with them. Though she did not like any of her choices, Destry seemed to be the most sympathetic of the group. If she played along with the game, maybe she could make it out alive. She knew that Jimmy intended to rape her and that Harry be in line right behind him. The thought of sex with any of them made stomach turn. Her options were slim, and in the back of her mind, she thought that forced sex with any of the three was far better than death.

She decided that she would stay and play their game. The gash on her back was bad no doubt. Effie didn't think it was bleeding much anymore, though, and it probably wasn't life threatening. She would take the time to recuperate and while she did that, she would watch. She would listen to their conversations and observe how they interacted. She would learn their strengths and weaknesses and she would formulate a plan. Then, when the time was right, she would act on it. It was the only thing she could do. It was the only way she believed she could stay alive.

A movement out of the corner of Effie's eye broke her concentration. Jimmy had pulled back his right arm and swung at Destry with all his might. That was all Destry needed as an OK to come out fighting. His eyes never left Jimmy as he swung. First his right fist then his left plowed into Jimmy's stomach, causing him to stumble backward. Jimmy's eyes got big, as if he could not believe that Destry had actually hit him. He brought his fists up in front of his chest and ran forward like an angry bull. He rammed his head into Destry's stomach, causing him to lose balance and fall backward. A puff of dust erupted around him as he hit the ground. Jimmy began kicking Destry's left side.

Destry rolled away and covered his face. When Jimmy stumbled on some loose gravel, Destry took the opportunity to lash his arm out, wrap it around Jimmy's ankles and pull him to the ground. He crawled up Jimmy's body and began pummeling his face. After a few moments, Destry rolled backward and watched Jimmy. Jimmy started getting to his feet and Destry scrambled to follow suit.

Both men were covered in dust. Destry's knuckles were bleeding. Jimmy's lip looked like it had been split open and his face looked like it had been repeatedly beaten with a frying pan. Just about that time, Harry waddled over and leaned against the back of the car, next to the open door and chuckled a little bit. His body blocked Effie's view of the fight but not the cloud of dust the men were kicking up.

"Hey," shouted Effie. Harry turned around and leaned in the door. "Aren't you going to try to break them up?"

Harry just laughed. "No way! I ain't seen these two get in a scuffle this big since we was kids. This is too much fun."

"And you call yourself a brother and a friend!"

"Shut up, Cookie. You don't know nothin' 'bout my brother and Destry." Harry scowled at her. "They'll have a little fight like this then they'll be right as rain. It'll be jus' like nothin' ever happened. That's the way my brother is." He laughed again. "Sometimes Jimmy just needs a knock in the head and Destry probably just needs a swat or two to put 'im in his place." Harry turned around and leaned against the car to watch again.

Effie leaned forward to try to see the fight as best she could. She suddenly realized that her back did not hurt as bad as it had. She didn't know if it was just that it hadn't been hurt as bad as she had initially thought or if it was her body's way of showing that it recognized that hurting wasn't going to get it any help. Either way, Effie knew that she could not let on that the pain was subsiding. Playing that she was in pain was her best possibility of gaining any sympathy among the men. If she dragged the injury out as long as she could and faked that it was worse than it actually was, it might give her extra time to come up with a plan to escape. She just had to make sure that she was careful. If they found out that she was faking, who knew what they would be capable of?

When she leaned to the side and looked around Harry, it was obvious that Jimmy and Destry were both beginning to tire. Their punches were slower and it did not look like the impacts were as hard. Finally, Destry just swung and wrapped his arm around Jimmy's back and pulled him into a brotherly hug. Jimmy swung his arm up around Destry and the two began whispering to one another.

Harry began laughing again. He turned around and looked at Effie. "See? I tol' you they was gonna be right as rain once they got the fight out of 'em and I was right."

Effie just scooted as far as she could toward the passenger side of the back seat. She would try to leave as much room as she could for Jimmy so she wouldn't have to be too close to him. She had no idea what the fight would do to the way he was acting toward her. Maybe it would be like Harry said and it would knock Destry down a few notches. Maybe he would be OK with Jimmy's advances toward her.

Harry joined the two men and patted each one of them on the back. "Good fight, boys. I knew it'd fix things between the two of you. Always does. I'm gonna go get in the truck and I'll be waitin' until yer ready to get goin' again."

As he walked back to his truck, Effie was joined in the back seat by Jimmy as Destry slid back in behind the wheel. Jimmy grabbed the towel from behind Effie and he wiped at the blood on his face. He spied Effie's half empty bottle of water on the floor and grabbed it. He poured what was left of the water onto the towel and used it to clean off his face then handed it to Destry to clean off his hands.

Jimmy pulled the back door closed and not a word was spoken as Destry started up the car and pulled onto the road. The silence between the two was maddening. If they did not talk or interact with one another, there was no way that Effie could gage how or if the fight had changed the situation.

Finally, after miles of silence, Destry glanced over his shoulder and said, "It's too dark out here to look at your back right now, Cookie. I'll look at it when we get to the cabin."

He called her Cookie without hesitating!! Was that his way of saying that he was siding with Jimmy? Was the fact that he wasn't going to pester Jimmy to let him look at the wound his way of saying that he had changed his mind about the situation?

A thousand thoughts trampled Effie's brain, not one of them good. Now was not the time to panic but she didn't know where she stood and she didn't know what else to do. She glanced over at Jimmy and he was just sitting there staring ahead, not even attempting to put a move on her. She glanced out at the landscape speeding by then down at her lap. A dark feeling came over her heart. Who knew what would happen to her next?

Chapter 11

Finally, bright lights shown in the sky ahead. As they drew closer, Effie realized that the road they were on was about to cross under an expressway and the lights were an all night truck stop and fueling station. There were a few trucks parked off to the side of the stop but for the most part, the place was deserted. No people seemed to be moving about. And it made sense. It had to be at least midnight.

Destry pulled up next to a pump with Harry following suit behind them. Even before Destry climbed out of the car, Jimmy began thumbing through a wallet. He pulled out a credit card and handed it to Destry. When Effie looked closer, she realized that it was her wallet and her credit card! She opened her mouth to speak but quickly closed it again. Her initial reaction was to protest him going through her wallet. Then she thought for a moment. If he intended to use her credit card to pay for gas, even if he paid at the pump, it would leave a trail. When she didn't return to work on time, people would get suspicious and when they finally involve the police, they would have to check her credit card records. They would be able to tell where it was last used and then they would have some idea where to start looking for her.

Destry climbed out of the car, credit card in hand. He slid it through the machine on the pump then started filling the car. With that done, he went over and did the same thing for Harry. Effie covered her mouth and allowed herself a small smile. Wouldn't it appear suspicious if her credit card records were checked and two charges for gas came up at the same station, within minutes on the same night? Someone would have to look into it. Beyond that, a lot of gas stations kept hidden cameras at the pump. Maybe she would even be lucky enough that this station kept video tapes and they would be able to run it to the time of the charges and see that it wasn't Effie who charged the fuel on either pump. She allowed a small glimmer of hope to grow in her heart.

Effie looked toward the expressway. A car was exiting and heading toward the station. When it pulled up to the bank of pumps, a man and a woman not much older than herself got out. The man began pumping fuel and the woman bounded toward the building. Effie glanced over at Jimmy. His he had closed his eyes and it appeared that he as dozing off.

"Excuse me," she said. He didn't move. "Excuse me," she repeated a little louder as she reached out and touched his arm. He smacked his lips, opened his eyes and looked at Effie. When Jimmy made a grunting noise, she assumed it meant that it was OK for her to keep talking.

"I really need to use the restroom." He shook his head slightly in disbelief. "Please. I really gotta go. It's been hours," she pleaded.

He rolled down the window and motioned for Destry to come over. When he got there, he leaned over and Jimmy whispered in his ear. Destry looked from Jimmy to Effie, stepped back, then turned and walked toward Harry's truck.

Effie's heart sank. She was sure that the woman from the other car had run to use the restroom. If Effie could get Jimmy to let her go before the woman was done, she could say something to her—Explain her situation. She tried to catch his eye. "I really, really need to go, Jimmy. Please." He wagged his head a couple of times then closed his eyes and went back to sleep. Effie looked down at the floor, her mind racing.

When Destry opened the door she was leaning on, Effie nearly jumped out of her skin. She hadn't even seen him walking back toward the car. He was holding a dusty, denim jacket, covered with patches from all over the country in his hand. He held out his other hand to help Effie out of the car.

"You're gonna put this jacket on so it covers the blood on your back and any other scrapes you might have. The last thing we need is to raise suspicion." He helped her into the jacket which hung on her frame like a tent. Judging by the size of it, Effie guessed that it must have belonged to Harry. "I don't think I need to remind you that there ain't gonna be any funny business. You clear on that?"

Effie nodded her head.

"You know what'll happen if you do try something."

She nodded again.

With that, Destry looped his arm through Effie's and they started walking toward the building. Effie scanned the area to see who might be watching or able to help her. The only people she saw were the guy filling the other car and a clerk behind the counter in the building. She knew that the guy fueling the car would easily be over powered by Jimmy and Harry if she tried anything outside so she looked toward the clerk.

He looked young. He was absorbed in a book or something of the kind. That truck stop was probably the last place in the world he wanted to be that night. He was a bit scrawny. Effie thought for a moment. There was no way he would be able to help her if Destry decided to go after him. The kid was less than half his size. Effie wondered what kind of person hired a kid like that to run an all night truck stop by himself.

When Effie and Destry walked into the building, Destry asked, "Where's the bathroom, kid? My girlfriend needs to use it."

The kid never even looked up from what he was reading. He just pointed across the convenience store and mumbled something that Effie could not understand. Once again, Effie's heart dropped into her stomach. The kid would never be able to say he recognized them if the police ever questioned him. Effie doubted that he would even remember them asking where the restroom was if he was asked. At least it was likely that they had been videotaped entering the building together.

When they were halfway across the store, the door to the Women's restroom flew open and out walked the woman from the other car. Effie gave her a pleading look but the woman must have misinterpreted it. She just gave Effie a sympathetic smile as she brushed past, paid the clerk for fuel and left the building. Damn! Another hope dashed.

A thought entered Effie's mind. If she could not actually tell someone what was happening to her, maybe she could use the edge of a coin from her pocket to scratch a short message on the wall in the restroom. She could tell the clerk that there was feces smeared on the wall in the restroom and he would have to go in to clean it up. When he went to do that, he would see the message and he would have to call the police!! The plan was brilliant.

What if he ignored her and didn't go to clean the restroom? Effie shook her head slightly. Even if the clerk didn't clean it, someone else would have to use the restroom eventually and they would have to see the message. Someone would eventually know that she needed help.

When they reached the restroom door, Destry pulled it open and walked in with Effie. He looked around to make sure there was no other way for her to escape then told her, "Make it quick, Cookie. We ain't got all night." He nudged her toward a stall then stepped out and let the door fall closed behind him.

Effie stepped into the stall and closed the door behind her. She didn't know how long it had been since the last time she had used the bathroom. As she sat down on the toilet, she fished a quarter out of her pocket and started scratching a message onto the back of the door. The paint was hard to scratch at first but she found if she scratched over her lines several times, the paint would start peeling off. It was taking too long. She made it through, *Help. I've been*, when the outside door opened. She froze in place.

Destry spoke. "You're takin' too long. If you aren't out in 60 seconds, I'm comin' in after you." The door fell shut and Effie sat motionless for a moment. When she was sure he wasn't in the room, she feverishly began carving the word, "Kidnaped," into the door. The paint just was not coming off fast enough. There was no way she would even be able to carve in her license plate number or anything else in the next 60 seconds. Instead, she firmly pressed her fingers around the words. Maybe police would check for fingerprints and find a full set of Effie's.

The outside door swung open again and this time Destry came storming into the restroom. As the outside door closed, he pounded once on the stall door and it flew open, banging Effie in the knees. She was sitting on the toilet with her pants around her ankles and there stood Destry looking down at her. She tried to cover herself.

"I'm almost done," she sputtered.

"You're done now," he spat back. "Do what you have to do and get moving." He stood, towering over her, not moving. There was an uncomfortable silence between the two of them.

"C-Can you at least turn around so I can wipe and pull up my pants in privacy?"

Destry turned around but did not close the stall door. As soon as he heard Effie zip her pants and flush the toilet, he turned around and grabbed her arm, pulling her out of the bathroom.

"I have to wash my hands," she said.

He didn't even stop walking. "You wasted your time in there, Cookie. You shoulda thought about wahing your hands before taking so long to piss."

Before she knew it, Destry was pulling her out of the building. She did not get the chance to tell the clerk to clean the restroom. The kid never even looked up at them when they walked out the door. There was no way anyone would find out about her situation now. By the time someone finally saw her partial message, they would be long gone.

The car with the couple was nowhere in site. As Effie and Destry walked toward her car, she wondered if the couple would hear about a missing person. Perhaps they would see her picture on the news or in a paper and realize that they had seen her. Had they seen enough of her to actually recognize her? She doubted it.

When they got to the car, they could see that Jimmy was sound asleep. He was sprawled across the back seat. Rather than wake him, Destry scooted the bag in the passenger seat and made room for Effie to sit up front. She gave him a funny look but said nothing.

"Best to let Jimmy sleep off the haze," he said. "He really ain't such a bad guy. He just doesn't always make real good decisions when he's been drinking."

Effie stood, staring at him like he had lost his mind. Not such a bad guy?? He beat and murdered his ex-girlfriend after watching his brother rape her then shove her body into the trunk of a car. Beyond that, he kidnaped Effie and threatened to kill her too! Jimmy had mentioned that he'd been in jail before. Who knew what secrets his past held? How could Destry stand there and say that Jimmy was not such a bad guy?

Effie would have understood Harry saying those things. It would not have been surprising in the least to hear him going on about how wonderful his brother was. He didn't seem bright enough to light a match, let alone comprehend that even family members can do bad things too. She thought Destry was different, though. Yes, he had taken part in everything that had happened that night but he had also shown some sympathy earlier. He was a wild card. There was no telling how he would react or what he would do next. She looked away from him and rolled her eyes.

Destry gave her a little shove. "You gonna get in the car tonight or are we gonna stand here 'til the sun comes up?"

Effie climbed into the passenger seat and pulled the door closed behind her. As she did so, a pain shot through her back. When she reacted to it, she made it look like it hurt twice as much as it really did. Even if Destry was a wild card, he was still her best hope for sympathy. She watched him walk around the car and climb in beside her. He never took his eyes off her. As he started up the car, he pressed a button on the door and all of the door locks clicked into place. Harry had already pulled around them and was getting onto the road. She just stared at the back of the truck as they accelerated behind him.

It suddenly occurred to Effie that she still had no idea where they were. She looked over at Destry and whispered, "Where are we?"

He shook his head and laughed to himself. "Cookie, that ain't how it works. Even if it is wrong, we kidnaped you. That means that it's probably better if I don't tell you where we are and where we are headed."

"Oh come on," she argued. "I already know you are taking me to a cabin or something like that. Jimmy said that way back before we left that first little town. What's it going to hurt to at least tell me what state we are in?"

"I jus' don't think it would be a good idea to tell you."

"What's it going to hurt to tell me? Even if you tell me what state we are in, I still won't have any idea where in the state we are. I'm not from around here so I don't know the lay of the land."

Destry looked over at her for a few moments as if he was weighing what she had just said. Effie really didn't believe that she was going to be able to get any information out of him just yet. She was very surprised when he said, "Still in Oklahoma. We'll be getting to New Mexico pretty soon."

She smiled at him and said, "Thank you, Destry." He never answered. He just glanced at her a few more times then stared straight ahead and rolled down the road behind Harry.

An hour or two later, Destry sped up and passed Harry. They had long since crossed into New Mexico and maybe even another state. Now, Destry was forcing them onto a deserted, old two-track. Effie's first thought was that they were at the cabin already. As it turned out, that wasn't quite right. Destry had pulled off so he could catch a little sleep. They stopped in a little clearing and when they did, Harry got out to see what was going on. He tapped on Destry's window even as he was rolling it down.

"What wee stoppin' for?" he asked, sticking his head in the window.

Destry rubbed his eyes and replied, "It's been a long night, don't you think?" Harry nodded in agreement. "Well, I've been up since 5 a.m. Either I need a little sleep or I'm not gonna make it to the cabin."

"Yeah. I guess I could use some too. What are we gonna do with her?" he said, pointing at Effie.

"Just pull the truck up close enough on that side of the car so she can't open the door wide enough to get out. As long as you do it right, she'll won't be able to go anywhere without waking up me and Jimmy first."

Harry looked at Destry like he was a genius. Without another word, he did exactly as he was told. There was no chance Effie could open her door. In fact, she couldn't help but wonder how in the world Harry was able to pull that close without scraping against her car. Not that it mattered. Nothing really mattered right then. She was trapped in her own car with two strange men and there was a dead body in the trunk! It couldn't get much worse than that.

Destry didn't even bother warning her to be good before leaning his head back and closing his eyes. He just left her to her thoughts. Within minutes, it was obvious that he was sleeping.

Effie sat, staring straight forward into the night. It felt as though it had been an eternity since she had sat in the Coon Pit Bar, watching the group at the other end. She close her eyes and wished that she had never let her curiosity get the best of her like that. She should have just gone back to her hotel room and gone to bed.

As the rhythmic sound of Destry's breathing lulled her, Effie's thoughts settled on the last bed she'd slept in. It had been so comfortable and she'd fallen right asleep. Now, sleep was like a dream. How could anyone sleep peacefully, not knowing what would happen next? She knew she needed the sleep, though. She had to be able to stay sharp or she would never survive. Her mind wandered for a while and the last thing Effie remembered thinking was that it might be better if she never woke again.

Chapter 12

The next time that Effie opened her eyes, she was aware that the sky was growing pink and they were moving down the two-track. She wanted to open her eyes all the way so she could see where they were going but she just couldn't. Her eyelids kept sinking, drawing her back into sleep.

Nightmares had plagued every corner of her mind and she was beyond the point of physical exhaustion. She was mentally exhausted now and that was, perhaps, even more taxing. Her body knew what she needed. There was no reason to fight it. She welcomed the sleep and this time, she was greeted by a state of blissful nothingness.

When Effie woke, hours later, her first instinct was to scream. They were flying down an expressway and Jimmy was leaning against the seat behind her. His hand was wrapped around her throat so tight, she had to gasp for air. A terrible feeling spread through the pit of her stomach. Something had gone wrong—very wrong.

"You say or do anything to cause suspicion and I will kill you before you know what hit you," he hissed. She shook her head in compliance then he let go of her and flopped back in the seat.

Effie quickly realized that she heard a police siren and that Destry was slowing down. He heart skipped a beat. Maybe the kid at the fueling station had seen her note and called the police after all. She tried to hide her excitement. She knew she had to stay calm or the guys would know that something was up.

The car came to a stop on the shoulder of the road with the police car directly behind them. Effie turned her head so she could see the officer out of the corner of her eye. He began walking toward Destry's side of the car with a black ticket book in his hand. With each step he took, Effie was sure that her heart beat a little harder. As the office approached the driver side window, Destry cranked it down. The officer bent and looked in the car, his eyes resting for a moment on each of them. He was tall with broad shoulders. His name badge read, *P. Matthews*. Effie was surprised how young he looked. Her guess was that he was fresh out of college or an academy. She held her breath.

The officer smiled and tipped his hat at Effie as he said, "Mornin', ma'am." Then he turned his attention to Destry. A grim frown spread across his lips. "You were going pretty fast back there, don't you think?"

When Destry just gave him a blank look and did not answer, the officer asked, "Do you have any idea what your speed was?"

"No," answered Destry.

"No?"

Destry slowly shook his head. The officer stood studying his face for a moment. "You look tired, sir," he began. "How long have you been on he road?"

"I dunno." Destry shrugged. "I guess it's been quite a few hours. Drove most the night."

The officer sighed and shook his head. "Well sir, you were going 88 and ½ miles per hour back there. Driving that speed is dangerous as is. It's ten times worse if you're exhausted. Is it really worth it to risk the lives of everyone in your car?"

"No, sir," said Destry.

"That's right. Now, I'm gonna need to see your license and registration."

Destry began digging to get his wallet out of his back pocket. "Get the registration Cookie," he said, flipping his hand at her.

Effie reached forward with a trembling hand and pulled the latch on the glove compartment. It dropped open, displaying its contents. There on the top was a plastic baggy which held Effie's vehicle registration and proof of insurance. Her mind raced. The officer obviously had no idea that she had been kidnaped and really was pulling them over for speeding. More than anything, she wanted to alert him to her situation but nothing came to mind. If she said something, Jimmy would probably stab her or slit her throat. If she tried to run, he would probably catch her then he would kill her.

Reluctantly, Effie opened the baggy, slipped her hand inside and pulled out her registration. Then it came to her. The back of her registration was not signed. She could say she needed to sign it, then, instead of writing her name, she would scrawl a short note. "My—My registration isn't signed yet. I need a pen, honey," she said, looking at Destry with a smile.

He patted his pockets then turned around and looked at Jimmy who just raised his hands and wagged his head back and forth. "Sorry, Cookie. I don't have one."

The officer pulled a pen from the ticket book and reached toward Effie. She took it from his hand. Her eyes dropped to the paper in front of her. If either Destry or Jimmy found out what she was about to write instead of her name, she was as good as dead. She glanced up at the officer who was standing there smiling at her. Very quickly, she scrawled, "I've been kidnaped." She turned the paper over before anyone could see it and handed it and the pen to the officer. Destry held his license up between two fingers and the officer snatched it from him then turned around and walked back toward his car. Effie put the baggy back in the glove box and sat as still as she could, barely breathing.

"Yer doin' good, Cookie," said Jimmy. "Just keep it up, or else."

Not another word was spoken while they sat waiting for the officer. After an eternity, he finally got out of his car and walked back to Destry's window. He bent and looked at Effie. "You are Effie St. Martin and this is your car?" She nodded her head. "May I see some ID?"

"Yes, sir," she whispered, frantically searching for her wallet. She finally spied it sitting on the seat next to Destry. Effie grabbed it, flipped it open and handed her driver's license to the officer.

He stepped back and studied her license then compared it to the registration. "You're from Michigan?"

"Yes, sir."

"You're a long way away from home. What are you doing out here?"

Her throat seemed to close. She wanted to scream out that she'd been kidnaped and that there was a dead body in the trunk. She also wanted to live, so after coughing a few times she said, "Visiting friends."

The officer nodded then he just handed the licenses and the registration back to Destry. Without even glancing at the registration, he handed it and Effie's license back to her then looked up at the officer.

"You were going way too fast back there, Mr. Clare."

"Yes, sir," said Destry.

"Normally I would give you a ticket but I'm just finishing up my shift and I don't need any extra paperwork. I'm gonna to let you go with a warning this time." Effie's heart dropped through her stomach. "Slow—Down! And the next exit up the way, I want you to pull off and take a nap or switch drivers. OK?"

Destry smiled. "I'll be sure to do that officer."

"I have to go beyond there so I'll be following you up there. If you don't pull off, I will give you a ticket."

"I'll be sure to pull off sir," said Destry.

The officer gave him a half-nod then turned and headed back to his vehicle. Destry started up the car, shifted it into gear and pulled onto the road. As soon as they were back up to speed, Jimmy leaned forward and slammed his hand down on Destry's shoulder. "Damn! That was close!! Even I was shaking! Even Cookie here put on a good show."

Effie crumpled the registration into a ball and hung her head. Large tears began rolling down her cheeks as she choked out sobs. Was it possible that the officer hadn't even looked at the back of her registration? Maybe it was. He had stood there and watched her "sign" it. That small action was a big risk for her to take and it was all for nothing.

Jimmy sat back and slapped his knees a few times. "Wanna know the funny thing, Cookie? We was gonna get off at the next exit anyway!" He laughed. "That dumb cop probably thinks that we're doin' exactly what he said for us to do."

Destry shook his head. "I can't take that kinda stuff, Jimmy," he said. "I think I just about had a heart attack. What if he woulda asked to look in the trunk of somethin'?"

"Well he didn't," laughed Jimmy. "Now hurry up. Harry's gonna get way ahead of us and I don't want him runnin' around town by himself. Damn fool would probably open his big trap and let somethin' out."

The police car caught up and was cruising down the road behind them just like the officer had said he would. Finally, the exit came into sight and as they neared it, Destry flipped on his turn signal. He moved into the exit lane and began slowing down. The officer looked over and gave him a thumbs up sign then kept moving down the road. Jimmy let another round of laughter escape and he pounded his knees again.

As they neared the end of the exit ramp, there was a rusty, crooked sign that pointed left for Guffy and right for Hall's Bluff. No cars were anywhere around so Destry did not stop. He just slowed down a little then kept on going to the left.

Chapter 13

The next thing Effie knew, they were flying down a highway. The mountains had been looming ahead for quite a while but now they were much closer. Ahead, the road rose sharply from the valley and twisted along the mountain side.

If the pressure in her ears had been an annoyance from the slow rise in elevation earlier, this was Hell. It seemed like she had to yawn every few seconds or her head might explode. At times, it was almost painful.

Once they made it over the pass and back down to the valley floor, Effie nearly smiled. She was definitely a flat-lander. The rolling hills in the countryside of Michigan were nothing compared to the land in…Well, wherever they were.

"Excuse me," Effie directed at Destry. "Where are we?"

"Colorado," Jimmy said, leaning over the seat.

"Colorado? Last night when I asked, you said we would be getting to New Mexico soon."

"I did and we did go through New Mexico. You were sleeping," said Destry.

Effie tried to picture where they were but nothing really came to mind. She had never really taken the time to look at a map of Colorado so she couldn't even imagine how the major roads might cut across the state. Judging by the angle of the sun, she guessed that they were heading west. She couldn't even be sure of that, though.

After a while, they turned off the highway, onto a much more desolate road. Everything about the road felt different. The valley they had been in before was wide and even but this road quickly gave her the feeling that they were truly in the mountains. Trees and jagged rocks rose sharply from the shoulder. Occasionally, a car or beat up old truck driving in the opposite direction would roll by. Here and there, other mountain roads or two-tracks disappeared into the rugged terrain. The majority of the houses she saw were run-down old shacks with sagging roofs and broken windows. Even those with windows intact did not look inhabitable to Effie and she couldn't help but wonder if the cabin they were heading toward looked any different.

Effie wiped the back of her hand across her forehead. She had been so absorbed in the topography that she hadn't realized how uncomfortably hot she was getting. For once, it appeared that the weatherman had been correct. She wished she was back at the Coon Pit so she could razz that waitress for giving weather forecasters a bum rap. Heck, she just wanted to be back at the Coon Pit, period. If there was one day Effie could live over in her life, it was the previous day. Given the opportunity, she would ignore the group and just go back to her room for the night.

She couldn't go back, though, so there she sat, a prisoner in the passenger seat of her own car. Why hadn't she taken her car in to get the air conditioner fixed last summer when it broke? It was a really stupid thing for her to overlook and now she was suffering for it. Even with the windows down, it was uncomfortable. Everything was just plain hot, including the wind.

While watching the scenery fly by, Effie realized that she was not feeling well. It wasn't something that had happened all of a sudden. It had been building. Not too long after pulling off the expressway, they had stopped for fuel again and Destry had been nice enough to get Effie a bottle of water and a sandwich from the store at the gas station. That was all she'd had that day and either it wasn't agreeing with her or the lack of food wasn't. Either way, she was beginning to feel woozy, her stomach was churning, she was sweating like a butcher and her head was pounding. She wanted to melt into the seat and make everything disappear. The worst part was, she was just going to have to suffer through it. If the men were not willing to take the time to look at her back, she knew they would not bother doing anything if she told them she felt ill.

Finally, they pulled into a little filling station and Destry got out to fuel the car. Effie was amazed at the building and gas pumps. She had never seen working pumps that looked so old. It was like she had stepped into an old movie. The building did not look much different than the shacks she had seen along the road. The peak of the roof dipped in the middle and old green shingles were missing in different places making it look like a crooked smile with missing teeth. A rusty sign that read *Webb and Sons* dangled from the eve at an angle. A small covered porch with tall pieces of grass growing up between the floor slats ran the length of the building. At the far end, the boards were warped and breaking apart. A tree grew up through a hole in the floor and nearly reached the ceiling. One board in the center of the porch, directly in front of the door looked new. The rest looked as though they had been there for countless years. A wooden bench sat on either side of the door and Effie doubted that they would support a child, let alone a weary adult.

The wooden exterior of the building was gray and weathered. Even a big piece of wood that covered an old window looked like it had been there for years. The front door stood open and as Effie squinted to peer into the darkness, a Native American man came out and leaned against the door-frame. He said something to Destry that Effie could not hear then pulled out a pocket knife and began digging under his fingernails.

Effie studied the man. An old, straw cowboy hat crowned long, flowing black hair. He had a strong brow with dark eyes and deep bronze skin. His red t-shirt was tucked into his blue jeans and both looked comfortable worn but clean. A beautiful pair of snake skin cowboy boots graced his feet. The man was tall—easily a head taller than Jimmy, Destry or Harry. Effie's best guess was that he was in his early 40's.

Jimmy, who had been staring at Effie, turned to see where her gaze fell. A look of recognition spread across his face and he began rolling down the window. "Ahanu Webb," he shouted.

At first it appeared that the man either did not hear Jimmy or he was ignoring him. He just kept on digging under his nails. Then he snapped the knife shut and slid it into his pocket as he stepped away from the doorway. He stood at the front edge of the porch, looking toward the car.

"Jimmy Roth?"

"Sure is," said Jimmy as he hung his arm out the window and banged is hand against the door a few times.

Ahanu stepped down off the porch and approached the car. "It's been a long time, my friend. I was beginning to think you had sold the cabin."

"It ain't my fault you ain't seen me in a while. Last two times I been up here, jus' your dad was workin' and you was out on a job or on some trip or something. Where the hell is your dad today?"

"He's away for a few days. Went to pick up some things for the store." He looked in the car at Effie. She nervously looked away. He kept looking at her as he said, "I saw your brother a while ago. It's been about 20 minutes or so since he stopped."

Jimmy laughed lightly and reached over the seat to pat Effie's shoulder. "This here is Cookie, Ahanu. She's my new girlfriend. Thought I'd bring her up here for a nice little vacation at the cabin. We're gonna do a little partyin'," he said as he winked. "You know what I mean."

"Cookie," echoed Ahanu.

Jimmy leaned out the window and lowered his voice as if he had to worry about crowds of people listening in on a secret. Ahanu leaned closer to listen. "She don't look like it but she's real wild when it comes to sex Ahanu—likes makin' up wild stories and actin' and bein' tied up and other stuff. Since I known you for a long time, you come out the cabin after a couple of days and I might be willing to uh, *introduce* you to her a little better." He smiled and winked at Ahanu.

The blood drained from Effie's face at the thought of Jimmy passing her around to his friends. What kind of person treated another human in that manner? Furthermore, what kind of person took their friend up on something like that?

Suddenly she realized that everything was too much for her. Effie got a familiar feeling that rose from her stomach to her throat. With everyone looking at her, she flung her door open and heaved. Nothing but a little water spattered on the ground next to the car. Her eyes were pinched shut but tears worked their way out. Finally she pulled the door closed and sat back, wiping her mouth with the back of her hand.

All three men had been watching in silence and finally Jimmy broke it with a loud guffaw. The other two men joined him with a peal of light laughter.

"Must be the heat," said Jimmy.

Ahanu chuckled and shook his head. "I may or may not take you up on your offer."

The gas pump clicked off and Destry returned the nozzle to the holder. He dug into his pocket and pulled out the wad of money Jimmy had given him back at the first gas station. He silently looked Ahanu in the eye for a few seconds before peeling off a pair of bills and handing them to him.

Ahanu patted Destry's arm then reached out and squeezed Jimmy's outstretched hand in a brotherly handshake. "Have fun with your new girlfriend," he said. "I will see you in a few days, no doubt." Then he turned and walked back toward the building.

Destry climbed in behind the wheel and started up the car. Ten minutes down the road, they turned onto another mountain road. As they rounded the corner, Effie's eyes climbed up the mountainside. She was surprised to see a patch of dead trees along the top. When she looked back beside the roadway, her gaze fell fell on a single tree on a hill that seemed to stand taller than the rest around it. The bark on the tree was charred and suddenly Effie realized that there had once been a forest fire on the mountainside.

They traveled for another twenty minutes or so. At first, Effie did not see the two track jutting off the side of the road and she wondered why they were slowing. When they turned onto the two track, it felt as though the dense forest and brush was swallowing them up. There was no sign of any other shacks or people anywhere.

The trail was full of ruts, some of them so deep, Effie was sure they would get stuck. She closed her eyes tight. How would Jimmy react if they got stuck? Destry just kept moving at a slow, steady pace and in a few minutes, they came to a small clearing. The first thing Effie saw when she opened her eyes was Harry's truck, then her gaze fell on the cabin. They were finally there. She could not believe what was before her eyes.

Effie glanced at Destry with a look of horror on her face. That was the cabin where they were going to keep her? It was just as rundown as everything else she had seen since they had left the expressway. It was built on a steep hillside and the cabin leaned a little as if it was growing weak in its old age. Even from a distance, Effie could see that years of grime caked on the windows seemed to darken the cabin. The old growth of the forest loomed all around and above them, filtering out the bright sunlight. Everywhere she looked, deep shadows fell.

Up the hill, through the trees, there was a tiny shed. The bottom hinge on the door was broken causing it to hang at a slight angle. Down the hill a ways there was a meandering river. A rickety, old dock protruded from the bank and the far end dipped toward the water as though the wood had rotted and given way to the river current. Leaning against a tree next to the river was a dented fishing boat that looked like it had originally been painted green. Years of use had scraped away the paint and left a dull gray boat.

Effie's eyes traveled back up the hill and stopped at the cabin. The porch sat at a slight angle, leaning toward the ground. There were no boards to keep animals from getting under it and no railings to keep people from falling off it. Four steps lead from the ground up to the porch and compared to the rest of the cabin, they looked quite new. Though there was no handrail next to them, at least they looked sturdy.

A wooden rocking chair with one of the rockers missing sat at the far end of the porch. A long, dirty, gray window that was situated high on the wall started near the corner and ran half the width of the building. The door stood open and even in the daytime, only darkness filled the cabin. Next to the open door sat Harry on a sagging, wooden bench. With eyes closed and mouth hanging open, he leaned against the building, snoring. Effie just sat staring at the cabin in shock.

When Effie finally looked away from the building, she was surprised to see that she had missed Destry and Jimmy climbing out of the car. Destry was still standing next to the open driver's side door but Jimmy had stepped over to a tree. Though he was facing away from her, Effie could see liquid running down the tree and pooling between his feet. She knew he was urinating and quickly looked away.

Jimmy looked over his shoulder at Destry as he stretched and barked a command. "Get her out of that car and into the cabin."

Destry turned around and looked into the car at Effie. He nodded toward the cabin. "Best you get inside before you're told to do it again."

She climbed out of the car, over-exaggerating the pain in her back. When she turned around and leaned in to collect her bag and wallet from the seat, Destry shook his head. "Just get into the cabin."

"Christ, Destry," said Jimmy as he stomped toward Effie, zipping up his pants. "When you gonna learn that you can't jus' tell a woman what to do. You gotta grab hold of 'em and make 'em do what ya want or they won't never learn to listen." He hooked her arm and yanked her toward the building. Effie stumbled on an exposed tree root and nearly fell but even that did not slow Jimmy down. He just kept heading toward the cabin.

"You gotta train a woman just like you gotta train a dog, Destry."

Even when Jimmy stomped up the porch, dragging Effie, Harry did not stir. He flung Effie through the open door, causing her to trip over her own feet and fall. Then he turned his attention to Harry. Just inches from his face, Jimmy sucked in a deep breath and yelled at the top of his lungs. "GET UP YOU FAT TUB OF LARD!"

Harry's eyes snapped open and he stared at Jimmy for a moment. "I—I— took the stuff from the truck inside already and took care of 'em. I was just catchin' a little nap til you got here, Jimmy," he said. "Honest. I was." He shook his head up and down.

"Well we got other stuff to take care of," Jimmy said and walked into the dark cabin.

Effie tried to get up as fast as she could but Jimmy was already standing over her. He reached out and tangled his fingers into her hair then pulled upward as she struggled to her feet. A huge lump formed in Effie's throat and she tried to swallow it back. She sucked air in through her nose. The air was thick with the musty odor of a cabin which had been closed up too long and it assaulted her senses. Jimmy just stared into her eyes.

"Please," she whispered, looking down.

He let go of her hair and grabbed her chin, forcing her to look into his eyes. He wagged his head back and forth and smiled. "You're mine now, Cookie," he said. "You're mine and I'll do anything I want with you for as long as I want to do it with you. Now, you got some learnin' to do."

Destry and Harry joined them in the darkness. Jimmy did not let go of her chin and his eyes never left her. "Destry, you need to get the shovel and go out into the woods aways and start diggin' a hole. It don't need to be too deep an it don't need to be too big. Just big enough to fit that dead whore. Do it far enough away so if some animals come and try diggin' her up for dinner, she won't end up rottin' near the cabin and stinkin' the whole place up."

When Destry did not move to do as he was told, Jimmy turned and yelled. "Now, Destry! You get on it *now,* before I have to give you more of the same thing you got along the road back there." Destry turned and headed out of the cabin without a word, his shoulders slumped and his head hanging low.

Jimmy looked at Harry. "Gimme the truck keys," he said. Jimmy dug into his pocket until he came out with a small key-ring with only three keys and a beer bottle opener on it. He handed it to them to Jimmy. "You're gonna stay here and watch Cookie and I'm gonna go into town and buy some stuff that I need. Don't let her out of your sight and don't let her outside the cabin."

"What if she has to go to the bathroom or somethin'?"

"Hell, I don't care. Let her squat over a bucket. Just don't take your eyes off her." Jimmy bit his lip and thought for a moment. "You got some rope in the back of your truck?"

"I ain' got nothin' back there no more," replied Harry.

"Well go find some. We gotta have some 'round here somewhere."

Harry shrugged and turned to go look for some rope.

"Make sure it's long enough to tie Miss Cookie up," Jimmy called after him. "I don't want no chances of her escapin' and I don't know if you kin keep track of her good enough."

With Harry and Destry gone, Jimmy returned his attention to Effie. He looked at her and sneered. "Now it's just you and me, Cookie," he said and tilted his head to the side. He still had a tight hold on her chin. Jimmy pulled her away from the door and deeper into the cabin. Effie was not aware of anything around her but Jimmy. All she could see were his eyes and that awful sneer. He grabbed two chairs from somewhere beside them and forced Effie to sit down facing him. He finally released her chin and sat back in the chair.

For a moment, Jimmy did not say anything. He just stared. The look on his face made Effie uncomfortable. The way his eyes traveled over her body and lingered in some places made her feel like he was undressing her. She just couldn't keep looking at him. Effie dropped her eyes to the ground and crossed her arms in front of her chest.

Jimmy laughed. "You don't gotta worry about nothin' right now, Cookie. I don't got no time to do the things to you that I wanna do. I gotta get to town and get some stuff and I can't go to town all excited, can I? People would give me would give me a funny look if they seen me goin' around with a big, huge bulge in my pants." He rubbed his hand over the front of his jeans then grabbed Effie's hand and pulled it away from her body. He forced her to rub the crotch of his jeans too. "See? You got lots to look forward to." He threw his head back and laughed before releasing her hand. The instant he did, Effie snapped it back and crossed her arms in front of her chest again.

"How about I tell you the rules of the cabin?"

Effie did not respond or even raise her eyes. She just sat looking at the floor.

Jimmy chuckled. "Number one, we're far enough away from anythin', you could yell all day long and no one would hear ya and it would just piss me off. Number two, don't ya dare try to run away. First of all, you wouldn't have nowhere to run and second of all, we would hunt ya down and plant ya in the ground right next to Angie. Number three, if I tell ya to do somethin', ya best do it the first time I say so. If I have to tell ya to do things more than once, it's gonna piss me off and yer gonna know it. Finally, number four, ya ain't nothin' but a dirty whore and you ain't good for nothin' but pleasin' a man so ya better show me some damn respect. And what's more, yer my dirty whore and if I wanna share ya with another man, ya better do to him what I tell ya to do to him."

Effie mumbled something to Jimmy. His eyes clouded with anger. "You wanna repeat that Cookie?"

"I'm not a whore and if I was, I certainly wouldn't be yours," she spat.

Flames sparked in Jimmy's eyes and he jumped to his feet. He stood for a moment, clenching his teeth. Effie dared to look up into his eyes. Even before she said it the first time, she knew it was wrong. In one fluid movement, Jimmy drew his hand back then let it fly forward. The back of his hand connected with the underside of Effie's chin with so much force that it knocked her and the chair backward. Her chin felt like it was on fire.

Jimmy walked around the chair and bent to hit her again. She knew what was coming and tried to cover her face with her arms. His fingers dug into her forearm as he yanked it away from her face with one hand and swung with his other. This time his fist struck her cheekbone and she screamed.

"Don't ever talk back to me again, ya whore," he growled and spit in her face. He walked over to the door and leaned against the frame, looking out.

Effie just laid there and pressed her eyes shut, forcing a tear to roll out of the corner of her right eye. She tried to concentrate on breathing. In, out. In, out. In, out. Was it worth it to try to live through all of this? Was there even any chance of her escaping and making it to safety? No one even knew she had been abducted and she didn't have any friends who would notice that she was missing. Everything seemed hopeless to Effie.

In the back of her mind, she scolded herself for allowing curiosity to get her into the situation. If she had just minded her own business back in the Coon Pit, she would be happy right now—enjoying her vacation with hardly a worry in the world. What were those old sayings? Curiosity killed the cat? Ignorance is bliss? Why couldn't she have gone with the ignorance?

She patted her chin lightly, trying to see if it felt like there were any broken bones. Even the lightest pressure made her wince. There was a lot of swelling already and warm, sticky liquid felt like blood. From what she could tell, nothing felt broken.

Effie slid her hand up to her cheek. Even before she touched it, she could feel heat radiating from the place where Jimmy had hit her. She touched her other cheek, trying to compare the two and estimate the amount of swelling. The entire left side of her face was swollen and when she tried to open her eyes, she found that only the right one would open all of the way. She could see out of her left eye some but only a sliver.

The heat and pain from the two blows combined and when she looked up at the ceiling, the room started to spin. Effie closed her eyes, hoping to make the spinning stop. The more she concentrated on making the movement cease, the more the room circled around her. Before she knew it, it felt like her body was getting pulled into the spin. Around and around, faster and faster! Her stomach was churning and her heart was racing. Finally she rolled onto her side and her body convulsed as her stomach heaved into her throat, spewing clear mucus and stomach acid onto the floor. She squeezed her eyes closed as tight as she could, tears rolling down her cheeks. Her nostrils burned from the vomit and the flavor in her mouth caused her to heave again. This time nothing came out.

Effie didn't try to move away from the vomit. She just laid down next to it, her eyes closed and mouth hanging open, drool dripping onto the floor. Her arms and legs felt like dead weights. The last thing she remember was wishing that she could just sink through the floor.

Chapter 14

Cold water splashed down on Effie's face causing her to jump. She tried to open her eyes to see what had happened but found that she was no longer able to open her left eye at all. She rolled onto her back and looked up with her right eye. Everything was dark but she could make out the faint shape of someone standing over her.

A crusty towel was thrown into her face and a command was barked at her. "Clean up the mess you made before my brother comes back and beats you more." It was Harry. She grabbed the towel and attempted to look up at him.

Effie tried to speak but the instant she moved her lips, she felt a tremendous pressure from the swelling. She could only talk through clenched teeth. "I-can't-thee-it," she said.

"That's just tough. Ain't gonna be no light til Jimmy gets back with fuel for the generator or some candles or something. Only flashlight I could find had dead batt-ries. Yer jus' gonna hafta do it in the dark. I don't need it to stink the place up so just feel yer way around."

She thought about his words for a moment then it occurred to her that she had not seen any power lines running into the cabin. That meant no electricity and probably no running water. She frowned then leaned up on her right arm and dragged the crusty towel across the floor. The first two circles she made, it didn't feel like she'd run across anything. The third circle she made, Effie knew she had dragged it through the bile. The more she pulled the towel through the mess, the more it lost its rigid texture and became pliable.

Harry kicked a bucket, sloshing water onto the floor. She had not seen it sitting next to her but knew what he meant for her to do. She dunked the filthy towel into the water and jumped as she submerged her hand in the icy water. After she swirled the rag around a few times and wrung it as best she could, she flopped it back onto the floor in the general area she had been cleaning and scrubbed back and forth. After Effie repeated the process four more times, Harry reached down and grabbed the towel from her hand.

"Stay right where you are while I go dump this off the porch."

Effie moved so she was sitting upright with her back to the door and crossed her legs in front of her while Harry grabbed to bucket and walked away from her. There was a quiet sploosh as the water from the bucket hit the ground then Harry clomped back into the room. He tossed the bucket somewhere behind her and when it landed, the loud clatter of pans falling to the floor made Effie jump.

Harry moved so he was directly behind her and struggled to kneel on the floor. He was breathing hard and the air hissed as he began inhaling and exhaling through his nose. He leaned forward so his lips were pressed to Effie's ear and whispered. "Put yer arms behind yer back so I can tie yer wrists up ya stupid whore."

Effie jerked her head away and shook it. "No-pleeth-don't-tie-me-up."

"I have to," said Harry. "My brother said to make sure to tie ya up and we both know how he is when he gets pissed, don't we?"

She tried to scoot away from him but he put a gigantic hand on her shoulder to hold her in place.

"If ya want more of what my brother already gave ya, fine. I'll just tell him ya gave me a hard time and fought it when I tried to tie ya up and he'll beat ya till there ain't a breath left in ya. It's yer choice, Cookie."

Effie thought for a moment. Harry was probably right about Jimmy. If he came back and saw that she had not done as she was told, it was very likely that he would beat her to death. On the other hand, if she let him tie her up, she was giving up any means of protecting herself. She weighed out her choices. Render yourself helpless and do as you are told or do something that could seriously lead to death? She reluctantly moved her wrists around behind her.

Harry chuckled a little. "I thought ya'd see it that way," he said then began looping the rope around her wrists. It felt too tight and she wanted to ask him to make it looser but did not bother trying to make the request. The last thing he cared about was her comfort. He finished tying the rope and jerked on the end to make sure it was secure. When he was satisfied with the job he had done, Harry pushed his way onto his feet and stood beside her for a moment.

Effie could feel his eyes on her. She decided to try talking to him. "My nameth Effie," she said but he didn't make a sound or move. "I'm from Mithigan and I'm on vacathon. I'm not lucky like you. I don't have any kind of relathionthip with my brotherth or thitheterth." The floor creaked as he shifted his weight from one foot to the other.

She wondered if it was it worth it to keep talking with him. The more she moved her mouth, the more painful it was. Effie decided that even if he didn't say anything back to her, hearing what she had to say might make her more of a real person to him so she kept talking. "I don't like my job and I got in trouble for arguing with thomeone who wath more importhant than me tho I dethided to take thith trip acroth the country. No one ever treated me real good at work." She tried to find some common ground between herself and Harry. "I don't think anyone liketh me there becauth I'm fat. They don't underthand that I have feelingth too. I'll bet you know how that feelth too. People called me nameth to my fathe and I know they did it behind my back too." Effie fell silent for a moment and Harry scuffled his feet. Was she tugging at his heart-strings?

When she opened her mouth to speak again, Harry jumped in. "Shut up," he hissed and she snapped her mouth shut.

Maybe it wasn't such a good thing to try to hit home with him. Apparently, it upset him. She would have to think of something else. Then Effie realized why he had told her to shut up. She could hear it too. Heavy footsteps were coming closer. They stomped up the front steps and into the cabin. Effie braced in case it was Jimmy. She was afraid he would beat her again even though she was tied up. He hadn't said anything about talking but she was sure he was more interested in keeping her quiet than in listening to her chatter away at his brother.

Effie heard the person walk across the room behind her and drop something metal on a table or shelf but it was so dark, she couldn't see even with her good eye. She just shut her mouth and held her breath. Maybe it wasn't Jimmy at all. Maybe it was the Native American man from the filling station or another of Jimmy's friends. He had offered to share her with one friend. What was to stop him from doing it with others?

"Why in the hell is it so dark in here?"

It was Destry!! Effie exhaled in relief. It could have been fatal if it had been Jimmy. She decided to play it safe for a while and keep quiet—only speak when spoken to. She needed to listen and figure out how far she could push the boundaries without getting beaten.

"Jimmy ain't back from town yet," said Harry.

"Well find a flashlight."

"Already did. Ain't no batt-ries in it that work."

"How about one of the hurricane lanterns then? There should still be a bottle of oil right next to them."

There was silence for a moment. Harry scuffled his feet then said, "I can't see to find matches to light them with."

Destry sucked in a deep breath and blew it out. She was certain that if she could have seen him at that moment, he would be shaking his head in disbelief. "Harry," he said.

"Yeah?"

"How long have I known you?"

"I don't know. A long time. Why?"

"Of all the years that I've known you, I have never seen you without a cigarette lighter. Not even when we were kids."

"So?"

"So," said Destry in a sarcastic tone. "So couldn't you use that lighter to start the lantern?"

Another silence from Harry then, "Oh." Effie could hear him rustling through his pocket. He pulled something out of his pocket and after a few clicks accompanied by sparks, a flame leapt to life in his hand. He stood there, a faint glow lighting his face. "I didn't think abou't that."

Destry mumbled, "Christ," then walked across the room and grabbed something from a shelf. There was a sound of glass clinking together as he walked back across the room and set something on a table. Harry joined him and in a moment, two glass hurricane lanterns provided a warm glow in the room.

"See," said Destry. "Didn't even need to add any oil either." He left one lamp on the table and set another on a shelf near the door.

As he went to light two more lanterns, Harry picked up the pans that had been knocked down when he threw the bucket. After that, he stepped out the door, into the darkness. The bench on the porch moaned under his weight.

Destry sat one of the newly lit lanterns on a small table toward the back of the cabin, near a bed. The last lantern, he sat on the floor next to Effie as he kneeled behind her to remove the rope. Though her wrists had only been bound for a short time, it felt good to have them free again. She rubbed her wrists but did not move from her spot on the floor.

A few feet to her right, a tall, wooden support beam ran from the floor to the ceiling and it was almost inviting to lean upon. The combination of the gash on her back and the swelling in her face was too much pain, though, and sitting up was enough of a chore. Moving even an inch seemed like too much.

"Excuthe me," she whispered.

Destry was busy digging through something behind her and gave no sign that he had heard Effie. He just continued what he was doing in silence.

Effie repeated herself a little louder. "Excuthe me." She was confident he had heard her so when he did not answer again, she continued speaking. "I prefer not to be thied up but Harry thaid that Jimmy would be very angry ifth he cometh home and I'm not thied up like he thaid."

The way she spoke made Destry stop what he was doing and come around to look at her. His eyes opened wide. For the first time since he'd come into the cabin, he looked straight into her face. Half of it was swollen and purple and smeared with blood.

"What—How—Did Harry do this to you?" He had a look of disbelief on his face.

She shook her head slowly. "It wath Jimmy. I thalked back to him and he wath angry with me." Destry's face fell. "Doeth it look that bad?"

Instead of answering, he walked around the table to a large wooden sink in the corner. An old water pump was mounted on the counter next to it so that the water would pour into the sink when someone pumped the handle. Destry pulled a small bowl off a shelf next to him and began working the pump. After a few moments of squeaking, water came rushing out and he filled the bowl. From another shelf, he grabbed a pair of towels that were far from sterile then soaked them in the water and placed them on the floor near Effie. He retrieved a first aid kit and finally, he kneeled down in front of her.

"I don't have any ice for your face in here. The best I can do is soak a towel in cold water and give that to you for the pain," he said.

For a moment, Destry sat studying Effie's face and when she tried to smile, he looked away. Perhaps he wasn't such a wild card after all. He mumbled something but she couldn't understand what he said.

After a few minutes of silence, Destry opened the first aid kit. "I'm not sure what to take care of first." Finally, he picked up one of the towels and gently pressed it against Effie's face. At first, she pulled back but when he gave her a stern look, she allowed him to wash the blood away.

The hurricane lantern cast a glow on Destry's face. Beads of sweat formed on his forehead and temples. The sweat trickled through smudges of dirt and dripped onto his shirt. His glasses were thick and as Effie's gaze hung on Destry's eyes, she noticed that the glasses made his eyes look abnormally small. The more she looked at him, the more she felt that her scrutiny was making him uncomfortable.

"Hold up your arms," he said.

Effie lifted one arm then the other. Destry was so gentle as he washed each one then wiped peroxide across the scrapes. The sting made her jerk her arms back a little but if he noticed, he paid it no attention.

"Lay down on your stomach," he said, placing a cold, dripping wet cloth in Effie's hand and lifting it to her face. When she gave him a questioning look, he continued, "I need to look at your back and with this light and the angle, it would be best if you lay down on your stomach."

A brief moment of panic shot through her mind and her face paled. What if Destry took one look at her back and saw that it was not injured as bad as she had made it out to be? She shook her head.

"It's—it's fine for now," she stammered.

Destry let out a deep sigh. "Look," he said, "I don't know when Jimmy is gonna come back but you can be damn sure that when he does, he ain't gonna let me do anything for your back. At the very least, it needs to be cleaned out with antiseptic so it don't get infected. Right now could be your last chance to let me see it."

Reluctantly, Effie laid down on her stomach in front of Destry. He was right. Even if it was a minor cut, an infection could be bad. Very carefully, he took hold of her shirt and tried to peel it away from the wound. There was too much dried blood and it was almost like someone had melted the shirt to her skin, it was stuck so hard. Every time he tugged on the shirt, Effie whimpered. It was like razors digging into her skin.

Finally, Effie cried out. "Stop! Pleathe sthop! It isn't going to justh come off. You need to use thomething like a damp towel to soak it and moisten the dried blood so it will release it."

Destry struggled to his feet, grabbed another towel, ran it under the water pump, then returned to Effie's side.

"This is gonna be cold," he warned, then carefully placed the dripping towel on her back.

Her body jerked from the shock of the sudden feeling of ice cold water. After a few moments, though, the moisture started to loosen the blood and Destry was able to peel the shirt away from the wound.

Destry grunted when he realized how well Effie's suggestion worked. "You're pretty smart," he muttered.

Instead of answering, she just smiled slightly and rested her forehead on her arm. With Effie's shirt pulled back, Destry was free to clean up the actual wound.

The crusty blood wiped away to reveal a jagged gash on Effie's back. Destry frowned at what was in front of him. He had been hoping that the cut would not be deep enough to need stitches. It was quite a gash, though, and his best guess was that it did need them. He had never had them himself and really was not sure how to go about putting them in.

Destry fished around in the first aid box and pulled out a small bottle of peroxide and a square of gauze. After twisting off the cap and tipping the bottle to get some of the cool liquid on the piece of gauze, Destry paused and stared at the side of Effie's head for a moment. It was the least injured side of her face and with her hair fanned across her face, it looked almost as if nothing had happened to her.

The hesitation caused Effie to turn her head and catch Destry looking at her. For a moment, he just kept staring. When it sank in that she was looking back, Destry jumped and immediately pressed the gauze in his hand to the wound on Effie's back.

The peroxide on the gash fizzed up. The gouge was very tender and the pressure combined with the stinging from the peroxide made Effie jerk away from Destry. He grabbed hold of her and pulled her back toward him.

"I know it hurts but I don't know when Jimmy is gonna be back," he said. He pulled a short, thick stick out of his breast pocket. "I don't have time to mess around with you movin' around because of a little pain. Put this stick in your mouth, Cookie, and just bite down on it when it hurts."

Effie took the stick from his hand. She looked down at it for a moment then cautiously raised her hand to her mouth. It hurt just to open her mouth wide enough to put the stick between her teeth. How was it possible that biting down on it would help her make it through what Destry was going to do to her? It just seemed like there would be more pain than she could handle. In the end, Effie did as she was told and braced for what was coming.

Destry paused for only a moment before picking up the needle. Instead of pressing it to Effie's back, he removed the glass globe from the top of the lantern. Slowly, he passed the needle through the flame several times. When he was satisfied that it was sterile, he replaced the globe.

The thought of pressing the needle and thread through Effie's flesh made his stomach churn. Destry nervously looked from the needle in his hand, to the wound on Effie's back, to the darkness beyond the door. For all he knew, Jimmy was going to come walking through that door in any moment.

With one last deep breath, Destry gabbed hold of the loose end of the thread with one hand and pressed the tip of the needle into the skin on one side of the gash and out the other side. As he did, Effie bit down on the stick. For a moment, it seemed like the pain that shot through her mouth and jaw was worse than the pain in her back. She let loose a throaty scream. She spit the stick from her mouth and it rolled toward the door.

The scream startled Destry so much that he jumped, giving the thread a little tug. Immediately, he opened his hands and dropped the needle and thread then muttered a quick, "Sorry."

Even Harry was startled by the scream and he came waddling to the door. He stood with a confused look on his face.

"Whatcha doin'?" he asked.

"What does it look like I'm doin'?"

Harry gave Destry a funny look. "I thought Jimmy said we wasn't supposed to do no docterin' on her."

"Jimmy says a lot of things, don't he," Destry grumbled as he pressed the needle through Effie's skin again. This time her scream was not as loud. "Listenin' to Jimmy is what got us into this mess, isn't it?"

Harry gave him a look like he didn't know what to say. He wanted to agree with Destry but if he did, that would be going against his own brother. How could he go against someone who had told him what to do his entire life—his own flesh and blood.

"Harry," said Destry, piercing Effie's skin again. "Sometimes you gotta think for yourself." He paused for a moment to tie off the stitch and Harry just stood looking at him. "When are you gonna learn that Jimmy ain't always right? Look how many time he's been in trouble. Heck, look how many times *we've* been in trouble because of him. I know he don't see where some of the stuff he did was wrong. He wouldn't have gone to jail if he wasn't wrong, though. The world isn't like he says, Harry. They don't put you in jail 'cause they don't like you. They put you in jail 'cause you done somethin' wrong."

Harry frowned, a deep crease forming between his eyebrows. "You act like he's always wrong and you always know what's right," he snapped then turned to go back out on the porch. "He ain't always wrong and you don't always know what's right."

Before long, Destry was done stitching up Effie and he pulled some bandages out to cover up the crooked line on her back. Her eyes were wet with tears but at least it was over. Never in her life had Effie experienced so much pain.

"Harry," Destry called out.

No answer.

Destry knew he was out there sulking so he said, "Go out to the car and get a clean shirt for Cookie. This one has blood all over it and it's torn pretty bad.

Still no answer.

"Please, Harry—Please."

Finally, Effie heard Harry get up and walk across the porch and down the steps. A minute later, she heard him coming back.

He stood in the doorway and said, "Can't find no key for the trunk and there ain't no clean shirts in the car."

Destry had cleaned up the first aid kit and was putting it on a shelf near the door. He turned and looked at Harry. "What do you mean no keys?" he asked.

"You heard me. Ain't no keys unless you got 'em in yer pocket or something."

Destry's head sank with the thought of what that could mean.

"What now?" asked Harry.

"Don't you get it?"

"Get what?"

"If the keys ain't in the car and neither one of us has 'em, it means Jimmy has 'em."

"So?"

"So??"

"Yeah. That's what I said. *So?*"

"So it means that one, Jimmy don't trust you to watch Cookie alone and two, he don't trust me to keep her here either. You know how he is when he gets suspicious or don't trust people."

"Oh," said Harry, his head dropping too.

Destry drew in a deep breath. "You got any semi-clean shirts still hangin' around here?"

"I don't know," said Harry. "Maybe there's one in the trunk." He picked up the lantern near Effie and walked over to an old trunk sitting in the back corner of the cabin. A few minutes later, he rejoined Destry with a huge flannel shirt hanging in his hand.

Destry grabbed it and hulled it to his nose, inhaling deeply. He wrinkled up his nose. "This is the best you got here?" he asked.

"Yep. Best, cleanest shirt I got here."

"I guess it will have to do then. Help me get her up so we can get the shirt changed."

Effie was laying on the floor, motionless, her shirt still pulled up in the back. As long as she didn't move, her back just throbbed instead of burned with pain. The men stood on either side of her, each of them grabbing hold under an arm.

"Ok, Cookie," said Destry. "We're gonna get you into a cleaner shirt now. We just gotta get you standing up first."

When they lifted, Effie whimpered but forced herself to stand. When the men let go, Effie swayed a little then stepped back and her knees started to bend. Destry grabbed hold of her arm and quickly pulled her back up straight.

"You're gonna have to stand in front of her and I'll stand behind her and switch the shirts," he said to Harry.

Harry moved around in front of Effie and placed one of his mighty hands under each of her armpits and held her up. Destry dropped the clean shirt to the floor and pulled her soiled shirt up and over her head. With a little effort, he managed to work the shirt off her one arm at a time. As soon as the shirt was off, Harry's eyes fell to Effie's bra. Sweat began beading on his forehead and he licked his lips. He just couldn't tear his eyes from her chest. It was suddenly as if the temperature in the cabin was rising and the heat was spreading through his body. Destry was fighting to put the flannel shirt onto Effie but not even that took Harry's eyes away from her chest. It was as if he didn't care if Destry could see how turned on seeing Effie like that was making him.

"Christ," said Destry, shaking his head in disbelief. "She's had the crap kicked out of her by your brother and all you can think about is what's going on in your pants."

"Well I can't help it if she ain't bad to look at."

Destry was buttoning up the shirt. "Well just keep your pants zipped up cause you ain't doin' to her what you did to Angie. We ain't gonna repeat any of that. Not while I'm around, we ain't."

Aware that resting her back against him would probably hurt Effie, he still slid his arms under hers and took over holding her up. "Clean off one of the mattresses," he told Harry.

"I thought you just said we wasn't gonna do none of that to her."

"Just because we lay her down on a mattress, it don't mean that we gotta do anything to her Harry." Destry gave him a dirty look.

"Well ya don't have to get all angry with me ya know." Harry glared back.

"Just clean off a mattress so she doesn't have to lay on the floor. She's startin' to get heavy and I don't know how much longer I can hold her up."

"Fine," said Harry. As soon as he was done clearing off the mattress, he helped Destry lower her down. With Effie laying on the mattress, the men went out to sit on the porch until Jimmy came back.

"She sure was tired, huh," said Harry.

"I don't think it was because she was tired."

"Well if she wasn't tired, how come she was like that?

"I think it was too much pain for her to handle. She just went kind of loopy cause it hurt too much."

"Well why would she get like that if it hurt so much?" asked Harry.

"She just did, Harry." Destry sighed.

"I don't get it, though."

"Harry."

"Yeah?"

"Can we just drop this now? I haven't had hardly any sleep in over 24 hours and I'm gettin' pretty tired myself. I don't know when Jimmy is comin' back but you can be sure when he does, he's not gonna let me sleep. He's gonna have some sort of crappy project for me to do while he sleeps. Let me catch a few winks now, OK?

Harry agreed. "Yeah. I guess I could used a few too."

Finally, both of them were silent. The sound of the water running in the river was all they could hear. That was more than enough to lull Destry into a deep sleep, even if he was sitting up. Harry wasn't too far behind.

Chapter 15

Bright headlights illuminated the front porch, rousing Destry and Harry. Even though they were blinded by the light, the truck had a familiar rumble and they knew at once that Jimmy had finally returned. Destry shielded his eyes with one hand and tried to look down at his watch to see what time it was.

Inside the cabin, Effie, too, had been roused by the sound of the truck and the bright light shining through the open door. Her mind raced. Instead of laying in the middle of the filthy floor with her wrists tied, she was cleaned up, unbound and resting on a mattress. She pushed herself up into a sitting position and sat as still as she could, listening.

The headlights finally snapped off and the rumbling engine ceased. After a door opened and slammed shut, Effie could hear heavy footsteps coming closer to the cabin. She sucked in her breath and held it; hoping for the best but expecting the worst.

"Hey there, boys," came a heavy voice.

Then Destry spoke. "Where the heck ya been, Jimmy? Ya been gone hours."

"I went to the hardware then I went to the bar for a while. There's always time to wet yer whistle and besides, I wanted to see some of the ol' guys from around here. You gotta have yer priorities, Destry." There was a pause then Effie heard him go back to retrieve something from the truck.

So he had been out drinking. Effie could not help but wonder if this had worked to her advantage or not. On one hand, it gave Destry the time to tend to her wounds. On the other, though, she knew that Jimmy was capable of doing things that were much more horrible than if he had come home sober.

When Jimmy started climbing the porch steps, the bench that Harry was sitting on creaked as he leaned forward and asked, "Whatcha got there, Jimmy?"

"Just some stuff," Jimmy said, reaching his hand into a bag and giving the men a glimpse of a thick silver chain.

"Jimmy," began Destry, staring at the bag, "what do you plan to do with that?"

Instead of answering, Jimmy snorted and stumbled into the cabin. Just inside the door, he stood for a moment, swaying slightly. Effie pressed herself against the wall, ignoring the pain in her back from the pressure. Her eyes were fixed on Jimmy's face and the ugly smile of malicious delight on his lips.

Finally, Jimmy walked the rest of the way into the cabin without a word. Harry and Destry came in behind him and stood watching in confused silence. Even though they knew the bag had to be heavy from the chain, they both jumped when Jimmy dropped it on the floor next to the center support pole with a loud thunk.

Jimmy dropped to his knees next to the bag then reached in and began pulling out the heavy chain. One end, he wrapped around the center pole and snapped a padlock through the links to hold it in place. The other end of the chain already had a thick cuff attached. He opened and closed it a few times, testing the hinge. When he was satisfied with it, he dropped it on the floor then laid down another padlock next to it. He got up and walked over to stand in front of Effie. The blood drained from her face.

"Get up and take off yer clothes," he growled.

She gave a startled gasp and her gaze flashed from Jimmy to Destry with a pleading look in her eyes. She did not like being naked alone and the thought of being so exposed in front of someone like Jimmy as well as two other men seemed like a nightmare. She just sat there and did not move a muscle.

Destry broke the silence. "Come on, Jimmy," he said. "There ain't no reason for her to take her clothes off. Just—"

Jimmy held up a hand to silence him. His eyes bore into Effie. "I told ya to get up and take yer damn clothes off. Ya better do it now! Don't you dare make me tell ya to do it again or you'll be sorry I had to."

Effie gave Destry one more look, begging him to do something but the look in his eyes told her he was not going to argue with Jimmy. Fearing that

Jimmy would beat her again, she slowly got to her feet. She kicked off her shoes then peeled off her socks. Her heart was pounding in her ears and it was getting harder and harder to breathe. Very slowly, she brought her hands up to unbuckle her jeans. She glanced at the men then turned her back to them before sliding her pants down.

Suddenly, a hand on her shoulder spun her around. Jimmy was in her face. "There ain't no reason to turn away from us," he said. "Yer just a woman. You ain't got nothing we ain't seen before and I didn't tell ya to turn around!"

Effie began trembling and she suddenly had the feeling of spiders crawling up her back. She dropped her eyes to the floor. She couldn't look at the sick expression of happiness on Jimmy's face any longer. Finally he pushed her away.

"Jimmy, really," Destry stammered.

Jimmy turned to look at him. "I've had just about enough of your bull-shit, Destry. I don't know what's up with you but I'm pretty sick of yer pretendin' to be a good guy all of a sudden. If you don't like the way I do things, you got to feet and you can hit the road. Otherwise, just shut yer mouth and let me handle this."

Destry stepped away from Jimmy and for a moment, Effie thought he was going to leave. Terror filled her heart. She wanted to cry out and beg him to stay. As it turned out, she didn't need to. He just shut his mouth and stood a few feet from Jimmy like a well trained dog.

Jimmy turned back around to look at Effie again. He folded his arms in front of his chest. "Ok, Cookie," he said. "You can finish takin' off yer clothes now."

Effie kept her eyes cast downward as she slid her pants to the floor. Her hands were shaking as she moved them up to start unbuttoning the shirt. When she got to the last button, she just stood there holding the two sides of the shirt together. She was desperate not to expose her body to the men.

Instead of telling her to remove it, Jimmy stepped forward and yanked the shirt open then off. He dropped it on the floor then stood back to study her body. "For a fat chick, ya ain't too bad looking," he said. "I'll bet if ya lost some of them rolls of fat, ya'd even be a little good looking."

Destry had finally had enough of Jimmy and walked out of the cabin. He didn't leave, though. Effie heard the bench seat creak as he sat down on the porch and she was relieved that he had not left. So far, Destry was still her best chance for sympathy.

Jimmy was growing impatient with Effie. Instead of waiting for her to remove her bra and panties herself, he just ripped them off and tossed them on the floor with her other clothes. Never had she ever felt so exposed. Instantly, one arm went up to hide her breasts and the other down to cover her genitals. Jimmy back-handed Effie, causing her to stumble backwards.

"Don't disrespect me by coverin' up yer body. If I wanted ya to hide all that fat, I wouldn't a had ya take all of yer damn clothes off. From now on, Cookie, yer gonna do everything I say when I say it. I ain't gonna play like I'm a nice guy no more. Just play my way and you'll get along jus' fine."

He waved his hand at Harry and he stepped up to Jimmy's side. "Grab me that cuff and the lock next to it."

"What's it for, Jimmy?" asked Harry as he went to do as he was told.

"That, Harry, is so that Miss Cookie here don't get no ideas and try to run away."

"Oh." Harry had a funny look on his face. "You gonna clamp this thing 'round her wrist or somethin'?"

"Somethin' like that. See, the small ones they had was way to small for her fat wrist. Most of the rest was way too big for it. I figured this one could go around her ankle. If she's got that 'round her ankle, ain't no way she can run away from here and blab that big fat mouth of hers about what we did back at home."

"Boy, Jimmy, I sure wouldn't know what to do if you weren't here. If she went and told people what we done, we'd probably be in some trouble, huh?"

"Well, you don't need to worry about that, baby brother. I'm takin' care of ya just like I always do."

"What if she breaks the chain or somethin', Jimmy?"

Jimmy laughed lightly. "There ain't no way she's breakin' this chain. Even if she did, she wouldn't go runnin' nowhere. She ain't got no clothes on."

Jimmy wrapped his arms around Effie and pulled her to him, squeezing as tight as he could. "Clamp that 'round her ankle," he said.

Effie tried to hold her ankles together to keep Harry from placing the cuff around one. The more she tried to fight it, though, the tighter Jimmy squeezed. "Remember what I told you about doin' the things I tell you to do," he whispered into her ear.

Not seeing any other options, she gave in and let Harry clamp the cold metal around her ankle. It wasn't too tight yet it wasn't loose enough to slide off over her foot. Effie could tell right away that it wasn't going to be the least bit comfortable. The bottom edge dug into her skin. There was still a lot of slack in the chain and that meant that she could probably make it as far as a step or two out onto the porch.

Jimmy saw her looking at the doorway and it was as if he could read her mind. "Don't ya ever set one toe out on that porch. I don't even want to see ya standin' in the doorway. Yer place is in this cabin and that is where yer gonna stay. Yer my property now and yer gonna do every little thing I say woman."

Effie began to tremble. The only comfort she had was that Jimmy was standing so close that there was no way he or Harry could possibly see her exposed body very well.

"Aw, Cookie," he said. "You ain't got no reason to shiver like that."

"Harry," he shouted over his shoulder. "Go outside and get some wood for the stove and get a fire going. I don't like my Cookie cold."

Harry gave Jimmy a look as if his balloon had been burst. Apparently, he had other things he wanted to do. Instead of arguing with Jimmy, though, he went to do as he was told.

"Close the door behind you," Jimmy called out as Harry stepped out onto the porch. "Me and Cookie need a little privacy. You can just sit the wood by the door and wait out there with Destry 'til I tell you to come back in.

Effie's blood ran cold and her face became a mask of terror. There was not a doubt in her mind what Jimmy intended to do to her. She began to beg.

"Please, Jimmy...Please...Just let me go...I promise I will never speak a word of any of this to anyone...," her voice trailed off as tears began to form in her eyes.

"Cookie, ya ain't got no reason to be upset." He paused for a moment. "Yer pretty lucky if ya think about it. Bein' a fat chick, ya probably ain't never had any kind of a boyfriend who would pay ya any kind of attention when it came to sex before, I'll bet.

When Effie did not answer, Jimmy continued speaking. "Ya know what kind of cookies I like, Miss Cookie?"

No answer.

"I like the kind with the thick, gooey cream on the inside." He smiled suggestively. "You know how they get that gooey cream inside those cookies? They take this tube and they slide it into the cookie and just inject that cream right into the cookie. It's true," he said as if she had told him she didn't believe him. "I saw it on that food channel on television one night."

Finally, his grip on Effie loosened and he stepped back from her. When she moved her arms to cover herself again, Jimmy's hands shot out and caught her wrists, holding them away from her body.

"Tsk, tsk, tsk," he said. "I know it's hard to get some things through that fat head of yers but ya gotta learn fast that it ain't very respectful of ya to cover that body when I told not to. Don't make me correct ya again or the next place you'll find yerself is in the ground next to that dead whore."

As hard as it was, Effie stood there with her hands at her sides and eyes cast down. The last thing she wanted was to end up like Angie. Even if she had slept around or had not been the best person, she deserved better than to be buried in a shallow grave in the woods somewhere. She had to have parents or someone somewhere that cared about her. Someone would miss her and Effie had to believe that person would want better for her. There had to be a way to outsmart Jimmy, Harry and Destry and get out of there alive. Besides, if it had been so easy for them to rape and murder one woman then turn around and kidnap another, how many times had they done this before? How many times would they do it again?

Chapter 16

Jimmy grabbed hold of Effie's chin and forced her to look into his eyes. "What the hell is wrong with ya? Ya ain't been listening to a word I said! I ought-ta beat the crap outta ya right now!"

"I'm—I'm sorry, Jimmy," she whispered, trying to look down again. "It won't happen again."

"What was that?"

"I—I said, it won't happen again. I promise I'll listen better."

He gave her a curious look. "Well, I guess I'll let it slip this one time. Mind ya, if it happens again, I ain't gonna be so nice."

"Now," he said, "I wanna make a cream filled Cookie, if ya know what I mean.

"Yes, Jimmy," she said stepping toward him.

"That's better, Cookie." His eyes roamed freely up and down Effie's body. "Take my clothes off."

Effie took another step closer to him and it took every ounce of willpower she had just to keep from wrinkling up her nose at the stench of stale beer and horrible body odor. As she did so, she became uncomfortably aware of the cuff around her ankle. With that thing on, there was no running away so she had no choice but to do exactly as Jimmy said.

Her stomach contracted into a tight ball and she swallowed as she raised her trembling hands to undo the buttons on Jimmy's shirt. One by one, she slipped the buttons through the button holes and pulled the shirt apart. Thick brown hair covered his chest and disappeared down into the top of his pants.

As Effie pulled off the shirt and dropped it to the floor, he wrapped his arms around and placed his hands on her butt, pulling her against him. He ran his tongue back and forth between his lips then sealed them to Effie's. She hadn't expected the horrible flavor and it made her shudder. Jimmy misinterpreted this as excitement. He ground his hips against her, forcing her to feel how aroused he was.

When Jimmy finally broke the kiss, he moved to suck her ear into his mouth. "I got a big ol' surprise for ya, Cookie," he whispered. "Just take Daddy's pant's off, baby, and we can fill that cookie up with warm, gooey cream just like I like."

The knot in her stomach twisted tighter and tighter. She had to try to shut the thought of what was happening to her out of her mind. But how? The more she tried to think of other things, the harder it became.

Very slowly, Effie tugged on Jimmy's belt until it came unbuckled and revealed the snap on the front of his jeans. That too she tugged on. As it popped apart, the zipper slid down and she was faced with pulling his pants down to reveal dirty, gray underwear. As she bent to pull his pant-legs off, he hooked his thumbs into his underwear at his hips and slid them off as well.

Effie closed her eyes and turned away to avoid looking at his hard penis. Jimmy didn't want her to miss seeing it, though, and he thrust his hips at her, poking her in the side of the face with it. He grabbed her head with both hands and turned it straight toward him.

"Open yer eyes, Cookie," he said. "Open 'em and look at what ya done to daddy. If ya don't do it, daddy is gonna have to punish ya like the bad little girl that you are."

She slowly opened her eyes and looked at the rigid penis just inches from her face. She quickly looked away again but when she did, Jimmy slapped her in the side of the head.

"I didn't say ya could look away, did I?"

Effie's eyes snapped back to what was in front of her. This time, though, she tried to look past it. Her eyes focused on the thick mass of hair just above it. Jimmy thought she was staring at his penis and his mouth curled into a dirty little grin.

"Little Cookie likes looking at daddy down there, don't she?" he said. "I'll bet you've looked at boys' wee-wee's at school haven't you, Cookie?"

She did not answer. There was no way she would willingly play a part in his sick fantasy. Jimmy just went right on speaking. "It's OK, baby. You don't have to say anything. Daddy knows that's what dirty little girls like you like to do. I'll bet ya even kissed some of those boys' little peckers before." He stroked the side of her head with one hand.

"Show daddy how you kissed those boys down there," he said pressing his penis against her lips. "Come on. Open up and show daddy how ya do it. I have to know if yer doin' it right. Besides, ya got daddy all excited like a bad little girl and if ya don't help daddy take care of it, it could hurt me real bad. Ya don't want to hurt daddy, do ya?"

Effie refused to part her lips. She just pursed her lips all the more.

Jimmy's voice became angry. "Do what daddy says or I will bend you over my knee and spank ya like the bad little girl that ya are and then you will do what I told ya to do in the first place"

When Effie still refused to open her mouth, Jimmy took a handful of her hair and yanked her to her feet and over toward the old bed in the corner. With one swift movement, he tossed the blankets and everything else off the bed and onto the floor. Effie knew what was coming next and she fought to pull out of his grip even if it meant getting beaten senseless. Jimmy's hand was too tangled into her hair and she couldn't get away. In a split second, his other hand connected with her face.

He sat down on the edge of the bed and yanked on her hair to pull her down to lay across his lap. His free hand rose and came down on her exposed bottom so many times she lost count. Each time she writhed less and less. When Effie finally stopped moving, Jimmy stood up, tossed her onto the bed and climbed on top of her.

The violence had aroused him even more and he forced himself inside Effie. She opened her mouth to scream but no sound came out. It felt as though he was splitting her in half. Jimmy just kept pounding and pounding away and at last he froze, moaning as his penis emptied into her. He just laid there on top of her, sweating.

Finally, after what seemed like an eternity, he crawled off her and pushed her to the floor beside the bed. He laid on his back, staring at the ceiling for a few minutes, ignoring Effie completely. She had curled into a ball and was not moving. When he got up after a little while, he just stepped over her and walked over to the water pump. He worked it up and down a few times. Then, as cool water ran out of the pump, Jimmy ran a hand through the flow and splashed it against his face.

"You can come in now," he shouted.

When the door swung open, Harry lumbered in, carrying a load of firewood in his arms. "Sure sounded like you had some fun," he said.

"Where's Destry?"

Harry chuckled as he opened to old stove to start a fire. "He got mad about somethin' right after I went out to get some wood and he said he was goin' off for a walk so he didn't have to listen to ya." He laughed a little harder. "Truth be told, I think he's just jealous of you bein' the first one to do Cookie."

"Screw him," said Jimmy. "He'll be back later for his share of the prize. In the meantime, Harry, I'm kinda tired, if ya know what I mean. I'm gonna take a little nap. I want ya to keep an eye on Cookie."

He walked over to the pile of his clothes, found his underwear and pulled them on. Jimmy scooped up his jeans next and dug into the pocket, pulling out the keys to Effie's car. He tossed them to Harry.

"Go out and get all of her clothes out of the car. While yer watchin' her, I want ya to burn every last stitch of 'em so she can't get her fat hands on a single one. That'll make sure that she never runs if she ever gets loose. Ain't no way a fat whale like her would run away naked."

Jimmy walked over toward the bed and picked up a pillow from the floor. He tossed it on the bed then flopped down on top of it and drifted off to sleep with ease as if he had done nothing wrong. It was almost as if he believed he was right in forcing himself on Effie.

Chapter 17

Harry was kneeling near the little, metal door on the front of the stove, his face lit up by the glowing fire within. Little beads of sweat trickled from his brow. Every few minutes, he would prod the blaze with a long, thick stick then reach down to the pile of clothing next to him and toss in another piece. The pile had started out as a mountain and when he finally wadded up the last shirt to toss it into the licking flames, his entire body seemed to let out a sigh of relief. Before that shirt left his fingers, though, the cabin door burst open and he spun around to see who it was. He had been staring into the dancing flames for so long, all he saw was a purple blur in the darkness. Destry, however, could see Harry just fine.

Destry's eyes flicked from Harry, to Jimmy, to the crumpled body on the floor. "What the hell happened here?" he roared.

Harry's grip tightened on the shirt in his hands as he fell backward. Jimmy's eyes snapped open and he turned to look at Destry.

"It don't matter what happened here," Jimmy said. "It ain't none of yer worry."

"It's not my worry? Not my worry??"

Jimmy got to his feet. "You heard me right, Destry."

"It just wasn't enough to beat her and chain her up was it?"

"Cookie's just a worthless woman. It ain't like it matters."

Destry clenched his teeth. "Does the word rape mean anything to either of you?"

"That word was made up by fags who either didn't know how to screw or they couldn't get what they want from a whore. I know what I'm doing. I'll use a woman however I want, whenever I want. The only person who has to worry about what went on here is me."

"That's where you're wrong. Harry and me are part of this entire thing too. It doesn't matter if one person beat and raped her or if all of us did. We're all gonna get in just as much trouble. Don't you understand that we are all gonna get in trouble here? Everything you do to her just makes it worse for us."

"First off, the only thing Harry has to worry about is doin' what I tell him to do. Second, all *you* gotta worry about is what I tell *you* to do." Jimmy stepped over Effie and stood nose to nose with Destry. "Long as both you do what I tell ya, ain't no one has to worry about trouble at all."

"Look at her," Destry said, pointing at Effie. "You took all her clothes, you raped her and you beat her then tossed her on the floor. You keep that up and she is gonna die. If she dies, it's called murder. If she dies, we are gonna get it for two murders. Do you have any idea how long they are gonna send us away to prison for doin' somethin' like that?"

"We ain't gonna get caught for even one murder unless ya keep blabbin' that big, fat mouth of yers, Destry. Ya act like ya ain't even grateful for nothin' I ever done for ya." Destry seemed shaken by his words. "Just shut that mouth of yers. I don't want to hear ya say anything about murder or killin' anyone ever again!"

He turned around and looked directly at Harry. "What the hell is your problem?" he snarled. "Didn't I tell you to get all them things burned?"

Harry's stare was frozen on Jimmy. He could not seem to find the words so he just shook his head.

"Well then what the hell are ya doing with that shirt in yer hand? Ya saving it as a souvenir or something?"

Harry looked at the balled up shirt in his hand as if he didn't know where it had come from. As quick as a young boy who is afraid of getting cooties, he tossed it into the fire then wiped his hand on his pants.

"You're burnin' all her clothes?" Destry asked.

Jimmy turned back toward him, a cool look of confidence on his face. He puffed his chest out and flexed his muscles and wagging his head back and forth, he said, "It's all part of the plan. I know exactly how to handle this so you can just back off or get out."

The veins were popping out on Destry's temples and his face was turning bright red. "I don't know what kind of plan you got but you're gonna get us all in trouble."

"Destry, you been actin' funny since we left home. I think you're gettin' some of that repented up anger or something. Or maybe it's just been so long since you got any, you got that repented up sex tension." A sickening smile curled onto his lips. He stepped back and with a sweeping motion, he pointed at Effie. "I won't mind if ya do her. Might do ya some good. Might make ya calm down some."

"Screw you, Jimmy."

"Not me. Screw Cookie. I'll bet she won't even put up a fight when ya do her."

Destry practically hissed as he looked at Jimmy. "You're a sick man, Jimmy, and you need help."

"I already helped myself—To Cookie." Jimmy let loose a maniacal cackle.

"You really are sick."

Jimmy frowned. "I'm sick of listenin' to you tonight, Destry. I already told ya, if you don't like the way I'm doing things, get the hell outta my cabin. Just get the hell out and don't come back until ya had some time to cool down and come to yer senses."

Instead of arguing back, Destry stomped over and grabbed the truck keys off the table then flew out the door.

"What we gonna do, Jimmy?" asked Harry. He was still sitting on the floor with a look of horror on his face.

Jimmy looked at him like he was crazy. "What we gonna do about what?"

"Abou-about Destry. What if he goes to the cops or somethin'?"

"He ain't goin' to the cops, ya tard." Jimmy shook his head in disbelief. "Destry's just mad 'cause he didn't get to do her first. He'll calm down after a while and come back. There is a naked woman layin' on the floor of our cabin. How could he resist comin' back to that? He'll be back."

Harry gulped. "What if he ain't mad about that? What if he does go get the cops? We're gonna get in a lot of trouble like he says, ain't we? We're gonna get sent to prison for a long time."

Jimmy reached out his hand for his brother to take and helped him to his feet. He wrapped his arm around Harry. "I'm yer big brother, ain't I?" he said.

Harry nodded.

"Ya just gotta trust me then, don't ya? I would never do nothin' that would get my big, baby brother in trouble. I ain't never steered ya wrong before and I ain't gonna do it now. Ya just gotta trust me. I know what I'm doing. Ya do what I say and ya won't never have nothin' to worry about."

"I guess yer right," Harry said, calming down a little bit.

"Dang right, I'm right," said Jimmy. "Now you just get some sleep, baby brother. We gotta get that generator out and runnin' in the mornin' or we're gonna have to live with them damn flickerin' flames and we ain't gonna have the little refridgenator to use. Now I don't know about you but I like my beer cold outta the fridgenator. Them coolers don't seem to make things cold and even when things in them start out cold, they don't never stay cold for a long time."

He patted Harry on the shoulder then pushed him toward his mattress. "Get some sleep."

"Ok," said Harry cautiously, walking toward his bed to do exactly as he was told.

Chapter 18

The next morning, Jimmy got out of bed and stepped over Effie who was still curled up on the floor. He grabbed some food and crammed it into his mouth then walked around the cabin, making no attempt to be quiet. When he spotted a cooler near Harry's bed, he reached into the icy water and pulled out a can of beer.

Jimmy stood over Harry, letting the water from the cooler drip from the can onto Harry's forehead. "Hey!" he yelled. "Get yer lard-ass outta bed. We gotta get that generator up and running."

Harry sat up, rubbing the sleep out of his eyes and the water from his forehead. "Mm-k. I'll be right out," he said as he stood and arched his back. His eyes roamed the room then stopped on Effie. "She OK?"

"Who cares. Just get outside and help me get that thing going."

"Well, I—I was jus' asking. I know she's just a woman and all so it don't matter none. I just wanted to know is all. Sheesh. What put ya in such a bad mood this morning?"

Jimmy cast a dirty look at him. "Well if yer so worried and ya wanna know how she is so bad, go poke her or something. Do whatever ya want for all I care. Just get yer ass outside and give me a hand as soon as yer done. I don't want this project takin' all day and I know it's gonna take some tinkerin' to get that generator runnin' right."

Harry just stood looking at Jimmy until he stormed out of the cabin, beer in hand. With Jimmy gone, he crept over to Effie's side and got down on his hands and knees. He leaned forward and listened in silence for a few seconds. When his ears picked up a low, steady rhythm out of the still air, he was satisfied and got up to join his brother outside.

Forty-five minutes later, a loud buzz broke the silence and the two came bouncing through the door in triumph. Jimmy pulled the cord on the naked bulb hanging from the ceiling, clicking the light on and off. After that, he walked over to an ancient refrigerator that sat next to the stove and reached around behind it. Moments later, it too was humming. Immediately, Harry pulled the cooler across the room and started moving beer from it to the fridge.

"We done pretty good, didn't we Jimmy? That didn't take half as long as I thought it would."

"I told ya to trust me, didn't I?" Jimmy said.

"I never doubted ya for a second."

Neither of them spoke for a moment as Jimmy went over to look out the window. Harry cleared his throat. He was looking at Effie again. "She's OK, ya know," he said.

Jimmy turned and gave him a funny look. "What?"

"W-well she ain't dead, that is. I uh, checked her before I went out to help ya."

"Well if she ain't dead, I guess we better get the bitch up so she can make us some proper food, shouldn't we?" he said with an innocent expression. He walked toward the sink, snatching up a bucket on the way. As he worked the leaver up and down, water splashed into the bucket. When it was full, he carried it over and stood looking down at Effie.

"Get up, Cookie," he shouted.

When she did not move, he did not bother to repeat himself. Instead, Jimmy just tipped the bucket until the water poured over her face. In a flash, her eyes snapped open and her body jerked. Her eyes traveled up Jimmy's body and rested on his face. There was no sense in making him angrier just then so she pushed up off the floor.

"I want some food. Get up and make me and Harry something," he said as he walked away from her.

Effie's head felt like it weighed ten pounds and her body ached in places she didn't know existed. She was alive and she was still chained up in the cabin. Slowly, she got up and went to find something to make for the men while she thought about what had happened. The world around her melted away as her thoughts returned to the previous night. The last thing she remembered was Jimmy on top of her pounding away and the feeling that he was ripping her apart. And when he exploded into her and stopped moving, she remembered feeling like she didn't want to live anymore. It was like he had marked his territory by forcing himself on her. A feeling of nausea came over her and she ran to hang her head into the sink.

When she straightened up and wiped the back of her hand across her mouth, the men snickered. She turned to look at Harry but sealed her lips.

"Hurry up with the food, Cookie," said Jimmy. "I wanna eat today."

Effie walked back toward the stove and stirred a bubbling pot of soup. It seemed kind of early in the day for that. Had she put it there? It didn't seem possible but she must have. She must have been so wrapped up in remembering what happened that she didn't even realize what she'd done. She ladled the soup into two bowls and sat them on the table for Jimmy and Harry. Neither one bothered to wash-up. They just sat down at the table and started slurping away. Effie didn't know why but she went and silently kneeled on the floor next to Jimmy. He patted her on the head like a dog.

As soon as Jimmy was done with his soup, he pushed the bowl away and leaned back, his eyes on Effie. He reached out and stroked the side of her face. In a soft, kind voice, he started speaking. "We gotta get some rules into that fat head of yers so ya don't gotta get punished again, Cookie. I don't hafta be a mean guy unless you don't do what I say."

She just looked at him.

"That's a good way to start," Jimmy said calmly. "I don't wanna hear a word outta ya unless one of us asks ya something. And don't you ever—EVER—talk back or question us if we tell ya to do something. Just do what we say."

He looked toward the door. "Now, Cookie," he went on, "I think that chain is long enough, ya can just make it out onto the porch. Don't never let me catch ya even goin' near the door when it's daylight out. It ain't very likely that anyone would ever come back here but I don't wanna chance them seein' ya if they do."

"What about goin' to the bathroom?" piped up Harry.

Jimmy waved his hand at him. "Just quiet yerself, ya twit. I was gettin' to that." He turned his attention back to Effie. "Long as ya do everything we say and ya do all the cookin' and cleanin' and ya keep yer mouth shut, we'll take ya out to the pit mornin' and night so ya can do yer business. If yer real good—and I mean REAL GOOD, we'll take ya down to the river every day or two so you can wash off good. How's that sound to ya, Cookie?" he said and he reached out and pressed her nose. "All ya gotta do is be a good girl."

She stared at him with her mouth hanging open for a moment then she gave the slightest of nods.

"Good," Jimmy said smiling then he got up. "Now I gotta go to town and get some stuff for us. You can just get busy cleanin' this place, Cookie, and you listen to everything that Harry here tells ya to do. Just be a good girl or Harry's gonna have to punish ya."

With that said, Jimmy dug into his pocket and pulled out the keys to Effie's car. He swung them around his finger once then walked out of the cabin whistling.

Effie sat frozen, looking at the door, not sure what to think of what Jimmy had just said to her. For the moment, it looked like he planned to keep her around. She weighed it in her mind but could not decide if that was good or bad. Either way, it wasn't the time to think about it. She shook it off, and tried to figure out a way to make herself less sexually appealing to him yet good enough to keep alive.

After a while, Effie looked up from her spot on the floor. If Jimmy wanted her to clean, she would do it. She looked around the room, trying to figure out where to start first. Should she start at the floor and work up or the walls and windows and work down? One look at the thick dust and grime and she decided to start on the top and work down. Then it came to her. Maybe, just maybe, if she worked hard, cooked great meals and made the cabin cleaner than it had ever been before, Jimmy would want to keep her around. What's more, if she got really filthy doing all that, maybe he wouldn't want to touch her. Quickly, she found a towel and got ready to start cleaning.

"What's the rush, sweet Cookie?"

Damn! Harry was the last thing that Effie wanted to deal with just then. "Your brother told me I have to clean. I'm doing what he told me to do," she said in a voice just above a whisper.

"Well he also told ya that ya gotta do whatever any of us says ya should do."

Effie looked at him blankly. "I heard him say that."

"Well I got needs too," he said, licking his lips and shifting in his chair. "Jimmy ain't the only one who likes the feel of a woman."

"Please, Harry—don't. Don't be like him. You're better than that, aren't you?"

Harry frowned. "You sayin' that my brother ain't good?"

"No! No, no, no. I didn't mean that." Effie gulped. "I just meant that——

Well I meant that a nice guy like you wouldn't, uh, force himself on a lady."

"Oh, I ain't gonna force ya," he said then he patted his lap. "Least I won't force ya to do anything ya don't volunteer to do. Course, if ya don't volunteer, I might have to give ya a spankin' just like the one Jimmy gave you last night."

"But—"

He patted his lap again. "Just come over here and sit down. I wanna get cozy like with ya."

Reluctantly, Effie walked toward him. As soon as she was within arms reach, Harry stuck his arm out to grab hold. She froze in place, trying to will him to leave her alone. Over and over, she mouthed, "Leave me alone and go away. Leave me alone and go away."

If Harry saw her lips moving or understood that she wanted him to stop, he completely ignored it. Instead, he pulled her toward him until he could lay both his hands on her hips and pull her down onto his lap. Effie did not move or relax a muscle. She just sat there on his lap, looking straight ahead, barely breathing.

"Leave me alone and go away. Leave me alone and go away."

"That's it, Cookie," he said as he brushed her hair away from her neck. "I just wanna be friendly with ya." He ran his hands over her shoulders and down her arms.

"Leave me alone and go away. Leave me alone and go away." Had she whispered it out loud that time?

"Stand up and bend across the table, Cookie."

"Don't do that to me. Please, Harry. Please don't."

Harry wrapped his arms around her and squeezed her breasts. "You turn me on, Cookie. Can't you feel what ya do to me?" He bounced her up and down on his lap and to her dismay, she *could* feel how aroused he was getting. "Just get up, spread your legs and lean over the table. I ain't gonna hurt ya."

Effie made no attempt to stand up and Harry seemed to lose patience with her. He pushed her away then stood up behind her, grabbing hold of her wrists. She tried to pull them away but Harry was so much more powerful.

He whispered into her ear. "I ain't gonna let ya go til ya agree to do just what I said."

Effie sealed her lips.

"Just do what I tell ya to, Cookie. I don't wanna have to tie ya to the table but I will. I guarantee that you'll like it a lot more and you'll be way more comfortable if ya do it on yer own. I don't wanna hurt ya, Cookie. Really. Do what I tell ya to do."

A large lump was forming in Effie's throat and every fiber of her being was screaming, "No!" She swallowed that lump back. "I'll do it," she said. It was barely audible.

"What was that, Cookie?" Harry ground his hips against her.

Effie cleared her throat and repeated herself much louder. "I said I'll do it. Now let go of me."

Harry let go of her arms. Effie scowled at him then turned toward the table and bent over it as she was told. Immediately, Harry stepped up to her and with his hands on her hips, he ground his pelvis against her several times. He dropped to his knees. For a minute, Effie wasn't sure what he planned to do then she felt his breath, hot against the inside of her thighs. It traveled up until it was at the crest of her legs and she tried to move away from Harry. He just wrapped his arms around her legs and held her tight. Finally, she felt his nose touch the delicate skin and she couldn't take it.

"Stop, Harry. Please stop. Don't do this to me. You don't have to be like this." Effie began to sob. "Stop, Harry! Stop! Stop! Stop! Don't do to me what you did to her!"

The next thing either of them knew, Harry was flying backward and Destry was yelling at the top of his lungs. "Get outta here, Harry! I don't wanna see you back in this cabin until Jimmy comes back! There ain't gonna be any of this crap goin' on as long as I'm here. We're in enough trouble already. There ain't no reason for you to go makin' it worse!"

Effie slid onto the floor and curled up in a ball under the table, sobbing.

"Jimmy promised me—" Harry scrambled to get to his feet.

"I don't care what he said. He's not here right now. I am and I said there ain't gonna be none of this goin' on when I'm here."

"But I ain't had my turn yet!"

Destry laughed out loud. "What do you think she is?" he said, pointing at Effie. "You think she's a carnival ride or something?"

"But—"

"I don't wanna hear it. Just get out."

Harry shoved his hands in his pockets. "Where the hell am I supposed to go then?"

"I really don't care where you go. Go fishing or wack off in the woods or something. Just go!"

"Fine. I'm gonna tell Jimmy though."

"Go ahead. Do whatever you want. Just get the hell outta the cabin before you do it!"

Harry was mad but he stomped out the door anyway. He could tell that Destry meant business and there was no way he wanted to get in a tangle with him. The few times he had seen Jimmy get in a fight with Destry, Jimmy had come out looking like he got the short end of the stick. And Jimmy could whip him with one arm tied behind his back! No way was he going to tangle with Destry! No way!

Destry got on his hands and knees and crawled under the table next to Effie. He wasn't sure how to go about trying to comfort her. Very gently, he reached out and touched her shoulder, rubbing his hand back and forth.

"He's gone now," he whispered. "It's gonna be OK for now. I'm real sorry he did that to you. I'm real sorry about what Jimmy did last night too."

Effie kept crying and he kept stroking her shoulder.

"I—I know this must be horrible for you. I've been thinkin' a lot. I just want you to know how sorry I am for it all." He hung his head low. "I know that everything we did to you and—" Destry sucked in a deep breath. "—and—and—Angie—I know everything we did to both of you was wrong. It probably don't help to hear me say I'm sorry."

He just looked at her in silence for a few minutes. Effie stopped crying and lifted her head to look at him through wet eyelashes.

"I just want you to know, Cookie, if I could go back, I wouldn't have any part of this right from the get-go. I'll admit that I've done some not so good stuff in the past but I never done nothing even half so bad as this before. I was there with Jimmy, though, and I was part of it and I didn't try to stop him from hurtin' Angie. I'm kinda stuck in a bad situation now because of it, see."

Effie spoke up. "Why don't you just let me go while both of them are out?"

"I wish I could but I can't do that," Destry said, shaking his head. "I don't wanna go to prison and I know you'll go straight to the cops. Besides, I owe Jimmy and Harry too much to send either one of them to prison."

"But they are the reason you are in this situation."

"You just don't know them like I do. They might not be great guys all of the time but they can be good friends if you get to know them."

"What difference does that make? They took a woman's life. What about her family? What could they have possible done that erases a murder?"

"They saved my life is what they done."

Effie looked into his eyes and just blinked a few times.

"It was when we were kids. See, we were out huntin' and I thought I'd go by the river to see if I could see any deer along there. The leaves were kind of slippery and before I knew it, I was down in the river instead of up on the bank. The current was movin' pretty fast and I wasn't such a great swimmer back then. Anyway, they musta heard me callin' because next thing I knew, Jimmy was in the river with me and Harry was up on the bank with a rope. They pulled me outta that river and up the bank. I woulda died if it wasn't for them."

"So they saved your life. That's great. But they killed Angie. Wouldn't you agree that killing someone more than cancels out having saved one life?"

"Cookie, I can't be part of sendin' Jimmy to prison. He went to jail once for assaulting someone. He was real unhappy there—depressed even. If one of your friends had saved your life, you wouldn't turn around and repay them by taking part in sending them to prison, would you?"

"Actually, I would. If my friends had done anything half as wrong as Jimmy has done, I would." Effie scooted out from under the table and sat up and Destry did the same.

"Destry," she said. "I know you want to help your friend and everything but this isn't about that. This is about right and wrong and your responsibility to either let me go or go to the police yourself."

"I can't send myself to prison. There are too many things I want to do with my life that I won't be able to do if I'm sent away."

"Fine. So you don't want to let me go. What about Angie?"

"There's nothing I can do about her now."

"What about her family? You have to go to the police. If you don't, her family will never know what happened to her. They will always wonder. They will always have questions but they will never have answers. How can you put them through that kind of pain. They will sit home night after night, wondering if their daughter is ever coming home."

"I can't help it."

"Well don't you think she deserves better than to be dumped in a hole in the woods like an animal?"

Destry got to his feet. "Just shut yer mouth, Cookie. Just shut it—or else."

"Or else what, Destry?" Effie pointed at her face. Even with a little of the swelling going down some, it still looked horrible. "Or else you are going to do the same thing to me as your good friend Jimmy—Or Harry for that matter.

"Shut up," he said. "I'm startin' to see things Jimmy's way. I don't wanna talk about this anymore. You don't understand the way it is! Those two are almost like brothers to me. I just can't go doin' stuff to get them in trouble."

"Then you're no better than either of them. You might as well have let Harry do whatever he wanted to me."

"I came in here to help but I don't think you appreciate it very much. For all I care, he can come back and finish what he started! I'm gettin' outta here. No way am I gonna sit here and listen to you spoutin' off." With that, Destry grabbed a fishing rod from a rack behind the door and he walked out of the cabin.

Chapter 19

Effie's eyes were blazing with anger as she threw up her hands. "What was I thinking?" she barked at herself. "That man was the only one of the three I had any hopes of getting to help me. Now I've gone and pissed him off. How could I be so stupid?"

She paced back and forth then went to the window. The filth on it was so thick, she couldn't even see out. She stomped across the room and snatched up the rag she had dropped near the table then returned to the window and began rubbing. It had to have been years since the windows had been cleaned. When the damp rag touched them, the dirt turned to mud. Effie kept working at it until it was relatively clean.

When she looked out the window, she could see Destry sitting on a log by the river. Even from a distance, he looked agitated. Movement off to his right caught Effie's attention. Something was in a large clump of brush and it was moving. She pressed her face against the glass to get a better look. After a few seconds, Harry made his way into the open and began heading toward Destry. He looked up to see what the noise was and when he realized who it was, he carefully laid his fishing pole on the ground and stood up to greet Harry.

It did not look like Destry was so angry with him anymore. The two talked for a little while and every once in a while, one of them would look at or gesture toward the cabin. It was pretty obvious to Effie that she was the topic of their discussion. After a few more minutes of talking, Destry gave Harry a manly pat on his back and they both sat down on the log.

Witnessing the exchange was like flipping a light on in the dark for Effie. She suddenly realized that she had been fooling herself. There was no way Destry would ever see the situation from her point of view. He was too tight with Jimmy and Harry and he would always side with them.

It suddenly felt as though a trap door in Effie's stomach had opened up and every shred of hope she'd been clinging to was emptying out. Her mind began to wander. How had she allowed herself to end up there? Compared to her present situation, putting up with Rich Hale's teasing was nothing. Maybe she had overreacted to it all. Then again, if it wasn't for Rich's teasing, she would not have ended up as a prisoner in a cabin in the middle of nowhere.

An angry furrow formed between her eyes. What made him so special anyway? Effie knew she could out-write Rich any day of the week. The more she thought about it, the more her hatred for him grew. She tugged on her chain lightly.

"It's his fault that I'm here," she muttered out loud. "If that kiss-ass could see me right now, he'd probably laugh…Probably compare me to some filthy animal because of the chain. The monster gets away with everything."

Then it came to her. If Effie wanted to survive the ordeal, she had to be like Rich. Well, not the mean and nasty part. She had to be the same kiss-ass that he was, though. That's how Rich had made it through the ranks. He kissed up to anyone and everyone above him and people ate that up. That also had to be why he was such a mean person. Deep down, he had to know that there were a lot of people below him with tons more talent. Rich Hale was nothing more than a coward!

With a renewed sense of confidence, Effie began cleaning like a mad woman. Before long, she was covered in filth but the cabin was already looking better. As she was standing at the sink, rinsing out her rag, she heard footsteps on the stairs and she turned to see who was coming to the door. It swung open and in walked Destry, a whole slew of fish in hand.

He didn't look at or say a word to Effie. He just snatched up a knife and went to work cleaning fish next to the sink.

"I'm really sorry about the things I said earlier," she said. "I—I know I was out of line and I promise I won't talk like that again."

Destry stopped what he was doing briefly and studied the knife in his hand, turning it over several times. Effie saw the way he was looking at it and stepped backward to distance herself from him. She bumped into Harry whom she hadn't even heard come in. She turned and patted his chest, smoothing his shirt.

She began stammering. "I'm—I'm just—I'm—so sorry, Harry—So sorry. I didn't mean to bump into you. I'm so sorry…"

Harry gave Effie a funny look and stepped around her. He began babbling to Destry about how good the fishing was. Minutes later, Jimmy came lumbering in as well.

"What was that you was sayin' when I came in, Harry?" he questioned.

"Well me and Destry was just down the hill doin' some fishin' and I was just sayin' that he was real lucky. Them fish were really biting."

Jimmy walked over next to Destry and looked at the pile of fish in front of him. "Cookie, get the fryin' pan out," he said. "Yer gonna be cookin' us a feast tonight, thanks to my good buddy here." He walked over to inspect the window. "This window looks like shit," he said. "Wash it again after we're done eating."

Effie bowed her head as if to say that he was right.

"Well go get that pan like I told ya. I don't wanna wait all night to eat ya lazy whore."

Quickly, Effie moved to do as she was told. As far as she was concerned, the new name of the game was *Kiss-Up*, and that was exactly what she intended to do. She walked over next to Destry and crouched down to reach into the shelves in front of him. Was he really angry with her or was there a chance she could win at least some of his affections? Maybe if she came onto him…

The next thing Effie knew, she was pretending to lose her balance and she reached up to steady herself by grabbing hold of Destry's leg. For a moment, she just stared at the shelf, allowing her hand to linger. When he looked down, she looked up at him and slowly blinked, a small smile on her lips. She grabbed a pan and stood up, sliding her fingertips along the inside of his thigh as she did so.

Effie turned toward the stove but looked out the corner of her eye at Destry. He was openly gazing at her! It worked! That was all the license Effie needed to lay the flirting on thick. Maybe all hope was not yet lost!

When the fish was ready to serve, she asked, "Who is ready for dinner gentlemen?"

Harry grabbed some plates and forks from a nearby shelf and tossed them on the table as the men crowded around. Effie started serving with Jimmy. From there, she moved to Harry then onto Destry. When she got to Destry, though, she served him a little different. She leaned in a little farther, making sure that he knew her breast was pressing against his shoulder.

When she was done serving and getting the men cold beer to drink, she obediently took her place on the floor next to Jimmy. Before, she had spent the meal with her eyes cast downward, waiting for their scraps so she could eat. This time, however, Effie made a point of repeatedly catching Destry's eye. Each time she did, she would quickly look away then back again.

Harry let out a loud belch then pushed his plate away and said, "I had enough. I was real good though. I wouldn't mind eatin' like that every night."

"You done too?" Jimmy asked Destry.

When Destry nodded, Jimmy reached over and picked up his plate and scraped the little bit that was left onto his own. After that, he had Harry hand him the little piece of fish left in the pan and he added that to the plate too.

"You done cooked us a good meal tonight," Jimmy said to Effie then handed her his plate. "Tonight, you can have what's left of the fish."

"Thank you," she muttered. It had been hours since any food had gone into her belly and even little scraps of fish were a delicious treat.

Jimmy got up from the table and headed over to his bed to lay down. "When yer done eatin', Cookie, get those dishes done right away like a good little girl."

For the moment, everyone seemed to be in a good mood so Effie rushed to do as she was told. With the other men away from the table, she collected the dishes and started pumping water into the sink. One by one, she began scrubbing the plates. She only had the pan left when Jimmy interrupted her.

"Come over here for a minute, Cookie," he said and she jumped to do so. To her horror, she could see a large lump in the front of his pants.

Jimmy started getting up from the bed. "I want you to spread your legs apart then bend over and grab hold of the frame on my bed."

Effie looked around the room. Harry and Destry perked up when they heard his instructions. She could not help but notice how similar Jimmy's instructions were to those Harry had given her earlier in the day. Had he told Jimmy about it?

As much as she wanted to do as she was told, Effie could not bring herself to voluntarily let any of the men violate her. She gave Jimmy a look like she didn't understand his instructions.

He did not repeat himself. Instead, Jimmy called Harry over. "Help me spread her legs and holder so she's bent over."

Effie tried to pull her arms away and hold her legs shut. "No!" she yelled.

Jimmy growled, "Yes, bitch! You will do what I tell you!" He began spanking her. The more Effie fought, the harder his hand came down.

"Yer a naughty little girl, Cookie, and you make daddy real mad," he said through clenched teeth.

Suddenly, Destry was up next to them as well. He grabbed Jimmy's arm and tried to stop him but it did not work. Jimmy just yanked his arm free and smacked Effie even harder.

"Come on, Jimmy," said Destry. "Give it a break. You don't have to do this."

"I know I don't gotta. This is fun! I wanna do it. Besides, she likes it. All whores like it."

Effie choked out a cry of pain.

"Stop it now, Jimmy! You're hurting her."

"I told ya, she likes it."

"No she doesn't. Just stop."

Jimmy looked up at Destry. "She likes it and if she don't, she damn well better learn to like it because I do and this is the way it's gonna be."

Destry tried to grab at Jimmy's arm again. "What you're doin' is wrong!"

"Screw you, Destry. If you don't like the way I'm doin' things, then get the hell out. I just can't believe you, boy! I just can't believe the mouth on ya anymore. You owe me and ya still talk all disrespectful to me. Just get out—NOW!"

Destry's face flushed with indignation. "Yeah," he said. "I keep tellin' myself that I owe you and that's why I always go along with everything you say when you get us into these messes."

"Now yer seein' things my way."

"Don't even start with that, Jimmy. One of these days—"

"—One of these days, what?" Jimmy interrupted, his eyes narrowing with disdain. "You will do what I say for the rest of yer life because that's how long you'll owe me. How about you get the hell out of my cabin until you can get that mouth of yers in line and shut the hell up? I don't want ya givin' me no lip about anything. I'm sick of it."

Destry snatched the keys from the table and stomped toward the door. He pulled it open, gripping the handle so hard, he could have crushed it in his hand. "One of these days, enough will be enough," he yelled then walked out, pulling the door closed so hard, the entire cabin shook.

Jimmy and Harry were still holding Effie in place and no one moved even a hair. Finally, after what seemed like an eternity, Jimmy began laughing. Harry looked into his face an joined in too.

"Screw him," said Jimmy as he ran his hands up and down the inside of

Effie's thighs. He pulled down his pants and began grinding his pelvis against her. "He'll come around soon enough.—Always does." He raised his hand up high and brought it down on Effie's back side with a loud crack. "Until he does, that's just more of this fine bovine ass for me."

Effie tried to squeeze her legs together and pull her arms loose. The men were much stronger than her and they were holding her so tight. The more she squirmed, the more turned on Jimmy seemed to get. Even Harry seemed aroused.

Jimmy decided that he'd had enough playing around and with one ruthless thrust, he forced himself into her. Effie's face contorted grotesquely as her voice exploded in agony. It felt as though she was being torn to shreds. She began thrashing in pain and when she pulled one of her hands free, she dug into anything she could get her hands on, including Harry.

Harry's fist connected with the back of Effie's head in an attempt to get her to stop clawing at his side. He caught her hand but with his attention on that, he was too busy to notice her teeth closing on his stomach. Harry howled as her teeth sunk into him and he let go of her arm and grabbed her hair, yanking her head away from his body.

Finally, Jimmy bucked a final few times then froze, trying to hold Effie's hips still. She gave up her fight, figuring if Jimmy did not kill her now, Harry surely would. Her body went limp and as she knees bent, Jimmy pulled out of her, letting her fall to the floor. He wiped the sweat from his brow then pointed toward Harry's mattress.

"Get her outta here," he said. "Take her over to your bed and do whatever ya want with her.

"Bitch," muttered Harry as he got up and dragged Effie toward his bed.

Jimmy chuckled. "She just need to be broken. Women are like animals. They're wild 'til ya get 'em trained up. She'll learn. We just gotta keep on her." He flopped down on his bed and within minutes, his breathing fell into a steady rhythm and he began snoring.

Harry dropped Effie onto his mattress and began peeling off his clothed. She knew she could have gotten away from him easily but what was the point? With that damn chain around her ankle, Harry would just catch her again then beat her senseless before raping her anyway. Her head was already throbbing from his harsh blows so she just laid there, waiting for him.

When Harry laid down on top of Effie, it pressed the breath out of her lungs. She began gasping for air as he began plunging in and out of her. Sweat dripped from his forehead onto her face. She squeezed her eyes shut, hoping that everything would disappear. The world started spinning. All Effie was conscious of was the lack of air. She sucked and sucked at the air but it was so hard to get it into her lungs. Each breath brought in a little less than the last.

Cool air suddenly filled her lungs. Effie was laying on the floor next to the mattress. Harry must have satisfied himself then rolled off and pushed her away. She just laid on the floor, sucking in the glorious air and as she did so, the spinning gradually slowed until everything stopped moving.

Effie was overcome with a feeling of filth. She had to clean her skin. Anywhere Jimmy and Harry had touched was tainted. She rolled onto her stomach and forced herself to crawl toward the sink. It seemed like every inch of her body either ached or felt like it was on fire. Tears poured from her eyes.

After getting to her feet, Effie began pumping cold water onto a cloth. She scrubbed and scrubbed but the filth just would not come off. She kept telling herself that if she scrubbed a little more, she would be clean but it didn't work and after a while, her skin began to get raw. When she could not stand any longer, she sat on the floor near the sink and kept scrubbing until she cried herself to asleep.

She didn't know how long she had been sleeping when the sound of the door opening roused her. Effie immediately began rubbing her arm with the damp cloth, her eyes glued to the door. Destry struggled to get a thin mattress in then he flopped it down next to the post in the middle of the room.

He followed the chain from the post over to the sink then he crouched down next o Effie, a look of pity on his face. Gently, he pulled the cloth out of her hand then got her to her feet. As he wrapped his arm around her to walk her toward the mattress, she began shaking uncontrollably and tears spilled onto her cheeks.

"Sorry," he whispered then laid her down.

Effie half expected Destry to take his turn with her but he didn't. Instead, he unbuttoned his shirt and laid it over her then went and laid down on his own mattress. She curled into a ball, pulling his shirt tight around her.

She could not close her eyes and fall asleep. Effie laid there thinking about Destry. Where had he found the mattress at that hour of the night? It certainly didn't smell new. Not that it mattered how old it was. Even a thin mattress was a thousand times better than laying on the floor.

Sometimes it really seemed like Destry wanted to do the right thing. Then he kept turning around and siding with Jimmy. There had to be a way around it. There just had to be a way to make him not only see how wrong Jimmy was but go against him too.

Effie began thinking about people in general and after a while, a thought popped into her head. What broke up more friendships? Romantic Relationships! Maybe it was not enough to just kiss up to Destry. Maybe the answer was to really make him fall for her. If she could get him to care—to fall in love with her, maybe, just maybe Effie could drive that wedge between Jimmy and Destry and break up their friendship. After that, she could get him to go to the police.

She kept going over the scenario in her mind until her eyelids became heavy and she couldn't keep them up a moment longer. Though she did not want to fall asleep for fear of what she would wake to in the morning, she couldn't help it. Soon enough, Effie had slipped over the edge into a deep sleep.

Chapter 20

The next morning, Effie woke to find the shirt she had been covered with missing and all three of the men out. The door was standing open and she could hear their voices. At first, she could not understand all that they were saying but when she sat perfectly still, barely breathing, the words became clearer.

"What's the deal with the plates on the car?" Destry asked.

There was a loud guffaw from Jimmy. "See? That's a good example of my smarts at work."

Harry interrupted," One of the smartest guys around, my brother is."

"I don't need you to say nothin' about me. Destry already knows how smart I am."

"I know, I know. I was just sayin' it anyway, though."

"Yeah but you don't need to do it."

"Fine, I won't never—"

"GUYS," Destry broke in. "Enough bickering already. Just tell me about the plates, Jimmy."

"I will just as soon as ol' blabber mouth over here stops his lips from flapping."

"You don't hafta worry about that. I ain't gonna say nothin' to ya even if ya ask me to."

"Good," both Jimmy and Destry said.

"Anyway," Jimmy began, "I was sayin' that it's my smarts at work." He paused and when no one said anything, he went on. "See, when I was in town yesterday, I saw this car sittin' in a yard with a for sale sign in the window. That's when I got my idea. I asked the old coot who owned it if I could take it for a little test drive. I just stopped and took the plates off when I was out driving. When I got back, I told the coot I'd get back to him on the car. He'll probably never even notice them plates are missing. Pretty smart, huh?"

"What did you do with the old plates for this car?"

"Oh, I just tossed 'em down the shit hole in the outhouse. Ain't no one ever gonna look down there." Jimmy laughed again but he was not joined by Destry.

"What? What? What in the hell is wrong now, Destry?"

"There's no way I am ever driving or riding in that car again."

"Why not?"

"Think about it, Jimmy." There was an edge of arrogance in his voice.

"Just tell me what you're gettin' at. I don't feel like playin' games today."

"First of all, what if that old guy does report the plates on his car missing?"

"He won't."

"Well even if he doesn't, what's gonna happen if one of us gets pulled over drivin' that car? The records attached to those plates ain't gonna match up with that car. They keep track of the make and model and color and all of that stuff, ya know. Second, the registration papers in that car are from Michigan and they have Cookie's name on 'em. Sooner or later, someone's gonna start lookin' for her. When you get caught with that car, it ain't gonna take much for the cops to put two and two together and figure out what you done. Ain't no way I'm gonna be any part of that. No sir."

Jimmy stood there mulling it over in his mind. After a long silence, he said," Maybe you're right on this one, Destry. Maybe we should just get rid of the car. We could dump it somewhere."

"I know where," piped up Harry.

"The river is too shallow. We gotta find someplace they won't find the car right off."

"It ain't a really long ways from here."

"If we leave it on some back road that's all deserted, someone could still find it."

"I could show you the place."

Jimmy stopped thinking out loud and looked at Harry with a confused expression. "What the hell are you goin' on about?"

"We could go there right now even."

127

"What? Where could we go, Harry?"

Harry rolled his eyes. "I said I know a place where we could dump the car. There's a good size lake up from town a ways. I been up there fishin' before and there's hardly ever anyone up there. I could show you where it is."

Jimmy looked at Harry with respect. He looked at Destry as if to see if he was as surprised at Harry's token stroke of genius and saw a reflection of his own reaction. "Why don't you take me up there, Harry, and Destry can stay here and keep an eye on Cookie." He held out his hand for the truck keys and Destry tossed them to him. "We can take the truck. If it really is a good place, we can take the car back tonight and put 'er in the drink."

Harry was already climbing behind the wheel of the truck when Jimmy turned around to hand him the keys. Destry did not say anything to either of them. He just turned around and walked back to the cabin. As he stepped through the door, the truck rumbled to life then pulled away from the cabin.

Effie's eyes followed Destry across the cabin to the table. He sat down with his back to her and as soon as he did, she hurried to get him a drink. This was the perfect opportunity to start working on him.

As Effie handed Destry a cool glass of water, his eyes rose and for the briefest moment they connected with hers. She let her fingers linger on the glass, touching his then shyly pulled her hand away.

"Thank you," said Destry then his eyes turned toward the floor.

He was obviously deep in thought about something. Perhaps it was not the perfect time to start working. Effie turned to walk away. The last thing she needed was to anger him further. She was about to pick up a rag and start cleaning when she stole one more glance over her shoulder and saw Destry rubbing his neck with his head rolled back. His eyes were closed.

Quickly, Effie crept up behind him. She reached out her hand to touch his neck but hesitated. What if he didn't want a neck or shoulder massage? What if he got angry for her touching him without being invited. Then again, maybe he would like it.

She reached out her hands and gently laid them on either side of his neck. Destry jerked his hand away as if hers were on fire. He just stared ahead. It was too late for Effie to go back so she started rubbing her fingertips in small circles and gradually, he began to relax. Her hands moved down to his shoulders, kneading the tense muscles. As she became more daring, she ran her hands into the top of his shirt and began massaging his chest.

Destry turned to look up into Effie's eyes. It was almost as if there was electricity in the air and as much as she wanted to look away, she couldn't.

Instead, she leaned toward Destry and closed her eyes, brushing her lips on his.

Suddenly, Destry pushed her away and got up to walk away. "No," he said. "I can't do this. I can't be like Jimmy and Harry. It's not right."

"I'm sorry," Effie whispered.

He turned to look at her again. "It's not your fault, Cookie. None of this is. You're just tryin' to do what Jimmy told you to do. That ain't right, though, and when he ain't around, you don't have to do that. Not when you're with me."

Effie was suddenly very conscious of her nakedness and she dropped her eyes to the floor. Maybe it was not such a good idea to try to get him to fall for her.

"I know I ain't any better than either of them. If I was, none of this woulda happened. But that doesn't mean I have to be like them. I ain't gonna take advantage of you. It's wrong."

She didn't bother saying anything back to him. What could she say? Effie didn't even know where to begin. Instead, she picked up a rag and started cleaning shelves. Not a word was spoken. Destry turned his back on her and spent the afternoon in deep thought. Several hours later, when Jimmy and Harry came rolling back, she was covered in filth and she was still cleaning. And to make matters worse, Destry still hadn't uttered a syllable.

Jimmy burst into the cabin with Harry tagging behind, a new spring in his step. Jimmy was smiling from ear to ear. "My brother is the smartest man in the world, right after me," he announced. "We drove right up to that lake and found the perfect spot to get rid of that car. No one is ever gonna find it even if they look for fifty years!"

He bound over and hooked one arm around Destry's neck and the other around Harry's. "Here's our plan, boys," he said. "Me and Harry are gonna take that car up to the lake after dark tonight and we're gonna put her right in. You can stay here with the lovely Miss Cookie, Destry." He winked. "Long as we're real careful drivin' up there, no one will ever know we ever had that car."

Chapter 21

Effie had been curled up on her mattress for hours when she became aware of the scent of alcohol wafting through the air near her. Her eyes popped open in the dark. It only took a second for her to realize that Jimmy and Harry were just getting in. Their return meant that her car was gone forever. With the car gone, her chance of ever being discovered by the police was drastically decreased.

It did not take long for Jimmy or Harry to fall asleep. Effie, however, could not find her way back to dreamland. She just laid there, staring at the moon, shining through the window. The night seemed to drag on forever. Even when the sky began turning pink, Effie did not move. There was no reason to risk making noise that could wake and anger Jimmy. She was left to drift through her thoughts.

What if they never let her go? Would it be possible for her to give in and allow them to violate her as they pleased? How long would they keep her alive before Jimmy got sick of her and tossed her into a shallow grave in the woods next to Angie? Why had any of this happened to her? What had Effie done wrong to deserve it? The questions kept building and building and she couldn't find an answer for even one of them.

After what seemed an eternity of questions running through her mind, Destry rolled over and looked directly at her. Maybe he could see the despair behind her eyes and maybe it was something else. Either way, he gave her a comforting smile. Even as low as Effie was feeling, she couldn't help but smile back. To her, that smile was like a ray of sunlight shining through the clouds on a dark, stormy day.

Effie got up from her mattress and tried to tip-toe over to the stove to make some coffee. The chain binding her ankle seemed to rattle louder than ever as she moved. With each step, she looked at Jimmy to see if he was aware of it. At the stove, she tried to stand as still as possible as she prodded the glowing embers and placed a new log on the fire. Before long, the flames were licking and the water in the coffee pot was boiling.

Destry got up and stretched before taking a seat at the table. For a while, neither he nor Effie said a word. She just stood near the stove, not moving.

"Sit with me," Destry said and Effie moved to sit on the floor next to him.

"I mean in the chair, Cookie."

Effie looked at him like he was crazy. Sit in a chair? She was sure that Jimmy would beat her to death if he woke up and saw her sitting on one of his chairs.

"They were out drinking pretty late last night and they were both pretty drunk when they came in," he said. It was almost as if he could read her thoughts. "They won't wake up for hours."

She was still uncertain about sitting in a chair and began moving to sit on the floor again. Destry caught her arm and pulled her toward a chair.

"They're sound asleep." He motioned toward Jimmy and Harry. "There's no reason for you to sit on the floor right now. Besides," Destry gave her a half-cocked grin, "I would like it if you would sit in the chair."

Effie sat down, ready to spring from the chair at the first sign that Jimmy and Harry were stirring. Destry took a sip from his cup then held it out to offer her a drink. Hesitantly, she took it and brought it to her lips, her eyes flicking from Jimmy to Harry to Destry. For a moment, her eyes rested on Destry and a faint glimmer of hope sparked in the pit of her stomach. Perhaps all hope was not yet lost.

Effie leaned forward and pressed her lips to Destry's. At first, he tried to lean back and break the connection but she was intent on kissing him. Slowly, he raised his hands to her face and began kissing back. It was a gentle, tender kiss. It was different from the drunken kisses Jimmy had planted on her. A little jolt of electricity danced through her stomach and then it was over. Destry pulled back and stood up.

Without another word, Effie stood up to take care of the coffee cup. Destry took it from her hands and began cleaning it himself. She could only look at him. Something had changed. Something was suddenly different. Effie smiled to herself then went to work reorganizing the shelves. When Destry was done cleaning his cup, he wiped his hands on a towel then went to stand next to Effie.

"I did a lot of thinkin' last night. I've been doin' a lot since I woke up today too. I want to do the right thing with you and everything here," he said, motioning around him. "I've always gone along with everything they said, though. That's the way things have been since we were kids. I had to make some decisions—"

Effie knocked a stack of pans from the shelf and they went clattering to the floor. It couldn't have been louder. Jimmy rolled over and fell off the bed.

"You damn clumsy cow! What the hell do ya think you're doing?," he yelled as he collected himself from the floor.

Effie did not answer. She was frozen in fear. Any second now, he would be on top of her, beating. She squeezed her eyes shut when she heard him get to his feet and lumber across the cabin. When his fists did not begin pummeling her, she peeked out of the corner of her eye. Jimmy had gone out on the porch and was holding onto the wall, peeing off the edge.

Immediately, she crouched down and began picking up pans. Destry hunkered down too. "I'll tell you later," he whispered.

"Well, well, well." Their attention snapped to Jimmy who was leaning against the doorframe. "Don't you two look like the cozy couple?" Destry started to stand up as Jimmy stepped toward them.

"Don't get up on my account," Jimmy said with a crooked grin. "Go right ahead and stay there. Diddle her for all I care."

Destry stepped around Jimmy and made for the door. "I was just headin' out to go fishing. I'm gonna catch us some dinner again."

Jimmy ignored him and turned to look at Harry who had not moved or waken through any of it. He walked over and nudged him with his toe a few times. Harry tried to roll over and ignore him but Jimmy would not be deterred. He kept nudging Harry until he sat up, rubbing his eyes.

"What's the big idea, Jimmy?" he whined. "I'm tired. I wanna sleep."

Jimmy gave him a disapproving look. "I got somethin' for you to do today so get up. Cookie'll get some coffee goin' for ya."

"Can't you have Destry do whatever it is? I didn't get enough sleep yet."

"I don't want Destry to do it. I want you to do it."

Harry pouted like a little boy. "Fine. I'll get up."

Effie already had the coffee pot going again and by the time Harry was finished peeing off the edge of the porch, she had two steaming cups of coffee for the men. Being careful not to spill a drop, she carried them over and set them on the table. Jimmy just pushed his cup away, slopping it on the table.

"I didn't say I wanted that crap today." He pointed toward the refrigerator. "Bring me a beer, Cookie."

Not wanting to anger him, Effie hurried to do as she was told. She returned to his side and handed him a cool can. He snatched the can from her, popped the tab and began guzzling. She took that to mean he was done with her for the moment. When she started to walk away, Jimmy wrapped his arm around her waist and pulled her onto his lap. He bounced her up and down a few times before stopping to wink at Harry.

"Harry," began Jimmy. "I want ya to take the truck and go back home."

"What?" Harry had a look of surprise on his face.

"Don't worry. Yer comin' back. I just want ya to go pick up some clothes and stuff for us."

"Well why can't Destry go do that? I don't wanna drive all the way back home then back here. Even if I go straight there and back, it means I'll be on the road all day today and most of the day tomorrow."

"I don't care what you want. *I* want you to go and I don't want no arguin' outta ya."

Harry finished up his cup of coffee and pushed the empty mug away. He stood up and held out his hand in front of his brother. Jimmy struggled to dig the keys out of his pocket then he laid them in Harry's hand. Harry looked around the room and held out his hand again.

"What?" Jimmy questioned.

"I need some cash. That truck ain't goin' nowhere if it ain't got no gas in it."

Jimmy gave him a disgusted look. He stood up, shoving Effie away. "Go clean the floor or something," he said as he dug into his back pocket and pulled out his wallet. Flipping through it, he pulled out a credit card and a wad of bills. "Only use the card if they have that pay at the pump thingy. They ain't gonna let ya use it if you try to pay inside. It has her name on it and if ya use it, they might call the cops or something. Long as ya use it at the pump, you'll be just fine with it."

Harry made one last attempt to change Jimmy's mind. "Are ya sure Destry can't go instead?"

"I said I want *you* to go. I don't think he's feelin' right. He's been actin' funny lately. Me and him gotta talk." He patted Harry on the shoulder. "Just get going."

Jimmy ushered Harry out of the cabin then watched until the truck was out of sight. He did not say a word to Effie, who was busy working. He just tossed the empty can toward the table and headed back to bed.

Several hours later, Destry came back to the cabin with at least a dozen fish and started cleaning them. Effie had finished scrubbing the floor so she offered to give him a hand.

Destry shook his head slightly. "Just get the pan ready for them."

The scent of the frying fish woke Jimmy. "It's about time someone made me some food," he said, glaring at Effie. "I thought I was gonna hafta go hungry all day." He grabbed another can of beer and cracked it open before taking a seat at the table so he could be served.

"Where'd Harry get off to?" asked Destry.

"I sent him back home to get some clothes and stuff this morning. He'll be back tomorrow afternoon or so."

"You sent him for clothes?"

Effie was just finishing up with the fish. She set two heaping plates on the table in front of the men then took her place on the floor next to Jimmy. He reached out and patted her head like a dog.

Jimmy laughed. "She's learning!"

"Hey," said Destry, pounding his fist on the table. "You sent Harry home to get clothes?

"Well yeah. Ya don't expect me to go without clean clothes for too long. I gotta have my stuff."

Destry growled and pointed at Effie. "You had every stitch of her clothes burned and you won't let her even cover up with my shirt at night and you are worried about clean clothes for yourself? You're insane!"

"Don't you dare take that tone with me, Destry Clare," Jimmy said, shaking his fork at him. "I done told ya why we had to take all her clothes the other day. I am tryin' to make sure that we don't get in trouble but ya must not care about that. What's yer deal with her anyway? You been actin' funny right from the start of all this."

"Did you tell him to stop at my place and get anything for me?"

"Nope."

Destry let out a deep sigh. "Well why the hell not?"

"Ya wasn't here when I sent him."

"Christ, Jimmy. I don't know what's wrong with you. Hell, I don't know what's wrong with me for listenin' to you for all theses years. You never did nothin' but get me in trouble."

"You ungrateful—" Jimmy was sputtering. His face grew red and the veins in his neck stood out in livid ridges. "I saved yer life! I could of let ya drown but I pulled yer sorry ass outta the river."

"Oh give up that saving my life bit! You bring that up every time I disagreed with you. I was stupid enough to get caught up with it when we were kids but I sure as hell ain't gonna fall for it now."

Jimmy's expression went from anger to shock. He could not believe that Destry would talk back to him like that.

"Don't give me that look either," Destry went on. "Any debt I've had to you was paid off a long time ago. And if it wasn't, the second you killed Angie, anything you ever did that was good was erased. Not that it would matter. You've done so many crappy things to people over the years—"

"As if she was the first!" It was Destry's turn to look surprised. "Anyway, don't you go actin' so proud. You been along and helped do plenty stuff with me and I ain't never heard ya complainin' before."

Their voices were raising to an ear-splitting level. Effie ducked down and covered her ears.

"What do you mean 'as if she isn't the first?'"

"That ain't what I said and it don't matter anyway."

Destry pounded his fist on the table as he spoke. "You know what, Jimmy?" he said. "From now on, you aren't gonna lay a finger on her so long as I'm around. Every time you do that you're just makin' this whole thing worse."

"As if you could stop me. You ain't never tried to tell me what to do or ever complained about the way I ever done anything before and now yer gettin' all big headed about it. I'm gettin' kinda sick of ya."

"I never complained before because I was too stupid to see what a sick, crazy person you really are."

"Lick my ass, Destry! Yer the one who's crazy. You changed. You ain't the friend ya used to be. I was always good to ya. I treated ya like my brother."

Destry pushed his plate away. "Yeah, you did," he said, nodding. "You treated me just like your brother and you crap all over him too. Boy, I'll tell you what, just as soon as he gets back here, I'm leaving. I ain't gonna have any part in any of this anymore."

"That's just fine with me. If you go, that's just more of her fat ass for me to enjoy," Jimmy said, pointing at Effie. "I won't have to put up with yer tryin' to stop me from enjoyin' what's mine no more either. I'll be able to take her any way I want, whenever I want."

"Maybe I'm gonna take her with me when I go."

"And maybe you can kiss my ass if you think I'm gonna let you take her outta here alive."

The tension in the air that afternoon was thick. Jimmy was so mad, he didn't even bother looking at Effie. He spent most of the day sitting on his bed, staring out the window or sleeping. Destry scarcely left the cabin either. It was almost spooky. The silence was so deafening. The afternoon just dragged on and on and when the evening finally arrived, it seemed to last even longer. Going to bed that night almost seemed a relief. It was an escape from the quiet.

Chapter 22

The next morning proved to be exactly like the previous evening. The resentment Jimmy and Destry now had for one another was like a wall. No one spoke or even moved around the cabin much. The quiet was uncomfortable.

By mid-morning, Effie couldn't stand sitting still on her mattress anymore so she got up to clean and organize the shelves again. When the silence became too much, she knocked a stack of pans from a high shelf and sent them crashing to the floor. Instead of yelling at her like she expected, Jimmy stomped out of the cabin. Destry stood in the doorway, watching him go. When he was satisfied that he would not be back soon, he joined Effie in picking up the pans.

He looked at her for a moment, smiling. Her cheeks turned pink and she had to look away.

"Your face looks much better," said Destry. "Well, I mean that the swelling is going down and the bruises are starting to fade a little. You might heal up OK."

Effie laughed lightly. "I'm just glad there aren't any mirrors here."

"Why is that?"

"Well I wasn't much to look at before. I must look ten times worse now."

Destry took her hand in his. "You don't look bad at all," he said.

She rolled her eyes. "Oh come on. You don't have to pretend with me. I know what people think. I've heard it my entire life. The only difference is, you have to see me naked and covered with scrapes and bruises and I haven't had a brush through my hair in days. I must look worse than a monster."

"I think you're beautiful." Destry's voice was too low for her to hear.

"When I was a kid, even my mom used to tell me that no man would ever love me or want to be with me."

Destry shrugged. "Your mom was wrong."

"Well so far, she's been right and she's not the only one. Lot's of people think that way, you know. It's like they think I can't hear or I don't have feelings."

"Who else?"

"Lots of people."

"Name one person besides Jimmy and Harry."

"Ok," said Effie, thinking for a minute. "There was a bunch of men at that bar—The Coon Pit. They kept turning around to look at me and they were laughing."

Destry smiled. "Those guys don't count. They wouldn't recognize beauty if it walked through the door and beat them over the head."

"Well they weren't doing anything that wasn't completely normal."

"You know what they were doing?"

Effie shook her head.

"They probably were cracking jokes about you—"

"See? You admit it!"

"—But they were only doing that because they knew they didn't have a chance with you. They were making jokes because they didn't want to admit that they knew they weren't good enough. They were trying to save face. That's just the way guys are."

Effie shook her head again. "That's a bad example then. Trust me. If people didn't find me unattractive, I wouldn't even be here."

Destry gave her a funny look and asked, "What do you mean by that?"

With little hesitation, Effie began telling about her problem at work with Rich Hale and Raymond Ludgreen. Destry listened in silence until she was completely done with the story. At first he did not say anything and Effie panicked, afraid that he would laugh and agree with Rich. Then he began speaking.

"That guy you work with couldn't be more wrong. I mean, uh—" Destry nervously ran a hand through his hair. "Well, I ah...I just think that you're one of the prettiest women I ever met. That guy probably thinks so too. That and he probably thinks you have more talent for what you do than he does and he's afraid you'll end up with his job. And that boss—he's wrong to handle the whole thing like he did. He doesn't deserve to have someone like you workin' for him."

Effie gave him a sad look. "I guess that's the way the cookie crumbles."

"Look," said Destry. "I know…Oh heck. I don't know what to say. Let's just go sit down on my mattress. You should take a break from all the cookin' and cleaning. Besides, we'll be more comfortable and we can see out the door pretty good so we can tell if Jimmy's coming back. I promise, I'll be nice."

Effie couldn't help but smile. "How about I fix us some lunch. After that, we can sit on your mattress all afternoon and do whatever you want." She winked at him then set about getting some food for them.

After eating lunch, they sat on the mattress all afternoon. They talked, told stories, even joked, and when the afternoon ran into the evening, they curled up and dozed off. The next thing either of them knew

It was dark in the cabin and Jimmy was standing over them, lantern in hand. It cast a sinister glow, distorting his features. His eyes bore into them as if he thought they were keeping something from him.

"Where ya been all day," asked Destry.

Jimmy ignored his question. "He been back here yet?"

"Who?"

"Harry. I told him to get his fat ass back here today. I walked up to Webb's fillin' station 'cause I figured he'd stop there on his way back then I could catch a ride home. That piece of worthless shit never showed up. I had to walk all the way back here. I get my hands on that boy and he's gonna be sorrier than a sheep 'round a queer after dark."

Destry laughed lightly and shook his head. "The whole world revolves around you, doesn't it?"

"You'd be a lot better off if you could see it that way," Jimmy answered as he walked over to get a beer before laying back on his bed.

"Damn," he went on. "He better get back here soon. We're almost outta the ol' brewski. I don't wanna hafta try to carry some all of the way back from the store. It's too damn heavy."

"Well here's an idea for ya," Destry said as he pulled Effie closer. "Why don't you either take it easy on them or just go without if it runs out before Harry comes back."

Jimmy completely ignored Destry's statement and changed the subject. "I was talkin' to Ahanu. Says he's lookin' at some land up in Montana. He's thinkin' about movin' up there. I guess there's some fine huntin' up that way."

"That's nice. How about you just zip it for a while. Some of us wanna get some sleep."

"I'll bet you're real tired," Jimmy said laughing. "I would be too if I spent all day long screwin' around with ol' red too."

"Whatever, Jimmy. Sounds like you've had too much to drink already. Get some sleep."

"I'll do whatever I want," Jimmy barked.

"Fine. Do anything you want. We are going to sleep now."

"*We are going to sleep now*," he mimicked. "*We* are going to sleep now. *We* are going to *sleep* now…" He just kept babbling until finally, he nodded off.

Chapter 23

"I need some breakfast," Jimmy howled the next day when he finally crawled out of bed.

"Fix it yourself," Destry replied. "We've had breakfast and lunch already."

Jimmy walked over next to Effie and frowned. She was sitting on her mattress, pulling a needle through an old, worn shirt as fast as she could. After the previous day, she was not as afraid of Jimmy as long as Destry was in the room. She didn't even bother to look up at him as he stood there grunting.

"What the hell is she doin'? It sure don't look like nothin; that can't wait while she gets me some food."

"What does it look like she's doing?" asked Destry. He rolled his eyes when Jimmy just shrugged. "She's mending some of your old clothes."

"So."

"So? I am going to need something clean to wear soon and she volunteered to mend a few shirts for me.

A furrow formed on Jimmy's brow. "Oh. She's all talented and stuff. Well, ya ain't gonna let her mend all day long. I ain't gonna let none of that go on. Where the hell'd she get that needle and thread anyway?"

"When I found out that she could sew, I dug some old clothes out of the trunk and asked her to fix something so I could change me clothes. I just thought it'd be kinda nice to not mell like a week old fish."

"And you wanna wear my old clothes?" Jimmy was looking at Destry like he had some kind of disease.

"What else can I do with?" Destry said.

A loud growl escaped from Jimmy's stomach. He looked from Effie to Destry. "Well I don't see why she can't stop for a couple of minutes and get me some food. It ain't like mendin' clothes for you is important."

"It ain't like you've never fixed your own meals before." He was getting fed up with Jimmy. The expression on his face was of pure annoyance.

"Yeah but I have her around so she can do stuff like that for me." He slowly ran his hand in circles on his stomach. "It's a woman's job to do all the cookin' anyway. She should just do what she's meant to do."

Effie laid down the needle and thread then started to get up. There was no sense in sitting there listening to them argue again. Neither one of them was in a horrible mood and if she could help them avoid getting really angry, she was going to do all she could. The noise they were making was too distracting anyway. Their bickering was just as bad as being in the middle of a three ring circus. As far as she was concerned, there was no concentrating with the two of them awake and in the same room.

"I'll get something for him," she said in a dry voice. A triumphant smile formed on Jimmy's lips when he heard her say it.

Destry stuck out a hand. "Please don't bother, Cookie," he said. "I'll get the lazy bump on a log something to eat."

He got out a can of beer and thrust it into Jimmy's hand. After that, he pulled out two slices of bread and a hunk of cheese. Very quickly, he sliced off a few thick slabs and smashed them between the bread then walked out and sat the sandwich on the bench on the front porch.

"Go outside and eat," he said when he came back in. "I'm already sick of listening to you today."

"Screw you," said Jimmy and he walked out the door.

Effie had picked up the mending again and sat with the needle poised over a small tear in a shirt sleeve. Her ears perked up as she listened to hear if Jimmy was going to stay on the porch or go away. The bench made a creek and her spirits sank as she realized that he wasn't going anywhere. How much more unlucky could she be?

Maybe after Jimmy was done eating, he would decide to walk back to the store or something. That would be perfect! Effie really felt that she had a good connection with Destry. He had mentioned that he might take her with him if he left. If Jimmy took off for the day again, it would be the perfect opportunity for her to get Destry to just run off with her.

Who cared if they didn't have a vehicle? If Jimmy had it in him to walk all of the way back to that filling station, Effie could certainly walk even farther if she had Destry to help her. Maybe when they got out to that main road, instead of turning and heading toward that station, they could go the other way. There had to be something. It did not matter what. One house or shack with a phone and Effie could call the police.

Well, all of that was possible if she could get Destry to help her get free. Effie was pretty sure she had him seeing things the right way. Then again, there was a lot at stake for him. Except for forcing her to have sex, he was just as much a part of all of it as Jimmy and Harry were. Maybe she could talk him into helping her if she promised to bend the truth about him when she finally made it to the police. Maybe.

When Jimmy was done eating, he tossed his empty beer can off the porch and went back into the cabin. Effie began stitching as fast as she could. Maybe he would get bored watching her and decide to go away.

No such luck. Effie stopped what she was doing and looked up at him.

Jimmy looked over at Destry. "Why don't you go fishin' and get us somethin' for dinner? You might as well do somethin' if yer gonna keep hangin' around here."

"Why don't you go do it," Destry said without looking up.

"I ain't like you——"

"Thank God!"

"You know somethin', boy? I don't know where you get off havin' such a big head all of a sudden but I think I've put up with just about enough of yer crap and I ain't gonna do it no more."

Before she knew what was happening, Jimmy was on his knees beside Effie with one arm wrapped around her head and a knife jabbing into her throat with his other hand. She scarcely took a breath for fear that moving a fraction of an inch would force the knife through her skin.

Jimmy's eyes were on fire and he spoke through clenched teeth. "I ain't gonna repeat myself on this one, Destry, so listen up good." Destry's gaze froze on the pair as he placed his hands in his lap and silently listened to Jimmy. "Get up off yer good for nothin' ass and go down to that river and catch some damn fish so I can at least eat good for dinner tonight. If you don't do that or if you take off, I swear on my dead momma's grave, I will run this knife through Cookie's throat so fast, there won't be a damn thing nobody can do about it."

Destry's face went white. It was obvious that there was no arguing with

Jimmy. He stood up, grabbed his fishing pole and tackle box and rushed out of the cabin. He didn't even look back as he walked down the hill to the river.

Jimmy pulled the knife away and eased his grip on Effie. As soon as he did, she sucked in a jagged breath. Her eyes were glued to the knife. Wasn't he going to put it down? It was like he was frozen. He just stared straight ahead, his face twisted into a maniacal expression, the knife clamped tight in his hand.

Effie knew if one wrong word came out of her mouth or even if she looked at Jimmy the wrong way, it could easily mean the end of everything for her. He was at a point where he could not have cared less if he ran that knife through her or if he let her live. He really did see her as nothing more than a piece of property that could easily be replaced.

Suddenly, it became clear to her, that for him, it had never just been about keeping her quiet about what she had seen him do to Angie. Effie belonged to Jimmy. In his eyes, she really was no different than an old, used toy. If she could not do the things he wanted, he wasn't about to think twice about getting rid of her.

Her voice was shaky and almost soundless when she began speaking. "I was wrong to ever talk back to you. I—I'm just stupid sometimes. I promise, I really will try harder to do exactly what you say when you tell me from now on."

Jimmy turned his gaze toward Effie. He tilted his head sideways as his eyes raked over her body. The corner of his mouth twitched.

Effie couldn't look into his face. Her eyes dropped to the floor. A prickling sensation ran up her spine and she suddenly found herself gulping spastically. This was it. He was going to slash her to bits and it was all her fault. She should not have said a word. If she had only kept her mouth shut, she wouldn't have drawn his attention away from whatever he saw glazed over in his mind.

Jimmy's lips curled into a snarl and he pushed her away with all his might. "Get away from me you fat, dirty whore," he growled. "Go hide in the corner or behind the table—I don't care where. Just get yer fat ass away from me. You poisoned my friend's mind and that pisses me off. I'm gonna kill you for doin' it but first I'm gonna make ya suffer. I'm so mad, I could kill ya right now but that's too good for you, ya fat cow. Just get away from me."

Effie hurried to get on her hands and knees and she crawled over behind the table as fast as she could. She had been so intent on trying to get Destry on her side, it had never occurred to her to even think about how angry Jimmy would be if she succeeded. How could she have overlooked that? What a stupid mistake! Of course Jimmy would be furious. They had been friends for years and she had taken Destry away from him. For the time being, all she could do was hunker down behind the table and hope he wouldn't change his mind and kill her right away.

Silent tears ran down Effie's cheeks. She was not going to make it out of that cabin alive. She was never going to see her beloved newspaper again. She was never going to get her big break. She was never going to get the chance to make a difference. She was just going to disappear from the face of the earth and no one was even going to miss her.

Chapter 24

That evening after dinner, Jimmy loaded up his arms with beer cans wand went out onto the porch to drink himself into a stupor. The second he stepped out the door, Destry was at Effie's side with a flurry of hurried questions.

"What happened after I left this afternoon?" he whispered.

Effie did not want to answer. If Jimmy heard her talking to Destry, she knew he would be angry. Instead, she looked into his eyes and shook her head as if to say that her lips were sealed.

Destry frowned. "Come on," he said. "We don't have time to mess around here. You need to answer. I need to know. Did he say anything more?"

She shook her head but did not part her lips or utter a syllable.

"Did he force himself on you or beat you again?"

Another shake.

"Everything is OK then. He just needed some time to cool down then, right?"

She shook her head again.

"Well what then? You need to talk to me. I have to know where we stand."

Effie looked toward the door then quickly pulled Destry's head closer so she could whisper in his ear. "He said that he is going to kill me eventually but first he is going to make me suffer."

"Jimmy was just tryin' to scare you. He ain't really gonna do that." He gulped. "At least I don't think he will. He's gonna get sick of this soon and let you go. I just know it. I know he seems like a real bad guy but if you get to know him, he isn't all that horrible. We're gonna hafta go back home soon anyway or we ain't gonna have jobs anymore."

Effie looked directly at him with a no nonsense expression. "Please don't try to lie to me, Destry," she whispered. "I know he wasn't joking. He's extremely mad about you and me. He thinks I did something to you to make you change the way you think. Jimmy said that I poisoned your mind."

"Well that's just bull. You didn't do anything to me. It just took me a while to see how bad he's been treatin' me and Harry all these years."

"It doesn't matter. Jimmy is going to see things the way he wants to. He's mad and I am the one he is directing it towards. He really intends to kill me."

Destry wagged his head back and forth. "That isn't true."

"Listen, Destry," said Effie. "If you want to do what's right, you have to go to the police. That is the *only* chance we have to stop Jimmy from killing me."

"No way. I can't."

"You have to."

"No. Cookie, you heard what he said he would do if I tried to take off. Besides, if I leave, there isn't gonna be anyone here to stop him from hurting you."

Effie rolled her eyes. "Destry," she began. "I don't think you quite understand what is going to happen here." She looked away for a moment and sucked in a deep breath. "First, Jimmy is going to hurt me anyway he knows how and then, he is going to kill me whether you're here or not. You can't stop him. The only chance I have of not ending up like Angie is if you go get the damn police!"

Destry sighed. He knew she was right. "Fine. But I can't just take off. I have to find another way. The second I just leave, he'll gut you like a fish then he'll come after me too."

Bright headlights shown into the cabin and a familiar rumble filled their ears. Harry was back.

"Good," Effie quickly whispered then sat down behind the table again. "Until you come back with the police, we better not talk. The more we talk, the angrier Jimmy is going to get. If I'm really good, I might be able to buy a little bit of time."

Almost as soon as she sealed her lips, Jimmy came swaggering back into the cabin.

"Where's Harry?" asked Destry.

Jimmy grabbed another beer then sat down at the table. He pointed over his shoulder with his thumb. "Out gettin' stuff from the truck."

Destry went out to help unload the truck. Effie sat, back pressed against the cupboards, hoping that Jimmy would not look at her. She sucked in her breath and watched as he guzzled down the beer then crushed the can in his hand.

Jimmy got up to get another can and as he prepared to crack it open, he stopped. His eyes were glued to Effie. His tongue poked out of his mouth and ran over his lips. "Go kneel next to my bed, Cookie."

Effie wanted to do as she was told but she was afraid to move and instead, she shook her head ever so slightly.

"I mean it. Go over there and kneel down and wait. Soon as they're done gettin' the stuff outta the truck and we get settled, you are gonna willingly join me in my bed and satisfy me."

Effie shook her head again. What was wrong with her? So what if she didn't want to be violated again. Wasn't it better to be violated than dead?

"I ain't jokin' with you, girl. Why do you have to make everything so hard for yourself? You just get over there and do as you're told or you'll be sorry. I don't have no problems diggin' a hole for you out in the woods."

She got up and began walking toward his bed. Effie stuck out her chin defiantly and began grinding out words from clenched teeth. "No matter what you make me do or what you do to me, I will never, NEVER willingly join you in bed or satisfy you. You are nothing but a sick, crazy piece of white trash shit, Jimmy."

The moment the words were out of her mouth, Effie regretted saying them. Jimmy only stood still for a moment, his eyes smoldering. Suddenly, he dropped his can of beer and sprang forward, hurling himself at her. His fists were flying wildly and in no time at all, they were in a jumbled mass on the floor. Effie tried to cover her face but he just kept pummeling, a continuous flow of profanity, flying out of his mouth.

As soon as he heard the commotion, Destry dropped the bags from his hand and went flying into the cabin, Harry hot on his heels. He grabbed hold of Jimmy and yanked him off Effie.

"Get your hands off her!" he screamed as his fist connected with Jimmy's face.

Harry dropped an armful of bags and the keys to the truck then rushed over, his chest heaving laboriously. He pulled Destry away from his brother. Harry looped his arms under Destry's and around behind his head. Destry couldn't move to defend himself or fight back.

Jimmy stood up and wiped a trickle of blood from his cheek. He studied the smudge of blood on the back of his hand for a moment, opening and closing his fist.

"I don't know what's wrong with you but you've changed. You used to be like us but now yer gettin' soft toward the whores," he hissed.

He pulled his arm back and then let loose, punching Destry in the stomach over and over. When he was satisfied that he had caused enough pain, he brought his face up to Destry's, their noses almost touching. He clenched his teeth together.

"Get outta my cabin or I will kill you and that whore right now. I don't ever want you to come back here neither. And if you try bring the cops out here, the whore will be dead before they can break down the door. Yer lucky to get outta here alive so don't you go tryin' no stupid shit. Just get the hell out."

Destry looked at Effie and saw the terrified look on her face. He wanted to take her with him but he knew that Jimmy was serious. He cast one last look of hatred at Jimmy and Harry before snatching up the keys to the truck and running out the door.

Jimmy was shaking, he was so angry. He looked at Harry and pointed at Effie. "Tie her wrists around the post," he snarled.

Harry did not stop to ask questions. It was obvious that Jimmy was not someone to be argued with at that moment. He just tossed her mattress away from the post and rushed to get Effie's wrists bound as he had been told.

As Harry finished up tying the last knot, Jimmy unbuckled his belt and slid it from the loops. "See what trouble you caused, Cookie?" he growled. He folded the belt in half and snapped the leather together a few times before continuing. "Well now yer gonna pay, you fat, piece of shit whore."

Harry stepped back several feet and covered his ears. Jimmy brought the belt up then cracked it down. Effie screeched as it licked at her back. Jimmy repeated the action a dozen more times and each time he did so, another red line appeared.

By the time Jimmy finished whipping Effie, her back was covered with blood. Through tears, she was begging him to let her join him in bed. He ignored her request and grabbed a fresh can of beer then flopped down on his bed by himself. While he drank the beer, Harry took care of a few bags of supplies then closed the cabin up for the night. As soon as Jimmy was done drinking, the lights were out and the only sound was Effie's muffled cries.

Chapter 25

The sky was already growing bright when Effie woke the next morning. Jimmy and Harry were still sleeping so she dared not make a sound. The thought of another whipping made her shudder.

Really, it had been her own fault. What in the world made her think she could talk that way to Jimmy. It was as if she couldn't control her mouth and it was exactly the same temper that had gotten her in trouble at work.

Not only had she screwed up and mouthed off but now she was alone. True, it was the opportunity that they had been talking about just moments before Harry came home. Effie just hadn't expected it to happen so fast. Destry was gone but at least he was free to contact the authorities.

Effie tried to stretch her sore muscles. Laying face down on the floor with her hands tied around a post was far from comfortable. But then uncomfortable was better than dead. At least the quiet left her to her uninterrupted thoughts.

A small bit of doubt began to creep into the back of her mind. She wondered if Destry was going to call the police and bring them back to get her. Maybe he would. Then again, Jimmy had warned him not to bring the police or he would kill her. Maybe it wouldn't be so good if he came back with the police.

Effie knew she was lucky to be alive. One more instance where she mouthed off or did something wrong and Effie knew she would be dead. Jimmy was capable of it and with Destry gone, so, too was the voice of reason. Why had she pushed him to go?

Everything had changed the night before. Effie had to change too. She had to find a way to make herself let Jimmy and Harry use her at will. That much she knew. If she couldn't make herself do that, she might as well be dead already because that would mean zero chances of surviving the ordeal. Above all, she had to remain calm.

Although Effie had lost track of the calendar, her best guess was that she had been gone for twelve or thirteen days. If she was right, that meant at least a couple more days until she was due to report back to work. Hopefully, when she didn't return when she was supposed to, someone would contact the police. With any luck, the police would check her credit card records among other things. Those would at least give them some clue as to the area of the country where she was being held.

If the police did look at those records, maybe they would think that she was still in Colorado. All they would have to do then is check for information about her car. Even though the officer who had pulled them over said that the reason he wasn't giving Destry a ticket was because he didn't want to do the extra paperwork, he might remember that he pulled over a car from Michigan. Maybe he even had to keep a log of all the vehicles he pulled over even if he didn't issue a ticket. Maybe they would check the video surveillance at the filling station where they had fist used her credit card. Maybe they would go there and see her partial note scratched into the paint in the restroom. Maybe, maybe, maybe. Maybe she was just getting her hopes up too high.

Effie wanted to roll over and get more comfortable and put all of the maybes out of her mind but she couldn't. Maybe he wasn't going to help her. She knew that just laying there and waiting for someone to come rescue her wasn't going to help her survive any longer. Something had to give. She had to change the way she was thinking. Calm, cool and collected was the way it had to be.

She tried to roll as far to the side as she could and pull on the ropes. They were tied so tight! Harry had done a very good job binding her wrists. The rope wouldn't give at all so there was no chance that she could pull her hands free. The edges on the post were not sharp so trying to wear through the rope was out of the question as well. There was no way she was going to get loose unless one of the men let her go.

Fine. They were going to have to untie her sooner or later. It was only a matter of time until she really had to go to the bathroom and the bucket they had been making her use wasn't going to work with her laying on the floor.

Jimmy obviously had some sort of plans for Effie. All she had to do was formulate some sort of plan herself. Knowing that she had to have a plan was the easy part. Actually coming up with it was a whole other animal. There was no telling how long Jimmy would keep her alive so she had to be ready to act if an opportunity arose.

Effie's mind was on overdrive. Unfortunately, nothing good was coming of it. The more she tried to think up a survival plan, the more she dwelled on the fact that time was slipping away and she really could not do anything to help herself. Then there was the pain.

The pain from the gouge in her back was nothing compared to the pain from the whipping. It even hurt to lay still. On top of the pain, now she had to worry about infection. What if there were open wounds from the belt? It sure felt that way and if there were, she was much more likely to get an infection.

Her thoughts were starting to run into one another. As long as Jimmy and Harry were still sleeping, nothing was going to happen. It would probably be best if she tried to get a little more shuteye while she had the opportunity anyway, Effie reasoned. There was no telling what would happen when they woke and when they did, she had to be sharp.

Even if Effie was a little tired, it was hard to fall asleep again. Every time she closed her eyes, she pictured a different form of torture she was going to have to endure. She just had to clear her thoughts and in the end, concentrating on numbers and counting backward from one-hundred finally did the trick.

Chapter 26

Effie woke with a start. How long had she been asleep? Heavy footsteps. That's what woke her. Quickly, her eyes darted from one bed to the other to see who was up already. Both were empty. How in the world had she slept through Jimmy and Harry getting up and around?

She had only heard one set of footfalls, though, and try as she might, she couldn't see to whom they belonged. Either way, it was surprising that either of the men had left her to sleep late. Did she dare speak and risk angering someone?

For the moment, Effie remained silent. At that point, speaking out of turn or saying the wrong thing could have dire consequences. It was better to try to figure out who was there with her and quietly let them know she was awake.

Fifteen minutes later, after making it quite obvious that she was no longer sleeping, Effie realized that she needed them to acknowledge her right away. There was a pressure building and if she didn't get to a bucket soon, there was going to be a mess on the floor. She squeezed her legs together and tried to think of other things. The more she tried to concentrate, though, the more she heard the sound of rushing water in her head. In a last ditch effort, she tried clearing her throat several times to draw attention. Finally, when nothing else worked and it felt as though her bladder would burst if she did not relieve the pressure soon, she was forced to speak without first being spoken to.

"Excuse me," she said in a quiet voice.

The person behind her scuffed his feet but did not answer.

Effie repeated herself. "Excuse me." Someone was definitely back there listening. "Listen," she said, "I know that I'm supposed to wait for you to talk to me first but I have a little problem here."

"So yer gonna play by the rules, are ya?" It was Jimmy. "I sure hope you don't think that's gonna change the game. I've had enough of ya. Doin' what yer told ain't gonna change nothing."

Someone snickered. Was that Harry? Was it possible that they were both back there, waiting to mess with Effie?

"I said I'm sorry. I know that nothing is going to change and I know that you are going to do whatever it is that you want to do to me. Right now, however, I have a problem and if you don't listen to me, it is going to become your problem."

Jimmy got up and walked over in front of her. "What? Yer uncomfortable? You want a pillow? Well, I don't give a damn about yer problems."

"Please Jimmy. Just listen to me for a second. Humor me," she said.

"My brother don't gotta do nothin' for ya, Cookie." Harry joined his brother and stood at his side.

Effie was losing patients and getting close to losing control of her bladder. She sucked in a deep breath. "I need to go to the bathroom and if you guys don't untie me and help me get to the bucket, it is going to be all over the floor. I don't think you want that."

"Oh, Miss Cookie," began Jimmy, clutching his chest and doing his best impression of a damsel in distress. "You still don't seem to understand that yer nothin' more than a animal. That pretty much means that I don't care if ya piss and shit all over yerself. Just don't be gettin' nothin' on my floor!"

Harry burst into fits of laughter, slapping his knee. He leaned over and whispered something in Jimmy's ear then they both began laughing. Jimmy whispered something back and they laughed even harder.

"Please. I really need to go," begged Effie.

Harry disappeared behind her but she could hear him rummaging around. Something clattered to the floor and all she could think about was the rushing water and the agony of the pressure building in her lower abdomen. He must have held something up for Jimmy to see.

"That ain't gonna work. Try gettin' somethin' like a long log. Has to be longer than anything we got split for the stove so ya might hafta look in the woods a little bit."

What in the world were they up to? It made Effie very uneasy to think about what Jimmy and Harry might want with a log. Any number of things could be done with it. They wouldn't beat her to death with a log, would they? Maybe they were planning to tie her to it. Effie didn't have to wonder long because Harry was back in a flash with something that pleased Jimmy.

"Perfect," he said as Harry dropped an object on the floor with a loud thud.

Effie did not like the feeling that something was going on. There was no telling what they were up to. She knew it was no good and being chained and tied to the post, there was nothing she could do to defend herself against whatever it was.

"Please, Jimmy. Please untie me so I can use the bucket," she pleaded.

"Spread yer legs apart."

"What? I can't do that," said Effie. "I'm going to lose control if I do."

Jimmy gave her a cockeyed look. "You wasn't never in control, Cookie, and I don't know what ever made ya think that ya was."

"That's not what I mean."

"Then why did you say it?" Jimmy questioned as he put a full teakettle on the stove then stoked the fire.

Effie began to whimper. "I mean that I have to go to the bathroom *that* bad and if I uncross my legs, I am not going to be able to stop myself from going."

Jimmy moved do she could look up at him while he talked. "I told ya once, whore, you ain't no different from a common animal. You been bad and I ain't gonna untie ya. I don't care if yer eyes are floatin' in piss."

"Jimmy, please let me up to use the bucket. As soon as I'm done going, you can tie me up again or do whatever you want to me." She did her best to give him a pleading look.

"No," he shouted then turned away from Effie.

"Harry, we got more rope sittin' around here somewhere?"

Harry had been quietly waiting for Jimmy to tell him what to do next. As soon as he knew what to look for, he began digging through the trunk in the corner. After a few minutes, he pulled out a coil of rope in triumph and handed it to Jimmy.

"Good," said Jimmy. "Now get that log over here by where her feet are gonna be. You and me are gonna get her legs apart if I hafta rip them off. We're gonna tie 'em to the log so she can't put 'em together again. We'll see how Miss Cookie likes that. Damn whore. We're gonna teach her a lesson about control."

The men set to work doing exactly what Jimmy had said. When they pried

Effie's legs apart, she thought for sure, that was it. All she could do was concentrate on controlling the urge. For the moment, it seemed to work. For how long, though, she was not sure.

"Aww," said Jimmy as he and Harry burst into laughter. "I thought you was gonna piss all over the place as soon as yer legs wasn't together no more. Looks like ya lied to me, Cookie."

Harry grabbed the kettle from the stove. "Won't it burn?" he asked.

"I don't give a damn if it does."

"Yeah, but if we mix it with some cold water, we'll have twice as much warm water."

Jimmy looked at Harry like he would an alien. "Sometimes you surprise me little brother," he said. "I think it's a fine idea to have lots of warm water instead of just a little. It'll work better if we do.

As soon as Harry had the hot water from the kettle mixed with cold water in a bucket, he walked over directly behind Effie. Neither of the men could suppress giggles. Jimmy dipped a coffee cup into the bucket and slowly tipped it so its contents washed over Effie's genitals. Again and again, he dipped the cup into the water then dumped it on her. He and Harry were nearly falling on the floor, they were laughing so hard.

Effie tried to squeeze her legs together but with her ankles tied to the log, it was no use. The sensation of the warm water was terrible. There was no way Effie would be able to control herself if they kept doing that.

"Stop," she moaned. "I can't hold it much longer."

That only made the men laugh all the harder. Harry had a cup now, too, and was pouring water on her.

"What's wrong, ya fat cow? She must not like the water Harry," Jimmy laughed.

"Please, please stop," Effie cried. "Just let me use the bucket."

She had reached a point where she could not take it any longer. When they wouldn't stop pouring the water on her, Effie just relaxed the muscles she had been clenching so hard. It felt both euphoric and beastly to relieve herself.

The pressure of a full bladder was no longer a problem. Urinating on the floor, in front of two men was far beyond the humiliation she felt from being naked in front of them. It lowered her to the level of a filthy animal. It made her into the very thing which Jimmy kept telling her she was.

He looked at Effie as if he had no part in making her lose control of her bladder. "You filthy whore," he growled. "Now ya done gone and pissed all over my floor. That ain't very respectful. Now I gotta teach ya what happens when ya do somethin' like that."

Effie squeezed her head between her arms and bracing herself for another beating. It was like time had gone into slow motion. She kept waiting and waiting for the fist to pound or the belt to lick. It didn't happen. Instead, Effie heard a zipper then a stream of warm liquid began pelting her head.

At first, Effie though Jimmy was just pouring another cup of water on her. After a moment, when the stream of liquid did not stop, she realized what was happening. Jimmy was urinating on her head! She struggled in her bindings but there was no way she could move away from him. The next thing she knew, another stream of liquid was hitting the other side of her head and the men were gasping for air, they were laughing so hard.

Finally, it stopped. Jimmy and Harry headed out to the porch, still in a state of hysteria, leaving Effie alone. Her head was soaked with their urine and when she lifted it, the urine ran onto her cheeks and forehead. The stench was sickening. She wanted to retch but the thought of a puddle of vomit just inches from her face kept her from it. Effie had to do something to keep her mind off the smell.

Thoughts were whirling through her head and the one that seemed to come to the surface was of Destry. He had been gone long enough that Effie knew he wasn't coming back. Deep down, she really wanted to believe that he would think up something and come through for her. She also wanted to believe that the feeling in her heart was right about him but now she saw that he was no different than everyone else in her life.

If there wasn't anyone who would ever be there for her, why was Effie even bothering to fight Jimmy? The more she thought about it, the more she knew it made sense to give in. She may as well do exactly as she was told and figure that she was going to spend the rest of her life (however long or short that was going to be) there in the cabin.

Then again, Effie had never done as she was told. Mr. Ludgreen, Rich Hale, other coworkers—none of them ever thought she would amount to much. That's why she was never given the opportunities that other people were. Even her parents never believed in her and always told her she would never amount to a hill of beans. She proved them wrong. She had put herself through college and landed a decent job. So what if none of it came easy. She put her mind to it and got what she wanted. If Effie gave up now, everyone who had ever been mean to her or tried to keep her down won. No way could she let that happen!

So what if she was currently chained and tied to a post and soaked in urine with her ankles bound to a giant log. There had to be a way out of it. Maybe Jimmy would not untie her. Sooner or later, though, he was going to leave her alone with Harry. He was the dumb one. She knew if they were alone together, she would be able to talk him into untying her. All she had to do was figure out what to do after that.

After a while, Jimmy came back into the cabin, Harry at his heels like a puppy. When they began talking about lunch, Effie's ears perked up. Her stomach had been rumbling and if there was a chance of Jimmy untying her, it was to prepare food for him. To her surprise, however, he and Harry pulled out some food and began preparing it themselves.

Effie did not want to speak out of turn again but she couldn't help it. She could hear them eating, rather noisily, behind her and it only made the pit of hunger in her stomach grow. The more she thought about the food they were eating, the more her stomach rumbled. It was loud enough, they had to have heard it.

She licked her lips and tried to dampen her cottony mouth. "I'm sorry for speaking out of turn again, Jimmy," she said.

His mouth was full so his words came out sounding more like a grunt than anything else. Effie took it to mean that he was listening.

"I couldn't help noticing that you and Harry are eating lunch." Effie paused for a moment to see if one of the men would pick up on her hint. If they did, they were both too busy shoving food into their mouths to say anything. "It's been a while since I've had anything to eat or drink."

Jimmy gulped down a mouthful of food. "So," he said, wiping the back of his hand across his face and staring at her with a blank expression.

"I was just wondering if you would be willing to show me your kindness again and share a little food and water."

"And why should I be worried about you getting anything to eat? It ain't like yer gonna die if you don't get nothing. With all that fat, it'll take you a long time to waste away."

"Uhhh," Effie began. That was something she had heard a thousand times while she was growing up. She had to get Jimmy's brain away from that frame of mind. She racked her mind. What would make the most sense to him? Then a thought occurred to her. "Well I *am* your prisoner and even in jail, they make sure that all of the prisoners get meals each day."

Jimmy's eyes were like burning coals. "If I fed you, that would mean that I care whether you live or die and I really don't give a shit. Besides, if you hafta eat, it's just gonna make our food supplies go down faster. To tell you the truth, there ain't no way in hell I'm gonna walk to town and haul groceries back here just to make sure that yer fat ass gets enough to eat."

"Please, Jimmy," she whined, her stomach growling again. "I'm so hungry and it's not like I'm asking for a lot of food. Just a little bit?"

"I'll tell you what," Jimmy said, his mouth full of food again. "If my baby brother feels like it after he's done eatin', I'll let him decide if he wants to give you a bowl of water."

Effie rested her head on her arm. It didn't matter if she was hungry or not. She had to accept whatever Jimmy was willing to give. At least water would keep her hydrated. It was better than nothing and it was a step in the right direction.

"Thank you, Jimmy," she muttered.

When he was done eating, Jimmy pushed his chair away from the table and waited to see what his brother would do. For the first time ever, Harry had slowed down and was taking his time eating his meal. It was obvious that he was trying to make it last as long as possible. He was unsure if Jimmy really wanted Effie to have some water or not.

Eventually, the time came when Harry could stall no longer. There was not a crumb left on his plate but he kept staring at it just in case one would appear. If it was up to him, he would let her have a drink. He did not see any harm in it and their supply of water was unlimited. If he gave her a drink, though, and it was not what Jimmy wanted, he would get mad at Harry for not making the right decision. The last thing he wanted was to be stuck in the cabin when Jimmy was mad at him.

As it turned out, Harry didn't have to make a decision. When he looked up from his plate, Jimmy was sitting there with his arms crossed in front of his chest and an amused look on his face.

"Well, go get Miss Cookie a bowl of water," he said as if it was the most obvious thing in the world.

Harry hurried to grab a bowl, he filled it with water then hurried across the room, sloshing water on the floor the entire way. He carefully sat the bowl on the floor next to Effie. She looked from it to him.

"How am I supposed to drink out of this?" she asked.

Jimmy got up and walked over to her side. He crouched down and began whispering. "See, ya whore? You just don't listen, do ya? I already told you that yer no different than an animal. Since you ain't no different, you can drink like dog."

"I can't do that," Effie scoffed.

Jimmy shook his head. "Well if you wanna drink so bad, yer gonna hafta drink that way. Otherwise, you ain't gonna get nothing."

"Well I at least need the bowl over where I can reach it. I can't reach it where it's sitting right now." She looked up at Harry. "Could you please put the bowl between my arms?"

Harry carefully moved the bowl. It was too far forward, though, and in order to drink from it, Effie had to pull it toward her with her chin. Jimmy stood with his arm braced against the post, watching in obvious delight. The movement of the bowl caused water to splash up into Effie's face and he laughed, his eyes glinting with pleasure.

Effie thought about how a dog drinks for a moment then she slowly stuck out her tongue and lowered it to the water. She began lapping at the surface. It felt good to get a little of the cool water into her mouth but she wanted more. She wanted to gulp down the entire bowl. It was frustrating lapping just a little into her mouth at a time.

After a while, Jimmy grew sick of watching Effie licking at the water and he went out to sit on the porch, leaving Harry alone with her. She continued on with the water for several minutes. Every few moments, she would glance up into Harry's eyes and find him staring right back at her. She stopped drinking and slowly ran her tongue over her lips. Harry gasped.

"Can you keep a secret?" Effie whispered with a smile.

Harry gave her a funny look. "Why?" he asked.

"There's something I really want to tell you but I have to know that you won't tell."

At first, she did not think that Harry was even going to say anything back to her, let alone agree to keep a secret. His brow dropped and he studied her face as if he was trying to figure out if she was trying to trick him. It was clear that he did not want to do anything that would jeopardize the standing he had with his brother.

"Why should I keep yer secret, Cookie?"

"Well," began Effie, "I'm afraid that your brother would get jealous and I don't want him to get mad at you." She caught his gaze for the briefest moment then looked away.

"I don't know," said Harry. "Jimmy would probably get mad if he even knew we was talking."

"OK, Harry. I understand. If you don't want to know, I won't say anything. I certainly don't want to get you in any kind of trouble."

He quickly looked at the door. "I probably shouldn't but I guess there ain't nothin' wrong with one little secret, it there?"

Effie smiled wide. Triumph! "There is nothing wrong with this kind of secret."

"Well?"

"Well now that I know I can trust you, I'm a little bit nervous. I mean, what if you laugh at me?"

Harry bent and gently brushed her hair away from her face. "I won't laugh," he said. "I promise."

"Ok," Effie said and took a deep breath then exhaled. "Here goes." She looked directly into Harry's eyes. "I want you to know from the first time I laid eyes on you, I liked you better than any of the others."

"Really?"

"Really. You've been much nicer to me and you are far more handsome."

Was Harry blushing? He looked away from Effie.

"Yer just sayin' that so I'll untie ya or something," he said.

Effie's smile fell. "No, Harry. That's not true. You have no idea how hard it is for me to say that I find you handsome. People aren't always very nice to me. I have a hard time talking to men especially because I know they never find me attractive. Please believe me when I tell you that I think you are very handsome."

Harry was blushing! He smiled as wide as Effie had ever seen anyone smile. Apparently women were about as nice to him as men were to her. She could almost sympathize with him. Well, if he wasn't one of her captors and if he would just wash up, get a clean shave and some fresh clothes, she could at least think about sympathizing with him for a moment or two.

Effie looked down at the floor then back up at Harry again. "Promise me that you won't say anything about this to Jimmy."

"I promise," he said.

She began lapping the water again. How in the world did the animal kingdom survive, drinking like this? It was horrible. She stopped and thought.

"Do you think you could help me drink this, Harry?" she said.

"What do you want me to do?" She had him eating out of her hand as long as Jimmy wasn't in the room!

"Just pick up the bowl and lift it to my lips. This is kind of an odd angle to drink so just tip it a little at a time or my whole face will be covered in water."

Harry was staring at her lips as he reached out to grasp the bowl. Effie decided to take advantage of the situation so she tried to look as seductive as possible. She slowly licked her lips then smiled, running the tip of her tongue along her teeth. It felt ridiculous but it must have done what it was supposed to. Harry's eyes were wide and he let out an audible gasp.

He lifted the bowl to her lips and ever so carefully, he tipped it. The cool water rushed into Effie's mouth. Oh! How glorious! It almost made her forget how hungry she was. Almost. The water just gushed down her throat, washing away any dry, cottony feeling she may have had. A small trickle of water ran from the corner of her mouth and she hated the thought of any water going to waste. There was no telling how long it would be until Jimmy would let her have more.

"Thank you," Effie whispered when the bowl was empty and Harry placed it on the floor. She looked into his eyes again and licked her lips.

Suddenly, the lightbulb hanging over the table began to flicker and the generator began to cough. The light went out. The familiar hum was gone and an uncomfortable silence filled the air. Out on the porch, Jimmy began swearing.

"Dammit! Generator's empty. You was supposed to make sure that it was kept goin' Harry. Get yer fat ass out here and get to it!"

Harry rushed to get to his feet and he began running toward the door. Halfway across the room, he stopped and ran back to Effie. He leaned down in front of her.

"I won't say a word to Jimmy 'bout the stuff you told me," he said then headed back toward the door.

This new development with Harry was surprising. Effie had not expected to win his affections so easily. She knew she could not trust him to choose her over his brother. If the opportunity arose, however, she knew she could manipulate him enough to where she might be able to swing an escape. She would be able to get him to untie her if she put forth a little effort. The chain would be her biggest obstacle. There was only one key to either of the two padlocks and as far as she knew, Jimmy had them. There would be no sneaking them out of his pocket.

As Effie's thoughts began to wander, they were interrupted by arguing out on the front porch. It sounded like the generator was empty and the fuel supply was gone. She could easily imagine the deep crease between Jimmy's burning eyes from the tone of his voice.

"What do you mean there's no more fuel for it?" he snarled.

Harry was almost stuttering when the words poured out of his mouth. It must have been terrible to have a brother like Jimmy. "Well," he said then licked his lips. "Remember? Ya had me put the gas cans in the back of the truck so we could take 'em up to Webb's to get 'em filled? They must still be in it."

"Why in the hell didn't you take the damn things out? I told ya to put 'em over by the generator after ya had 'em filled. If ya woulda done what I told ya to do, we wouldn't have this problem right now, would we?" There was a short pause. Jimmy repeated himself louder. "Would we?" Harry nodded his head in agreement and there was silence for a moment.

All of a sudden, Jimmy screamed like a mad man. Harry came tumbling into the cabin and he kept clear of the door. Jimmy picked up the broken rocker from the end of the porch and smashed it against the cabin wall then threw the remains as far as he could

"Yer an idiot, Harry," he screamed. "None of this would have happened if you just woulda done what I told ya to do!"

Cups and plates crashed to the floor as Jimmy hit the wall with something else from the porch. He heard the noise and came flying into the cabin. Harry dove for cover in his bed. There was nowhere Effie could go and nothing she could do but bury her head between her arms.

Before she knew what was happening, Jimmy was standing over her, belt in hand. He grabbed a handful of her hair and yanked upward. He crouched down and pulled Effie's head toward his mouth.

"You shoulda kept yer fat ass in yer seat back at the Coon Pit. You didn't, though. You had to go stickin' yer nose in other people's business. Yer head is full of snakes just like all the other whores. Them snakes got into Destry's head and screwed him over. The truck would still be here and so would our fuel supply if it wasn't for you bein' such a fat whore."

Effie was in tears. There was nothing she could do to defend herself and no one around who would do it for her. Jimmy had shown his anger before but nothing like the fury at this point.

He stood up and as he did, he yanked Effie's hair as hard as he could. Effie screamed at the top of her lungs. The pain was horrendous. Jimmy answered the scream by bringing his belt down across her back. Her body convulsed as he brought the belt down again and again.

Finally, he let go of Effie's hair and tossed the belt aside. Jimmy was already across the room by the time it hit the floor. With one swipe of his arm, anything that had not fallen off the shelves already when hurtling toward the floor. He stomped out of the cabin and down the steps and then he was gone. The only sounds were Effie's gasps between sobs. Neither she nor Harry dared move a muscle for fear that Jimmy would come back and continue his rampage.

After a while, Harry got up and peaked out the door. There didn't seem to be anyone out there so he stepped out onto the porch to look around. Jimmy was nowhere to be seen. He went back into the cabin but did not bother to check on Effie. Instead, he began cleaning up everything that had fallen.

When the mess was cleaned up, Harry found a few flashlights and sat them on the table then lit one lantern. Without a word, he grabbed a fishing pole and headed down to the river. It was best to wait away from the cabin in case Jimmy was still in a bad mood when he returned.

Effie cried until she had no tears left. Her back felt like it was on fire and her head throbbed. At that moment, she wanted to give up and die so she would not have to suffer any longer. Why even bother trying to survive? Even if she did escape, Jimmy would hunt her down and kill her. He knew the area far better than she ever would and he would probably recapture her long before she had a chance to make it to safety. And even if she did make it to another cabin or town or even the filling station, who was to say that the people there would not be good friends of Jimmy's. They would probably just take Effie right back to him.

Her mind was swirling with thoughts and before long, Effie couldn't even seem to capture a single one of them. Her head felt like it weighed ten pounds and she couldn't even lift it. She just closed her eyes and followed the swirls behind the lids into a deep sleep, hoping that she would never wake up.

For a long time, she did sleep without waking. Harry tried to rouse her when he came back in from fishing. He had another bowl of water and was going to offer her a small piece of fish. Nothing he did could open her eyes, though. Even hours later, when Jimmy came stumbling into the cabin in the dark cover of night, she didn't wake. She just slept through the night.

Chapter 27

The next morning, Effie woke to the worst headache she had ever experienced and excruciating pain from the whipping. There was a vague memory of wanting to die still lingering. She knew she had to try to put the pain out of her thoughts or she could easily slip into that frame of mind permanently.

Effie suddenly remembered that Jimmy had stormed off the previous night but she had no memory of him returning. She raised her head to look toward his bed but all she saw was a haze. Her eyes were filled with the remnants of a night of tears. It was uncomfortable and she desperately wanted to wipe the gunk out of them but with her hands tied, it was impossible. Instead, she was forced to resort to try to blink the gunk away.

At first, no matter how hard she blinked or how fast or slow, it didn't seem to do anything. Several minutes later, however, images began to take form. She looked toward Jimmy's bed again and her heart sank. There he was, sprawled out just like every other morning. She pressed her eyes shut and laid her head on the floor. Jimmy was bound to be in a bad mood when he woke. Not that there ever seemed to be a time when he was not angry.

Effie lifted her forehead off the floor and rested her head on her arm, facing Harry's bed. If it had been possible, she would have jumped when she opened her eyes. He was laying there, staring right back at her in silence. He did not move when he saw her looking at him except for the occasional sigh.

"Good morning," Effie mouthed and put on her best smile.

Harry did not bother to move or say anything back. His eyes just began roaming over her body. It was like he was lost in his own little world and no one else could get in.

Effie tried to talk to him again. This time, she whispered. "When did he come back? I don't remember it."

"He came back in the middle of the night," boomed a voice.

Effie swung her head around to look the other direction. Standing right beside her was Jimmy. He had crept out of bed and she hadn't even heard it, she was so intent on getting something out of Harry. Now she had done it. He looked as angry as she had ever seen him.

She opened her mouth to talk but no words came out. What more was there for her to say? She knew there was no reason to beg or plead and no amount of talking would ever calm Jimmy down. She just laid there, trying to look up at him. All she could do was wait for the other shoe to drop.

Jimmy glared at Harry for a moment. "Idiot," he muttered then walked out of Effie's field of vision.

Effie heard the scrape of metal as he picked something up. When he came back into view, her eyes went to his hand. Her heart stopped and she couldn't seem to fill her lungs. Jimmy had a large knife clenched tight in his hand.

She tried to think of any as many reasons as she could as to why he would grab the knife. Only one seemed valid. Jimmy was angry and how many timed had he said he would kill her? It wasn't even worth it for her to try to count. This was it. Effie had gone too far and now Jimmy was going to kill her. There were so many things that she would never do and all because she had not been able to hold her tongue. She had screwed up in talking back to Rich Hale in the office and now she had screwed up in trying to talk to Harry.

Effie squeezed her eyes shut as tight as she could and pressed her head against the floor. She didn't want either of the men to see her cry. Jimmy and Harry were horrible, evil people and there was no way Effie was going to face her death pleading for her life to the likes of them. Instead, she began conjuring up the happiest memories she could think of. If she had to go, she would at least be thinking happy thoughts.

Then something amazing happened. Jimmy did not stab or slash at Effie. Instead, he crouched down in front of her and began hacking at the ropes that bound her wrists. When she felt the tugging rope, she lifted her head and opened one eye to be sure her mind wasn't playing tricks on her. It was true! Jimmy really was cutting her bindings. When he was done with her hands, he cut through the roped that tied her ankles to the log.

166

Fresh air rushed into her lungs and she had to try to hide a smile. "Thank you, Jimmy," she said.

"Don't be thankin' me. It's my brother ya gotta thank. I was ready to cut ya to bits last night when I came back but Harry was all whiney like a little girl. He ain't had much chance to screw around with ya yet so I told him I'd let him have some time with you today but after that, I ain't makin' no promises. If you wanna thank someone, thank that pussy over there," he said, pointing toward Harry.

Effie began stretching and rubbing her sore muscles. As she did, she studied Harry's face. He was still staring back in silence. Had telling him that she was attracted to him really been enough for him to talk Jimmy out of killing her right away? It must have been. What luck that she had played her cards the way she did.

Then another thought entered her mind. Jimmy was ready to kill her while she was sleeping. She never would have known what hit her. He would have snuffed her out like a candle without a second thought. A chill ran down her spine. After Jimmy's rage the night before and this new knowledge, Effie realized that time was running very short.

Jimmy hooked his hand under her arm and yanked her upward, breaking her train of thought. "I'm sick of makin' my own meals and my stinkin' brother can't cook worth shit," he grumbled. "Get yer fat ass in gear and get us somethin' to eat before I change my mind about lettin' you live."

Effie stumbled as she tried to get some food around. Every muscle in her body ached. She worked as fast as she could, though, telling herself that she had to please Jimmy. True, he'd said that he didn't promise to keep her alive until the next day. However, he had not said that he would definitely kill her either. If she could please him, it just might buy her a little extra time.

She pulled open the refrigerator. Even though the generator had run out of fuel the day before, the things inside still seemed to be a little cool. Luckily, no one had been in it since they lost their power source. There were some things in there she wouldn't use for fear that the slightly warmer temperature had spoiled them. There was a nice hunk of cheese, though, and with Jimmy's permission, Effie began preparing grilled cheese sandwiches. It may not have been a top choice for breakfast but it was warm and anything that made Jimmy happy was good.

By the time Effie was done cooking, Harry had crawled out of bed and joined Jimmy at the table. Effie served them then obediently took her place on the floor next to Jimmy. With any luck, one of the men would share some food with her. At that point, she was so hungry, she would have eaten moldy bread off the floor if Jimmy had told her that she could.

Much to her dismay, Jimmy made sure that every last bit of grilled cheese was gone. He made a point of licking his fingers clean when he saw the hunger etched on Effie's face. It was clear, he was not going to make anything easy for her.

When they were done eating, Jimmy stood up and Effie took that as her cue to begin cleaning up the dishes. He announced that he and Harry were going to go down to the river to catch lunch and maybe even dinner. Harry looked as his brother like someone had just told him his pet had been run over. He had been expecting to get some time alone with Effie and now Jimmy was taking him away and keeping him busy.

Jimmy looked around the room then his eyes stopped on Effie. "You better get yer act in gear and get this place cleaned up. I don't take it very kindly when someone pisses all over my floor."

Effie just bowed her head and said, "Yes, sir."

Jimmy practically had to drag Harry out of the cabin but in a way, Effie was glad he was going. If they were both gone, it would give her time to concentrate on an escape plan. Maybe she could pick one of the locks on the chain. But even if she did that, they would probably catch her before she got to the road. Surely, one of them would see her leaving the cabin and they would both be after her in a split-second. Even if she could outrun them, they knew the area better. They probably knew shortcuts. No, picking the lock and running off was not a very good plan. Effie would have to think of something better.

She stood at the window facing the river for a moment, watching the men get settled. There just had to be a way to outsmart them. What was it? She kept drawing a blank. Reluctantly, Effie left the window. Jimmy would be beyond angry if she didn't get the cabin straightened up before they came back . She would think while she worked.

With the dishes done, Effie straightened up the shelves then moved on to find the bucket and some rags so she could begin working on the floor. It made her sick to think that Jimmy and Harry made her go to the bathroom on it. They kept telling her that she was an animal. How could either of them say that? If Jimmy had one shred of humanity in him, he would have at least let her up to use the bucket. He was more of an animal than anyone!

Effie kept working and for a long time, she didn't notice how hard she was scrubbing the floor. Then she realized that the particular board she was working on was moving. She stopped scrubbing and pressed on a few of the other boards. Some of them moved very easily too. In fact, when she looked at them, many of the nails had been pulled out.

Her heart began pounding and beads of perspiration formed on her forehead. This could be the answer to her problem. Maybe she could pick one of the locks then climb down through a hole in the floor. If she could move the boards back into place from below, they might have no idea how she got out.

Effie closed her eyes and tried to concentrate on the day they brought her there. When she first looked at the cabin, she noticed that the part under the porch wasn't covered. Did the cabin walls go all of the way to the ground or was it open under there as well? Jimmy had not given her much of a chance to look around outside before sending her through the door. She seemed to remember seeing that the cabin walls went all of the way to the ground. That might not be all bad. They probably had some kind of door so they could get under the cabin if they needed to. She could pick the lock, climb down through the hole and replace the boards then wait until they either left or went to sleep. After that, she could sneak out and escape on foot.

She began clawing at one of the loose boards. A few times, she lifted it a hair but her nails kept giving way. She just couldn't get a good enough grip on the heavy board. Effie got to her feet and looked out the window. Both of the men were still down at the river. Frantically, she looked around the cabin. There had to be something that she could use to pry up one of the boards. After she had one up, the rest would be easy.

Her eyes stopped on the cooking utensils. A spoon! Maybe she could use the tip of the spoon to lift the board up high enough for her to get a good grip. Then she could move it! Effie grabbed a big spoon then ran over to look out the window again. It looked like Harry was reeling in a fish. They were both still down there though.

Effie ran back to the loose board and fell to her knees. She slipped the tip of the spoon into the crack between planks and pressed down on the handle. It bent. The board didn't even budge. She almost cried as she tossed the spoon aside. There had to be something else in the cabin she could use.

This time, Effie rushed over to the trunk in the corner. If Harry had pulled a shirt and a piece of rope out of it, maybe there was something in there she could use. She lifted the heavy lid and began rummaging around inside. That was when she found what she was looking for. Underneath a pile of clothes and blankets, she found an old box of tools. There was no pry bar but there was a great big screwdriver. The shaft of it was as big around as her little finger. That had to be strong enough th lift the floorboard without bending. She grabbed the screwdriver then buried the toolbox under the clothes again.

Again, she raced over to the window to check on Jimmy and Harry. The blood drained from her face. Jimmy wasn't sitting next to Harry anymore. Instantly, she dropped the screwdriver. He would be furious if he saw her with it. There was no telling what he would do if he caught her with it in her hand.

She glanced out the front door of the cabin and even dared to step closer in order to get a better view outside. Where was he? Then she caught some movement out of the corner of her eye. Effie turned and looked back toward the river again. The bush near Harry was moving. All of a sudden, Jimmy stepped out into the open. He was zipping up his pants.

Effie took a deep breath. What a relief! All that panic and Jimmy had just been in the bushes going to the bathroom. As he sat down next to Harry again, Effie dove for the screwdriver then went back to her place on the floor.

The first time she tried to lift the board, it moved quite a bit but then it slipped and fell back into place. Effie closed her eyes for a moment and concentrated on just breathing. She had to calm down. It felt like her heart was going to explode right out of her chest.

As soon as her heart slowed, she put the screwdriver down to the floorboard and pressed down on the handle. The board lifted and she slipped her fingers underneath then lifted. The board was heavy but she slid it aside. She grabbed another board and moved it too.

Effie looked down into the hole. It was dark. That meant that she had remembered correctly. The cabin walls did go all of the way to the ground. Where did they keep the flashlights? She looked around. There was one on the floor next to Jimmy's bed. She crawled over and grabbed it. When she pressed the button, the light came on. It was a little dim but it was better than nothing.

Back at the hole, she aimed the light at the ground. There was something down there. Effie leaned over and stuck her head through the hole so she could get a better look. She jumped and dropped the flashlight when she realized what she was looking at. The bag that she used as a purse was laying under there and her little journal was on the ground next to it. Not only that, but women's clothing, purses and bags was strewn all about. None of it looked familiar. It couldn't have been hers. Harry burned all of her clothes. Jimmy made him. But if that wasn't her clothing, whose was it?

It did not really matter who any of it belonged to. It was obvious that someone had put it there for a reason. From the looks of it, that person had saved her bag and had taken the time to read through her journal.

This was both good and bad. On one hand, that meant that there was a door to get under there because she hadn't seen anyone move the boards and they had to put all of those things down there somehow. On the other hand, the flashlight was now laying down there too—and it was turned on. Even if she leaned through the hole and stretched as far as she could, she couldn't come close to reaching the flashlight. She would have to climb down there to retrieve it.

Effie got up and looked out the window again. Shit! They were packing up! How long had she been at it? There was no time to climb through the hole to get the flashlight. They were already starting to walk up the hill. She ran back over to slide the boards back into place. Oh no! She'd put the boards in the wrong place and they didn't fit right. Quickly, she lifted one board out and slid the other one over. Then she laid the second board back in place. She had to get back to scrubbing.

The bent spoon and the screwdriver! They were still laying in the middle of the floor. Effie scooped them up then dropped them into her bucket. They disappeared into the dirty water.

Jimmy came up the steps and into the cabin and looked around. There, in the middle of the floor was Effie, on her hands and knees, scrubbing. She kept her head down and worked the rag against the floor as hard as she could.

Effie's heart was drumming in her ears. Her eyelid began to twitch as she struggled to keep her cool. What if they could see a glow from the flashlight emanating from the cracks in the floor when it got dark? Jimmy would know that she'd pulled up the floorboards. She knew that if Jimmy became angry with her again, there would be no more chance of escape. She was already far beyond any line he had drawn and he would not hesitate for a moment. Jimmy would kill her and that would be it.

"Cookie!"

Effie almost jumped out of her skin. She swung her head around and looked up at Jimmy. Shit! She'd zoned out. Had he noticed that the flashlight was missing from the floor next to his bed?

Jimmy repeated himself when he saw that he had her attention. "I said that I want you to hurry up and finish washin' the floor. Soon as yer done, I want you to get to work cleanin' these fish."

"Clean the fish?" Effie looked at him like he was speaking gibberish. "You want me to clean the fish?"

"Well they ain't gonna clean themselves," Harry said.

"You got a problem doin' what I say?" asked Jimmy. "If you do, I got an answer for ya and you ain't gonna like it."

"No, I don't have any problem doing what you say." Her hands were flipping all over the place as she spoke. "It's just—Well, I've never cleaned a fish before and I don't want to screw up your meal just because I'm an idiot. I want you to be able to enjoy the fish since you spent all that time and energy catching them—"

"You can't tell me that you give a tinker's fuck in hell about what I like or don't like," Jimmy interrupted. Effie's mouth just hung open. She licked her lips and swallowed hard as he went on. "That floor looks clean enough. Yer done."

There was no point in arguing with him. Effie got up and carried the bucket over to the sink so she could work on the fish. Before she started, she looked right into Jimmy's eyes and studied him.

"I just want to say that I'm sorry right now if they don't come out satisfactory," she said. "I'm going to try my best to do it right."

This time it was Jimmy's turn to look at the ground. "Just shut up and get the knife. This one time, I'm gonna tell you how to do it. Next time I tell ya to clean the fish, I expect you to know what to do."

That was that. He was not going to cut her any breaks. Effie grabbed the first knife she could find and went over to the counter where the fish laid.

"That's the wrong kind of knife," Jimmy said as he ripped it from her grasp and tossed it into the sink. He rummaged around in a drawer until he found a knife with a long, thin, slightly curved blade then he handed it to Effie and sat down.

"Now yer gonna start by makin' a cut near the top of the gill then you'll slice all the way down the backbone. Make sure you ain't cuttin' too deep or yer gonna slice the stomach right open. That'll make the fish taste like shit and I ain't eatin' it then."

Effie had no idea what she was doing but she wasn't about to make Jimmy mad by not trying. She pressed the tip of the knife in just above the gill exactly like he said. There was something hard in there, though, and even with a sharp knife, it was difficult to slice into it.

Jimmy was watching like a hawk. "No, no, no," he said. "Yer startin' in the wrong spot. There's cartilage and stuff in there. You gotta find the soft spot right behind the gill and cut there."

She picked up the knife and placed it a little farther back on the fish. This time, the knife when right in when she pressed down on it. She began sawing the knife back and forth, slicing toward the tail.

"Stop!"

Effie dropped the knife and stepped back with her hands in the air. "Slice along the backbone toward the tail? That's what you told me to do, isn't it?"

"Yeah but yer not doin' it right. I can tell that you already ruined a perfectly good fish. I told you to watch how deep ya cut so ya don't slice open the stomach, didn't I?"

She nodded.

"Well I can tell already that ya hacked yer way right through it. The acid from its stomach is gonna make it taste bad and I already said that I ain't gonna eat that crap. You done screwed it up so now yer gonna find out how awful it tastes."

"I'm sorry," said Effie. She didn't care what the fish tasted like, just as long as she got to eat it. "As I said before, I've never cut up a fish so I don't know anything about his anatomy. I have no idea where a fish's stomach is located."

Jimmy sighed and rolled his eyes. "Harry," he yelled. He looked around behind himself only to find that there was no one there. "Harry," he yelled again. "Now where in the hell did that idiot get off to. I coulda swore he was right behind me when I come in. He was, wasn't he?"

"Yes."

"Then where is the tard?"

"I'm not sure. I was listening to you tell me how to cut up a fish."

Jimmy got up and walked to the door. Harry was sitting on the porch with his arms folded in front of his chest.

"Didn't you hear me callin' yer name?" Jimmy asked.

Harry didn't look at his brother when he spoke. "Yeah. I heard ya."

"Then why didn't ya come or speak up or somethin'?"

"Why ain't you lettin' me have the time with Cookie that ya promised?"

"Oh hell, Harry," said Jimmy. "You know as well as I do that we have stuff we gotta do first. I ain't gonna go and sit down there by that river all day just so you can mess around with the fat whore. Yer gonna work too. I told ya when we was down fishin' that you could screw around with her when we get done with lunch." Jimmy gave Harry a dirty look. "I'm beginnin' to think yer turnin' on me just like Destry."

Harry turned around and looked at his brother. His lip was twitching and it was obvious that the words had hurt. "You know I wouldn't never be like him. We're brothers. Ain't nothin' ever gonna come between us."

Jimmy stepped out on the porch and held out his hand for Harry to take. Harry looked at his brother's hand for a minute before reaching out and taking hold of it. With a big yank, he was on his feet with Jimmy patting him on the back.

"How about you take over cleanin' the fish? Cookie don't know the first thing about it and she already ruined one."

Hesitantly, Harry agreed.

Inside the cabin, Effie was still standing by the fish. She had not bothered to begin cleaning fish again but she had picked up the knife. She was staring down at it in her hand. Would that work to pick the lock? As soon as she got the chance, she would have to try. Not that she had ever picked a lock before. She didn't even know where to begin.

Back inside, Jimmy took his seat at the table. Harry snatched the knife out of Effie's hand and pushed her aside then began cleaning the fish. She didn't know what to do. No one had said a word to her. What she did notice, however, was that there was some sort of renewed bond between the brothers and that could not be good.

With nothing else to do and not wanting to anger anyone, Effie began preparing the stove to cook. She grabbed a towel and wrapped it around her hand so she could pull the heavy metal door on the bottom open to check on the fire. It had burned down and was in need of more wood. She looked over toward the woodpile near the door. Only two logs remained. They would do for lunch but someone would have to bring in more in order to keep the fire going later.

As Effie walked past Jimmy to get the wood, he stepped on her chain then reached out and wrapped his arms around her waste, pulling her onto his lap. She was caught completely off-guard and didn't have time to react when he plunged his hand down between her legs then held them up in front of them. They were covered with a slight moisture and he rubbed them together then brought them to his nose.

"Christ," he said and pushed her away. She fell forward onto her hands and knees on the floor. "You smell worse than a whole load of hogs in the summer sun. I'll mind the fire. Go wash that stink off for my brother before you cook us lunch."

Clean herself up? The words were like magic to her ears. Effie tried not to let her excitement show for fear that Jimmy would change his mind. She didn't remember the last time she'd felt clean. Even washing with cold water would be wonderful.

Effie remembered seeing a sliver of soap floating around the cabin somewhere. She closed her eyes to think for a minute. She had last seen it…under the sink! She rushed over and began digging around. Triumphantly, she came up with a dirty little piece of soap in her hand. Harry gave her a sideways look like she was crazy. It didn't matter, though. Nothing mattered except that Jimmy was letting her clean up. Suddenly, it seemed like things were taking a turn in her direction.

After finding the cleanest rag she could, Effie began working the pump until water came gushing out. She rubbed the little piece of soap against the rag until a foam began to appear. Just running the rag over her skin was like a little piece of heaven. She had not realized how dirty she was. Cleaning the filth off was refreshing and it made her feel like a new person.

When Effie was done washing her body, she began dragging her fingers through her hair. It was worse than a rat's nest. It was so snarled. When she thought she had worked the knots out as best she could, she ripped off a strip of the rag and laid it down in front of her. She pulled her hair back to the nape of her neck and began braiding. At the bottom, she wrapped the strip of rag around and around then tied it, hoping that it would stay in place.

It felt good to be cleaned up and have her hair pulled back. Even though she tried not to, she had to smile as she began cooking the fish fillets. She fried them up and served Jimmy and Harry then began cooking her own fish.

With a few pieces of fish fresh out of the frying pan, on a plate for herself, she took her usual place on the floor. Yes, it did taste a little odd. But so what. It felt good to have hot food in her stomach. As far as she was concerned, she'd never had anything that was so scrumptious in all her life. She closed her eyes with each bite and paced herself to make it last as long as possible.

Lunchtime, however, was much too short. Before Effie could finish the little bit on her plate, Jimmy and Harry were done with their food and ready to go on with the afternoon. Quickly, Effie stuffed the few remaining bites of fish into her mouth and set about cleaning up the dishes.

"Well," said Jimmy, standing and stretching his arms toward the ceiling. "I think I'm gonna go out and do a little hunting. Just see to it that you do everything my brother tells ya to do, Cookie. If I come back and find that he ain't happy, yer gonna pay."

Effie did not answer him. She turned and gave Jimmy a simple nod then went back to washing the dishes. The bucket she had used to clean the floor was still sitting in the sink, full of murky water. She glanced over her shoulder then reached down in to check and see if the spoon and screwdriver were still there. Her fingers wrapped around the screwdriver. She wanted to take it out and hide it but it was too dangerous with both men still in the cabin. For the time being, she would have to leave the bucket full of dirty water to conceal it. Perhaps later, she would have the chance to move it to a better hiding place.

Jimmy and Harry stood together near the door, whispering back and forth. Effie could not make out what they were saying but she was sure it was about her. They were probably making plans to torture her in some new and humiliating way. Then again, maybe they were trying to decide how to kill her when Harry was done. Maybe one of them found out that she knew what was under the cabin. *Or*, they could be deciding how to keep her there as their sex slave forever.

Effie squeezed her eyes shut and took a deep breath. She had to stop thinking about those things. Wasting her time thinking about what they might do was stupid. She had to focus on escaping before it was too late.

Finally, Jimmy left and Harry came sauntering up behind Effie. He ran his hands over her hips and stomach as he wrapped his arms around her waist. She snapped to attention. She knew that he intended to have sex with her. There was no mistaking his arousal when he pressed his hips against her.

It felt like there was a rock caught in her throat and she kept swallowing and swallowing. It just wouldn't go away. How could she just shut everything out and let him violate her body without fighting back? And if she fought Harry's advances at all, wouldn't that spell out immediate death for her upon Jimmy's return?

Harry pushed her braid aside and began kissing the back of her neck. Effie cringed. It felt all gooey and slobbery. She desperately wanted to reach her hand into the bucket and get the screwdriver. She wanted to push him away then stab him over and over. Harry wanted to force his way inside her and the thought of it made her skin crawl. She couldn't let him do that.

As his hands snaked their way to her breasts and began fondling her nipples, Effie's hand slipped into the bucket. She found the screwdriver and squeezed her hand around it. Harry reached down between her legs and pressed his fingers in. His breathing was hoarse and labored as he slowly began grinding against her. Her hand wrapped tighter and tighter around the screwdriver.

A picture formed in Effie's mind. She was in the cabin, standing over Harry's lifeless body. She had struggled to fight him off and stabbed him again and again. Blood was everywhere; floor, table, sink, Effie. He had screamed and cried like a little boy when she punctured his chest with the screwdriver but she just kept doing it. Jimmy had heard his brother and was coming back to get Effie. She had no time to escape…

She was pulling the screwdriver out of the bucket when Effie realized that the picture in her head was exactly what would happen if she stabbed Harry. She opened her hand and dropped it back into the bucket. It was a bad plan. There had to be another way to stop him. Maybe if she started talking…Maybe if she asked him to stop…This was Harry after all. He was the dumb one. He was supposed to be easy for her to outsmart. She had to think fast or it would be too late.

Effie cleared her throat. "Harry," she said in a sultry voice. "We have to slow down. You've been waiting for this so long. You don't want it to be over before it starts, do you?"

"I can't help it," he said between kisses. "Yer just so hot. You got me on fire." To punctuate his words, her pressed his hips against her extra hard.

"But if you slow down and hold off a little, it can be so much more explosive. Take your time and enjoy every little part. You deserve it."

"I don't know as I can do that, Miss Cookie."

"Oh but Harry—You can! You must!"

Effie nudged her elbow against his stomach and at first, she didn't think it was going to work. To her surprise, however, he stepped back after a moment and wiped the back of his hand against his forehead and temples. She took a deep breath then turned around and looked at him. It was not over yet.

Harry reached out and brushed his fingers against the side of her face. They smelled awful and they left a little sweaty trail when he dropped them away. It was all Effie could do to keep from wrinkling up her nose in disgust.

"I wasn't gonna say nothin,' Cookie, but I gotta," he said. "See, when me and Jimmy was down fishing, we was talking about you some of the time. He said I could keep ya—Kinda like as a wife. I was thinkin' we could live here so no one knows about you. And me and Jimmy could take turns makin' runs with the truck and spendin' time with ya. That would be real good, don't ya think? I ain't never had no serious girlfriend or wife or nothin' like that before."

Effie's face was glazed over in shock as she gaped in stunned silence. Harry wanted to keep her? Kinda like as a wife?? And he wanted to take turns trucking and spending time with her—With Jimmy??? What in the world was she supposed to say to that? Words did not exist that could describe the horror. A sudden burst of adrenaline shot through her veins. She made a helpless gesture that Harry took to mean that she agreed with his plan.

He dove at her but Effie held up her hands to stop him. "Slowly! Remember? S-l-o-w-l-y!"

Harry stopped dead in his tracks and looked at her like an injured puppy. Effie flashed a false, flirty smile at him. She had come to a point where some sort of action was needed. There wasn't anymore time for thinking.

She put her hands on Harry's shoulders and guided him toward a chair. She pushed him so he was forced to sit down then walked around, letting her hand trail over his chest. Effie bent so her lips were touching his ears.

"How about we start with a nice massage?" she whispered then slowly ran her tongue up the length of his ear.

Harry gulped. "Yeah," he breathed. "I think that would be good. Real good."

Effie began kneading this neck then worked her way down his shoulders. Every so often, she would press her breasts against his shoulders and squeal with girlish delight.—Anything to take control of the situation. Her hands roamed farther and farther down his chest.

She whispered in a throaty voice, "Would it be OK with you if I unbuckle that belt and—s-s-s-slide your pants down?"

He was already thrusting his pelvis forward when he nodded and let a low moan escape. Effie moved around in front of him and pressed her body against his as she slid to her knees. Her hands ran all over the his chest and she pressed her head against his belly. She was gasping for air. She had to calm her nerves. Harry thought that she was incredibly turned on and was trying to hold back

She looked up and locked his gaze as she began unbuckling his belt. Everything was going so fast! She pulled at the top of his pants until the button popped loose and the zipper slid down. It was too late to turn back now. She closed her eyes and sucked in a deep, deep breath as Harry lifted his hips a few inches and she pulled his pants and underwear down to his ankles. Staring her right in the face was his hard penis. The thought of him putting it anywhere in her body made her stomach churn. She could not let that stop her.

"Ooooh," Effie breathed as she climbed up his body, letting her skin connect with every inch of his. When her face was even with his, she said, "You're so sexy, Harry…So sexy." He leaned forward to kiss her but as he did, she pulled away and stood up.

Her heart was beating in her ears. "Be strong. Be strong. Be strong," it seemed to be saying. Did she have the courage she needed or was she at the point where she was willing to give in and accept a life in the cabin? *Be strong. Be strong. Be strong.* Had the time come for her to do something that would make him kill her and end her suffering? *Be strong. Be strong. Be strong.* The time was now and she had to make a decision. In the blink of an eye, she did it.

"You're so h-h-hot Harry," she whispered.

Effie reached down and picked up her chain. She laid a large loop around Harry's neck as she walked back around in front of him. His eyes narrowed in suspicion and he began raising his hands to the chain. Before he could wrap his pudgy fingers around it, though, Effie threw herself forward and jammed her tongue into his mouth in the most passionate kiss she could muster. His hands fell away from the chain.

When they broke from the kiss, she looked directly into his eyes and let her hand wander down to his erection. "Feeling the heat from your body radiating next to the cold h-h-hard links of the chain turns me on."

If Harry had any intentions of removing the chain before, they were gone. Slowly, his eyes closed and he let his head lay back. She was sliding her hand up and down the length of his penis. And then she moved, as if she was going to let him slide into her.

Without warning, she wrapped her free hand around the chain and jumped back, pulling it tight. His eyes popped open and he tried to stand up and reach for Effie as he realized his mistake in trusting her. He tripped on his pants and was face down on the floor in nothing flat. He began clawing at the chain but couldn't get a grip. She was pulling with all her might. She put her weight into it and leaned backward so she was out of his reach.

Harry's face went red as he opened his mouth to scream. The only sounds to escape were a few little gurgling chokes. Effie wanted to stop or at least look away but she couldn't. If she stopped or lost focus of the situation, Harry could turn everything around and she would die. She just kept pulling and pulling. His eyes began to bulge and his face went from red to purplish blue. *Be strong. Be strong. Be strong.* She had to be strong. There was nothing else she could be.

Finally, Harry's fight began to melt away and he went limp, laying face down. Effie's hands were aching but she didn't let up on the chain. She couldn't. How long could a human survive without oxygen? She'd heard it somewhere. What was it? He was definitely unconscious but that didn't mean that he was dead. She had to make sure that he was dead. Maybe she should keep tension on the chain for a little longer.

She held tight for a while. Fifteen minutes was long enough, wasn't it? Effie carefully let up on the chain, ready to jerk it back if he was just faking. He didn't move. With a lot of effort, she rolled him over and recoiled in horror. His eyes were glassy. He didn't blink and his chest didn't rise and fall. He just laid there, his frozen gaze fixed on the ceiling. She didn't want to touch him with his eyes staring upward but she knelt down and pressed two fingers against the artery in this throat. There was nothing. No rhythmic beat. Just nothing.

Chapter 28

Effie looked down at Harry. She had done it. She had actually killed him. Her heart was racing as it began to sink in. She was no different from him now. Correction: She was *worse* than him now.

While Harry had helped Jimmy kill Angie, Effie had killed Harry all on her own. Now she was a murderer. This was not good.

She was in a cabin with the body of the person she just killed in the middle of nowhere—And his brother would be back sooner or later! Why hadn't she thought it out? She should have come up with a plan. Yes, Harry would have raped her but so what. Now Jimmy was going to come back and see what she had done and he would just kill her without a second thought. Not good!

She had to do something. She had to hide the body. But where? Where could she hide something as large as Harry? There wasn't a place. She was in a one room cabin, chained to a post. How could she have been so stupid? A sickening feeling welled up in her stomach and her mind reeled.

Wait a minute. This was not the time to panic and she couldn't just give up. Effie was a smart woman. She could figure everything out. She just had to calm down and think. If she just cleared her head, everything would be just fine. She took a few deep breaths.

Now think. What did she have to do? Effie made a mental list: One, hide the body; two, straighten up the cabin and get ready for Jimmy to return; three, come up with a believable story as to why Harry wasn't there. She could do that.

Oh no she couldn't! It suddenly felt like her throat was closing up. A drink of water. That's what she needed. A drink of water would help wet her mouth, cool her throat and calm her down. Effie walked toward the sink like she was blundering around in the dark. Her mind was now set on water. One thing at a time.

When she got to the sink, she leaned on the edge for a moment, looking in. The bucket was still sitting there and without really thinking about it, Effie reached out and plunged her hand in. The screwdriver! When her fingers touched it, it was like a buzzer going off, waking her up. Effie spun around, screwdriver in hand. She would pry the boards up again then push Harry's body into the hole. It was simple enough. It had to work.

She raced across the room and fell to her knees by the spot where she had pried up the floorboards before. Effie jammed the screwdriver in the crack between them and tried to press down on the handle. Her fingers slipped. Her hands were too wet and sweaty. She scurried across the floor, wiped her hands on Jimmy's blanket then went back over to try the screwdriver again. She hadn't really noticed how shaky she was. It was the adrenaline.

Carefully, Effie pushed the handle of the screwdriver down and the board came up. When she tried to grip it with her fingertips, it slipped and dropped back into place. Again, she jammed the screwdriver into the crack and slowly pressed on the handle. This time when the board lifted up, she got a hold of it and slid the screwdriver underneath so it couldn't fall down again. With the screwdriver holding the board up, she was free to use both hands to lift the board away from the floor.

When she lifted, the screwdriver flipped around and fell into the hole. Effie sat, peering into the darkness below. She shrugged. She didn't need the screwdriver anymore anyway. And the good thing was, the flashlight had gone out. That was a relief.

With the first board out of the way, she was home-free. One by one, Effie lifted the floorboards away and stacked them up in order. When she thought she had a large enough hole, Effie got up and wiped a few stray hairs away from her face. She was sweating like a pig but it was no time to take a break to cool down. Then she heard something that made her blood run cold. Thunder.

Effie went to the window and looked out. Nothing could go her way. It was overcast and it looked like rain. With that rumble of thunder, Jimmy was sure to be on his way back from wherever it was he had gone. Now it was time to panic. She had no idea how far away he was or how long it would take him to get back and his brother was laying dead in the middle of the floor. If he came back and saw that, all hell would break loose.

She charged over to Harry and tried to roll him toward the hole. She pushed with everything she had but he only budged a few inches. The hole had to be at least fourteen or fifteen feet away. It would take all night to move him that far and time was not on her side. There had to be another way.

Effie got up. Maybe if she pulled him across the room, it would work better. She took hold of his hands and yanked as hard as she could. When she did, he slid toward the hole. Her hands were sweaty again, though, and she lost her grip. Then an idea popped into her head.

Where was the rope they had used to tie her wrists to the post? She looked around and spied it laying over on the counter in several pieces. One of them looked long enough for her plan. There was a good length of it and it was pretty thick. There was no time to think about wether or not it would work, she had to just try it out. She grabbed the rope then tied the ends around his wrists. When the rope was secure, Effie realized that she had no idea how she'd done it, her hands were shaking so hard.

With Harry's hands bound by the rope, Effie stepped inside the loop that remained and lifted it to her waist. When she leaned back to pull, it cut across an area that was still painful from the last whipping. She only hesitated for a moment before working to pull the body toward the hole. Pain did not matter anymore. She wasn't ready to give up her life yet. Even if that rope cut her in half, she was determined to pull Harry's body across the room.

Every few steps backward, Effie would look over her shoulder to see how close she was getting to the hole. When she got right up next to it, she began pulling sideways like she was going to go around it. With Harry as close as she could possibly get him to the hole, she dropped the rope, went around and pushed until his head drooped in. Lightening flashed and there was another loud crack of thunder. It only broke her concentration for a moment.

Be strong. Be strong. Be strong. She could do it! She'd gotten that far, hadn't she? Effie mustered every last bit of strength she could find within herself and pushed. The body slid into the hole. Well, almost. The bottom half of his body was still sticking up. Harry was wider around the middle than she had anticipated and he got hung-up.

Ooooh. This was definitely a very bad thing. Effie took a deep breath. There was no way she could pull him out and make the hole bigger. That was completely out of the question. That meant that the only option she had left was to try to force him through. The heaviest thing in the cabin she could use to push him through was her own body. There wasn't a single other thing she could lift or maneuver.

Effie went to work. First she tried pushing with her hands and then she went on to try pushing with her feet. Neither approach worked. She did not have time for mistakes like that. She just knew that Jimmy was going to come walking in and catch her in the act. In a last ditch effort, she lifted his legs over her shoulders so he was as straight up and down as possible and pressed down. Little by little, it worked. Each time she pressed, he moved a little. Finally, the widest part of his body popped through the hole and he slipped the rest of the way through. Triumph!

As soon as Harry's body hit the ground, Effie was at work, replacing the boards. It did not matter how heavy they were or awkward it was to move each one, they were going back into place. Before the last two were back where they belonged, she realized something. There was a sound. Her heart skipped a beat as she turned to look toward the door. It was raining. When had the rain started? As fast as she could move, she put the last two boards back where they belonged and began straightening up the room.

It seemed odd that Jimmy had not returned. Effie was sure that he would have come back after hearing the first rumble of thunder. Then a thought occurred to her. What if he hadn't really gone anywhere? He could have been hiding under the cabin the entire time. He was probably just waiting to see exactly how far she would go before he came out and beat her to death. The more she thought about it, the more she was sure that he was down there.

Something else occurred to Effie and it sent shivers up and down her spine. Harry might not be dead. She wasn't a doctor and she had certainly never touched a dead body before. In her state of mind, it was very possible that she hadn't checked the right spot for a pulse. What if Harry was faking? Effie rubbed her arms. That's probably what it was. He was alive and now he was sitting down under the cabin with Jimmy and they were plotting some sort of torture for her.

Then again, Harry was kind of an idiot and when Effie thought about it, she doubted that he could act well enough to fool her. After all, she had watched him die. As long as she lived, she would never forget the pleading expression on his face; his eyes bulging out as he laid there trying to gasp for air. Beyond that, there was no way he could have faked his skin color. He had to be dead.

If Jimmy was anywhere near the cabin and thought something bad was happening to his brother, he would have come back in a split second. It was not possible he was hiding under the cabin. She was just being paranoid and she had to get it all out of her mind. She had a bigger problem to deal with.

Effie had accomplished most of her first two tasks. The body was hidden and the cabin was almost cleaned up. In fact, it was nearly as tidy as she'd originally had it. All she had to do now was think up a believable story as to why Harry wasn't there. She began flipping through the possibilities in her mind.

Unfortunately, she didn't have long to think about it. Jimmy stepped into the doorway, dripping wet from head to foot. He looked less than happy standing there in a puddle. Effie rushed as fast as she could to find something for him to use to dry off.

Without a word, she snatched a blanket from Destry's bed and handed it to him. What else could she do to make him more comfortable? That was the key: Keep Jimmy's mind off things. He was still standing near the door, peeling off his clothes. He must have been chilled to the bone. The storm seemed to have washed away the oppressive heat.

Effie stoked the fire in the stove then pulled Jimmy's chair over near it. He would want something warm in his body too. Her heart skipped a beat. She was sure he would take one look at her while she was working and know what she'd done. She put the teakettle on and waited for him to say something.

With his clothes in a pile on the floor, Jimmy walked over and sat down in his chair. Why didn't he say anything? It wasn't like him. It made Effie nervous. He had to know something. She stood back, watching and waiting.

When steam billowed out of the teapot, Effie picked it up and poured it into a cup with instant coffee grounds. She held it out for him to take. Instead of drinking right away, he held it in his hands, warming his fingertips. For the briefest moment, when she looked at him, Jimmy didn't look so menacing. He was almost as exposed as she was. Other than the blanket wrapped around his shoulders, the only thing that he had on was a pair of sopping wet underwear.

Finally, Jimmy brought the cup to his lips and took a long drink of the steaming liquid. He sat back and looked around the room then his eyes stopped on Effie. "Where's Harry," he said.

If the blood hadn't already drained from her face, it would have with that question. Was it a trick or did he really not know where his brother was? Effie did not answer. She pretended not to have heard him.

"I asked a question, whore. Are ya gonna answer?"

"I'm-I'm-I'm sorry," Effie said. "I, ah, didn't hear you. Could you p-please repeat it?"

Jimmy sniffed then asked again. "Where's Harry?"

Effie threw up her arms. "Oh, I'm sorry! I was, uh, supposed to tell you as soon as you got back. He said to say thanks and you would know what for and he was going into town to get something to celebrate."

"He said what?"

"Um, he said you would know and that's all he told me," she said then walked over to make Jimmy's bed.

"I would know?" Jimmy muttered. "What would I know?"

Effie shook her head. She could not look at Jimmy. He would be able to see everything in her eyes if she did. She was sure of it. And even if he did not figure it out from looking into her eyes, he was going to know in a day or so anyway. Harry wasn't going to stay fresh for long. There wasn't a chance in the world the planks on the floor would keep that kind of smell out of the cabin. It wouldn't take long for the scent of a decomposing body to get so strong, Jimmy would have to investigate the source. Worse yet, what if he went under there to look through all that stuff on a regular basis? He'd get a big surprise the next time.

Who was she kidding? There was going to be nothing but trouble ahead. There was no way Jimmy wouldn't find out about Harry. Either she came up with a way to escape in the next twenty-four hours or she was dead.

Think, Effie, think. This was it. There was no more messing around, trying to come up with the perfect plan. She had set the wheel in motion by killing Harry and now she had to come up with a way to escape, plain and simple. But what?

Chapter 29

The silence in the cabin that afternoon was maddening. Why wasn't Jimmy yelling at her or making crude remarks or threatening her? It was like the calm before a storm and every time Effie, heard a creek or a bump, she jumped. If he was trying to play with her mind, it was working

With all the quiet, Effie was afraid to even think about an escape plan for fear that Jimmy would somehow hear her thoughts. If he would just go out on the porch, she knew she would be more at ease. He just sat there by the fire, though, sipping coffee and watching her without uttering a word. Go away! Say something! Do something, dammit!

Effie had to talk and make that awful silence go away. She walked up beside him and cleared her throat. "You still look cold, Jimmy. There's a can of beef stew left. How about I warm it up for you."

His face took on a predatory expression then his lips twisted into a wicked grin. "Yer very observant, Cookie," he said. "I am cold but I don't want no beef stew to warm me up."

"Well..." She didn't want to ask what he wanted.

He didn't wait. "You know, fire is hot. People even say it's *red* hot."

Effie cringed at the thought of what was coming next. She didn't even need to imagine it. It was obvious. He was still in his underwear and they did nothing to hide what was on his mind.

"Do you know what else is red and can warm me right up, Cookie?" He leaned forward and sat his cup on the stove. "Do ya?"

She shook her head. "What, Jimmy? What else is red and can warm you right up?"

"Yer red, baby," he said, licking his lips. "My brother already got some fire from ya and now I think it's my turn. He shouldn't get to have all the fun." If he only knew! "I ain't had any in a day or two so why don't you just come right over here and sit right down on my lap like a good little girl."

Effie didn't know what to do. Jimmy was a lot stronger than Harry so there was no way she could use her chain on him too. If she didn't do what he said, he'd probably beat her. If that happened, she wouldn't be in any shape to attempt an escape if an opportunity arose. But still, voluntarily sit on his lap? Maybe if she got him drunk enough, he'd pass out and then she could make a break for it! No, that was silly. He only became meaner when he drank. She didn't really have a choice. Hesitantly, she went to Jimmy and turned around to sit on his lap.

Just as she was about to sit down, Jimmy grabbed her hips and stopped her. He ran his hand over her back, tracing the cuts and welts left from her last whipping. Effie gasped. She couldn't keep it in. It was like he was raking it with a razor.

"I'll bet my brother had lots of fun with you." He laughed for a moment then tugged on her hips to make her sit down.

She didn't like sitting on his lap and feeling exactly how excited he was. She didn't like his arms wrapped around her waist or his hands roaming over her body either but there was nothing she could do about it. Or was there? An idea popped into her head. Why hadn't she thought of it before?

Jimmy was into controlling people. When she fought his advances, it only seemed to make him more aroused. Maybe the key wasn't to fight back. Maybe what she needed to do was go along with his every whim and tell him how right he was. Nothing else had worked so maybe it was worth a try.

"You know, Jimmy," Effie said. "I know there's no reason for me to think."

"Yer right about that."

She licked her lips. "I've been thinking anyway and I think that you're right about women—Me included."

"And what is it you think about that?"

"Well," she began. "I just needed to be broken and taught my place. Lucky for me, you came along and did it." He pinched her nipple so hard, she winced and covered her mouth with her hands to keep from crying out in pain.

Jimmy grabbed Effie's braid and pulled her head back so he could talk into her ear. "Yer real lucky I came along. I know what I'm doin' with women. You ain't the first I've had to break and you ain't gonna be the last either."

"I, ah, don't know why I was so darn stubborn. I'm really sorry it took me so long to come around."

"It's 'cause of the red," he said. "Move yer ass around some. It feels good when you squirm."

"What?"

"Move yer ass around."

"No." Effie sighed. "I meant before that."

Jimmy moved his hands down to her hips and tried to make her move them. "I said it's 'cause of the red. Yer a redhead. All redheads are more stubborn than any other bitches. That's why it took ya so damn long to learn. I told you to move yer fat ass. Do it now!"

She wasn't sure exactly how he wanted her to move so she began grinding her hips in slow circles. Agreeing with him wasn't working at all. It didn't even break his focus. At least he wasn't swearing at her and trying to beat her. That was good. He didn't seem to be complaining about the way she was moving so she just kept it up. Maybe he would get off that way and it wouldn't go any farther.

"You really do know a lot about women. I mean you're a real pro when it comes to dealing with us."

"Look," said Jimmy as he pushed her so he could stand up. He grabbed her by the shoulder and whirled her around so she was looking at him. "I've had about enough of yer talking. Yer full of shit and if you think that I believe one bit of the crap you been tellin' me, yer an idiot too. You ain't any different than any whore whose been through here and yer gonna end up like every last one of 'em!"

Effie opened her mouth to ask what other women he was talking about but before she could get the words out, Jimmy had his hands around her throat and was pushing her toward the table. When she hit the table, he did not let go. He wasn't squeezing hard enough to stop her from breathing—just enough to make her uncomfortable. It was difficult to suck in the air and frankly, it scared the hell out of her. She was sure it was his way of saying that he knew what she'd done to Harry.

Jimmy pushed her onto the table. "Slide yer fat ass up there so yer arms are at one end and yer feet are down here when ya lay down," he said, pounding on the wood next to her.

She didn't ask. She just moved.

While Effie was worrying about making Jimmy lose his temper, he was doing it all on his own. He was tearing the cabin apart, looking for something. After several minutes, mad did not even come close to describing his state of mind.

"Where the hell is it?" he yelled and threw up his arms.

That drew Effie's attention away from one worry and settled it on another. He was over in the corner, digging through the trunk. Clothes, tools and other various items were flying everywhere. There was no way she was going to ask him what he was looking for.

Jimmy turned around and stormed over to the table. He glared down at Effie, his nostrils flaring. "Where's the rope, whore?"

"I-I don't know what you're talking about," she said. She couldn't look into his eyes or he might see the truth.

"I'll bet you don't," he growled. He twirled around and acted like a woman flipping her hair. "I guess I'll just have to use twigs and berries."

"What?" Effie asked, confused.

Jimmy stopped acting like a girl and got right down in her face. None of the pieces of rope on the counter are long enough to tie ya up and I'm pretty sure there was at least one long piece earlier. I guess that means I'm gonna hafta improvise and use blankets to tie ya up!"

Oh no! Not again! If he tied her up, she would never have a chance to run before he found out about Harry. She would die there for sure. Even if he didn't find out about his brother, he wouldn't bother to see that she got any food or water. No matter what, she'd be dead in a few days time.

Effie started to get up but he put one large hand on her chest and pushed. She was sure she felt a pop from her breastbone when she hit the table. Jimmy was pushing so hard, she thought he might be trying to push her right through the table. He didn't stop until she cried out in pain either. What was she supposed to do now.

"If you move a muscle, I will skin you alive, Miss Cookie, and I ain't kidding."

The second Jimmy turned around to get a blanket, Effie tried to move a little bit. Laying still, her chest felt fine but when she moved, it was a different story. She didn't know for sure if there was any kind of break but she knew something was wrong. Just moving her head and upper body a fraction of an inch shot pain through her chest that made her eyes well up with tears.

Jimmy snatched a blanket from Harry's bed, muttering, "He lost the damn rope so he can give up his damn blanket. Idiot can freeze to death for all I care."

He walked back over and stood looking down at Effie. He didn't say a word. He reached a hand out and dug into her shoulder, flipping her over onto her stomach. Effie wasn't expecting it and the sudden surprise of the movement felt like someone had stuck a knife into her chest and twisted.

Effie just laid there on the table, her arms hanging over the sides. For the moment, there was too much pain to even cry. If she took a deep breath, it was like having her chest ripped open. She had to get past it. If she took shallow breaths and concentrated on making the pain go away, maybe it would.

It was hard to concentrate on anything with Jimmy standing next to her. He was slashing at Harry's blanket with a long knife and cutting it into strips. He kept mumbling something while he worked but Effie couldn't quite make out what it was. From the words she could pick up, however, it sounded like her was having an argument with himself. Not once the entire time he was at it, did he look at her or say anything to her. He was in his own little world.

That was just fine with Effie, too. The more time Jimmy spent babbling to himself, the more time she spent alive. He had a great big knife in his hand and that had the potential to equal death. If she had to hold her breath all night, that's what she would do to stay alive.

When Jimmy was done cutting up the blanket, he threw the knife on the floor, sinking its tip into a board. Effie's eyes got big. Just one flick of his wrist and he'd sent it right into the floor! Where might he send one sailing next?

She let out a startled gasp when he bent over next to her. She was sure that he was picking it up to use it on something else. Her. Instead, he quickly secured one end of a strip of blanket around the table leg. I seemed like he knew what he was doing because when he tugged on the blanket to test it, the table moved but the knot did not come undone.

Happy with his work, Jimmy brought the strip up, across the top of the table, looped it twice around one wrist, twice around the other, then he tied the end around the other table leg. After that, he moved down to the other end of the table and repeated the process on her ankles.

"We'll see how you like that, ya fat wore," he growled.

Effie didn't move or make a sound. Was he a moron or did he think that she was? It didn't seem possible that Jimmy didn't know how easily she could get out of her bindings. Apparently he wasn't as different from Harry as she'd thought.

Jimmy admired his handiwork for a moment then stepped forward and began tracing the sores on Effie's back with his fingertips again. When he found an area that seemed particularly sensitive, he pressed into it and watched her writhe. She pressed her lips together, not wanting him to see how much pain he was causing but it didn't seem to stop him. He was fascinated by the fact that he could cause so much agony just by pressing on cuts and bruises.

Suddenly, Jimmy jammed his finger into the spot where Effie had been gouged by the brick. It felt like her was poking his finger right through her body. Her face twisted as she choked out a cry of pain. A wide smile spread across Jimmy's face as he laughed and turned his finger this way and that. He pressed harder, becoming more and more delighted the louder she screamed.

She wanted to pull her hands free and attack Jimmy. It was everything she could do to leave them bound. He was so strong. She knew she could never fight back and win. He would just beat her and tie her up again. While he wasn't the brightest, he certainly wasn't a complete idiot either. If he had to tie her up again, he wouldn't make the same mistake. If she had any chance of beating him, she was going to have to endure everything he had to dish out.

After a while, it appeared that boredom and hunger became enough to force Jimmy to stop. While he went about warming soup, Effie laid on the table, her face hidden between her arms. She had to come up with a new game plan. Nothing she'd tried so far had worked. There just had to be something.

Jimmy put his steaming bowl of soup on the table between Effie's feet then pulled up a chair and began eating. She turned her head to the side a little and inhaled deep. Her stomach rumbled. The soup smelled so good! Her eyes drifted shut as she imagined how nice it would feel to have warm food on such a cool, dreary evening. She snapped out of her daydream when Jimmy spoke up between slurps.

"It ain't like Harry to be gone so long by himself," he said. "'Specially in the rain. Somethin' like this makes me think that maybe you done somethin' to him."

OK, maybe he didn't know for sure about what she'd done. All she had to do was stick to her story no matter what. As long as he wasn't sure, she wasn't going to tell him.

She sniffed and laughed lightly. "What in the world do you think I could possibly do to him?" she asked.

"I'm sure there's stuff. Yer just like every other whore that walks on the face of the planet. Ya'll got snakes in yer head."

Effie sighed. "Don't you think you're giving me a little too much credit— being a woman and all? It isn't even remotely possible that I could do anything to a person of Harry's size."

"There's stuff," he said.

This wasn't going well. She had to get his mind off Harry. The problem was, she couldn't just change the subject or Jimmy would know he was right. The reporter in her went to work.

Jimmy had mentioned other women. If she could get him to start talking about them, the benefits could be twofold. Not only would it get his mind off such a dangerous topic, it would also giver her a little clue as to what tactics other women might have tried when they were held there. She might be able to use that information to her advantage in planning out her escape.

"Yeah, right," she laughed. "I could do something to him just like all those other women."

Jimmy scraped his spoon on the bottom of the bowl, getting the last traces of soup from it. Instead of just leaving it there or getting up and putting it in the sink, he threw it in from where he was sitting. Effie hadn't been expecting it and when it shattered, she jumped, almost pulling her hand out of the tether. She quickly pushed her hand back in place and tugged like she was fighting to get free. With any luck, he hadn't seen any of it from where he was sitting.

Jimmy got up and walked over to where the bowl had landed. He bent and picked up a large, triangular piece with a jagged point and a long smooth side. When he ran his fingers along the edges, he got a look on his face like the piece of ceramic was an old and trusted friend.

"Maybe there weren't any others," Effie said.

He spun around and grabbed her braid, yanking so hard, she was forced to look into his eyes. "Don't mistake it for a single second, Miss Cookie. There were other whores," he hissed. "Plenty of 'em seen there way through here and I personally picked up every single last one of 'em!"

"Like any of them would go with someone like you voluntarily. And then their families and friends would miss them. You would be caught in a second. You'd never get away with bringing many women here. Your own brother and friend are proof enough of that, aren't they?"

"You think yer so smart, don't ya? You think ya know everything."

"Well, come on. Look how easy it was to get Destry to turn on you. I know I'm not much to look at and it was easy for me to get him going. It would be twice as easy for any other woman. Besides, he doesn't have the kind of evil in his sole that it takes to kidnap multiple women and keep them in this cabin.

"And then there's Harry; your own flesh and blood. He was as sex crazed as a teenage boy. There's no telling how long it's been since the last time he got any. With the way you view women, though, I'm pretty sure that you would have forced every last woman you met to have sex with him. He wouldn't have been nearly so horny if you'd really had other women here."

"Why don't you use yer fat head to think, ya whore?" Jimmy said, bashing her head into the table. The impact rattled her eyes and gave her an instant headache. "It ain't like I need either one of them to get women. It ain't like I go pickin' them up from the same places all the time neither. I got my methods."

"Sure you do."

"Think about it, ya fat tub of lard. I drive a truck for a living. That means I get all over the country on runs, don't it? There's always whores who are runnin' away or there are prostitutes hangin' around truck stops. All I gotta do is just take my pick of 'em and bring 'em back here. Ain't no better place for trainin' a whore."

"So you bring all the women back here and do your little thing with them." She paused to study his face. What was going on behind his eyes? She cleared her throat. "Well, if it's really true about all these women, I just have one more question for you."

"Good. Hurry it up so you can shut that fat trap of yers!"

"If you brought all those throngs of women up here, and put them through your little boot camp, where the hell are they?"

"Same place yer gonna be if you don't shut up." He clearly enjoyed bragging about his conquests.

She rolled her eyes and smirked. "Which is?"

"Planted about fifty yards or so out behind the cabin."

Suddenly, Effie was no longer conscious of anything but Jimmy. She though she'd been calling his bluff about the other women. The look on his face was dead serious and deep down, she knew everything he's said was true. She wanted to ask how many had come before her. She couldn't form the words. Nothing would come out of her mouth.

Jimmy put his piece of ceramic on the counter next to the sink then climbed on top of Effie. Ordinarily, his weight wouldn't have bothered her very much. This time it was different. Her back hurt so bad. It was like he was poking her with a thousand tiny nails at the same time. To make it worse, she knew what was coming next and she was going to have to let it happen. She was going to have to put on a good show so he would think the bindings were secure.

Jimmy leaned forward and whispered in her ear. "I know you like it when

I do ya, Miss Cookie. You like it rough. All whores do." He slid his hand over her braid as if he was petting her. "Tell me that you like rough sex."

Stony silence.

He wrapped his fingers around her braid and yanked backward. "Tell me ya like it rough before I grab that knife and slit yer throat!" he hissed. "Now! I mean it!"

In a cool, even voice, Effie said, "I like it rough."

"What do ya like rough?"

"Sex. I like rough sex."

"Alrighty," he said, letting go of her braid. "Now tell me you want me to rip you apart havin' rough sex right now."

"What?" Did he really think she wanted that?

Jimmy grabbed her braid again. "Yo heard me," he said. "Say it, whore!"

"I—I want you to have sex with me right now," she said.

"That ain't what I said. Say it right."

"I didn't hear what you told me to say, Jimmy…Please…"

"Don't feed me no line of bull, ya whore," he said as he leaned over and reached toward the knife.

Effie gasped when she saw what he was doing. She began to sputter. "I—I—I—I want you to rip me apart having rough sex right now, Jimmy."

He let go of her braid and settled back on top of her. "See?" he said. "You did hear after all, didn't ya? I knew it." He paused for a moment. "Ask nice and I just might give you what ya want."

Ask nice? Effie felt like she was sinking in quicksand. She knew she had to go along with what Jimmy wanted yet every fiber of her being screamed, "No!" Her heart was pounding in her ears again. *Be strong. Be strong. Be strong.*

"Come on, whore. I ain't got all night and I ain't tellin' ya again. I'm just gonna get the knife. It'll save me a lot of headache."

"Please, uh," said Effie. It was hard to ask for something she absolutely did not want. She took a deep breath then began again. "I want you to screw me, um, right now. I need it."

That was all Jimmy needed to get going. In no time at all, he shimmied out of his underwear and began grinding against her. He grabbed hold of Effie's braid and pulled as he forced himself into her. The intrusion was unwelcome and as she couldn't help but fight against it. It had to stop. It just had to stop. She closed her eyes and tried to imagine herself someplace else. She had to let him finish but if she kept that in her mind, she would pull her wrists out of their ties and try to fight him off. That would be no good. She would never get a chance to escape and in all reality, he would probably get to the knife before her and then that would be that.

Effie pictured herself safe at home. She was in her apartment, curled up with a good book in someone's arms. This was good. Now who was she with? Someone tough. Someone who could defend her. Someone who would stop bad things from happening to her.

Before she could finish her thought, Jimmy was finished and rolling off her. His knees were weak and he stumbled. As he fell to the floor, he grabbed the edge of the counter and grabbed the piece of porcelain from the broken bowl. Effie missed what he was doing. Her eyes were closed and her head was pressed to the table. He had raped her yet again and she had survived it.

Jimmy got to his feet and began walking away, letting his fingertips trace the length of her body. When he got to her feet, he stopped. He brought the porcelain up to eye level so he could inspect it for a moment. Without a word, Jimmy jammed the jagged edge into the bottom of her foot.

Effie hadn't been expecting it and at first, there was just pain. It shot from her foot, right into her belly. Someone was screaming. By the time she realized it was her own voice that she heard, Jimmy had jammed the porcelain into her other foot twice as hard and twisted it around.

"Just in case you manage to get loose and yer thinkin' about runnin' away," he growled. "Oh, and Cookie—If my brother don't get back by the morning, yer gonna pay with yer life. You better start prayin' now."

Chapter 30

Effie lay on the table for hours after pretending to cry herself to sleep. Every inch of her body ached, from the top of her head, right down to the bottom of her feet. She had to get her mind off the pain and move on to an escape plan. Time was almost up and she still didn't know what she was doing.

She knew Jimmy was serious about killing her when Harry didn't return in the morning. Even if she could get loose from the chain, there was no way she could just run away now. Her newest injuries would slow her down so much, she doubted she could even make in off the front porch before Jimmy caught her.

The thought of doing to Jimmy what she had done to Harry wasn't appealing either. Then again, at that point, what options did she have? If she wanted to survive, she was going to have to put her conscience aside and just do what she had to do. She still had to come up with a good plan and wait for the right opportunity.

Jimmy had puttered around the cabin for quite a while after he finished up with Effie. At one point, he even went out onto the porch and sat waiting for Harry. It took every bit of willpower Effie had to keep from climbing off the table then. She had to reason with herself. Jimmy would kill her for sure as soon as he saw her up. She just had to wait for a better opportunity. That was all there was to it.

Eventually, Jimmy gave up on Harry and went to bed. Time went by so slow, waiting for him to fall asleep. It could have been minutes or it could have been hours before Effie heard the low, even breathing that she'd been waiting for, she didn't know which.

Scenarios kept playing in her head. In each one, she would undoubtedly end up getting caught or they just wouldn't work. Besides, she had neither the time nor the ability to do things like slip poison into the food or tie Jimmy up while he was sleeping or even pick the lock and run away in the night. It was just stupid and it was a waste of her time.

Effie turned her head to the side and gently laid her cheek on the table. She listened to Jimmy's snores for a while as she stared at the sink. Maybe it hadn't taken him such a long time to fall asleep after coming back inside. He was even snoring now. Too bad Effie couldn't afford the same luxury.

A thought floated around in Effie's mind. There was no way around it, it had come down to kill or be killed. So far, she had survived terrible beatings and rape in the cabin. Unless she wanted all of her suffering to have been in vain, she had to kill him. But how?

She pulled her wrists out of the binding then turned to look at Jimmy. He was definitely sleeping. He was sprawled out on his back with his arm dangling over the edge of the bed and his mouth hanging open. If ever there was a time that he was vulnerable, this was it. This was the opportunity she had been waiting for. She pulled her feet free and as she swung them over the edge and prepared to slip onto the floor, a glint of light caught her eye.

The knife. It was still sticking in the floor where Jimmy had left it. This was good. Effie could use that knife instead of rummaging around in the dark, trying to find another one. How fortunate.

As quiet as she could, she slipped off the table. A sharp pain shot from her feet through her entire body. She had not expected it to hurt so much to stand with the new gouges. Her knees began to buckle and as she began to go down, she caught herself on the edge of the table. *Be strong.* This was not the time to think about pain. She gritted her teeth together and pushed into a standing position. She was determined not to give in. Effie wasn't going to survive only for herself. She was also going to do it for all those other women buried out in the woods. This was it. It was time to be a new person.

Effie put the woman who put up with the teasing all those years beding her and brought out someone new. The new person was everything she always wanted to be and more. The new Effie had the strength and courage to handle any situation and she could not feel pain. She was going to do whatever it took to walk out of that cabin alive.

Confidently, Effie took one step forward then wrapped her hand around the handle of the knife and yanked. She turned around and looked at Jimmy sleeping at the other end of the room. As she took a few steps forward, he began moving and she froze. He rolled over onto his stomach, smacked his lips a few times and began snoring again.

Fine. She could still drive the knife in if he was laying on his back. It would probably be easier. With him laying like that, she would not have to look at his face when she did it.

Effie swallowed a lump in her throat. Her pulse was racing and she was very aware of her breathing as she bent to lift the chain. She did not want to risk the slightest sound. If Jimmy woke to find her standing over him with the knife, that would be the end of everything. As much as she didn't like it, this was her only option. Come morning, he would gladly sink a knife into her back.

Walking across the room was like walking on hot coals. Her feet hurt so bad and every step toward the bed was a step closer to becoming just like Jimmy. The very thought of it weighed on her conscience. The desire to live was greater and before she knew it, she was standing by the bed, gently placing the chain on the floor.

Effie stood looking down at Jimmy. She did not want to sink to his level. If only there was another way. There wasn't, though. Her time was up and this was the opportunity she had been waiting for. If he was awake, she would never stand a chance. She had to do it—For every woman Jimmy had ever tortured, abused or killed. Most of all, she had to do it for herself. The old Effie might not have been strong enough but this Effie was.

She clenched both hands on the handle of the knife and brought it up over her head. She glanced up at the blade then focused her gaze on the spot where she wanted to put it. With all of her might, she brought the knife down and sunk it into Jimmy's back. As she pulled it out so she could do it again, his head popped up and he looked at her in shock.

Effie brought the knife down again but this time, Jimmy rolled to the side at the last second. She missed, sinking the blade into the mattress. Before she could pull it out and stab at him again, he closed his hand over hers. For a split second, she thought it was all over. Somehow she jerked her hand free and she stumbled backward. When she caught sight of Jimmy again, he was getting up.

She scrambled to her feet and looked around. Effie had to find something with which she could defend herself. Jimmy had the knife now. The first thing here eyes fell on was a cast iron frying pan, sitting by the stove. Quickly, she grabbed it. One hand was not enough to support the weight so she wrapped her other hand around the handle and held it up like she was getting ready to swing a baseball bat.

Jimmy careened toward Effie, flailing the knife about wildly. She locked her gaze on the knife. *Be strong. Be strong. Be strong.* The only thing she could hear was her blood pumping.

When Jimmy stepped into range, she swung with all her might. The frying pan made a solid connection with his hand. As the pan swung through, the knife flew across the room and went spinning under a cabinet.

It was obvious that the impact had hurt Jimmy's hand and wrist but it was not enough to stop him. With each step that he took forward, Effie took a step backward. She lifted the pan and as he lunged forward, she swung again. This time, the frying pan slammed into the side of Jimmy's head. He stumbled to the side a few steps then stopped. He looked in her direction for a moment, his legs wobbling under the strain to keep himself up and then he toppled into a heap on the floor.

Effie began crying wildly as she stepped forward and brought the frying pan down on Jimmy's head another time. When she could no longer lift the pan, she simply let it fall on the floor and she collapsed next to it in a fit of tears. For the first time in a long time, they were not tears of fear or pain. They were tears of joy. Jimmy was dead and with him went the immediate threat of her death.

When Effie finally calmed down, she began looking around for Jimmy's pants. The key to the locks on her chain had to be in a pocket. She looked around and spied them, still in a soggy pile by the door. What relief. She picked herself up and hurried toward them.

As she reached the center of the room, the chain suddenly drew taught. Effie spun around. Laying there, holding the chain and looking at her with more fury than she had ever seen was Jimmy. He wasn't dead! She had been so sure. He began pulling her toward him.

"Fat whore," he growled.

She had to think fast. The knife was lost under the cabinet and the frying pan was right next to Jimmy. If Effie went for the pan, it was very possible that he would get to her before she could grab it and she would not be able to defend herself.

Something else…A chair! That was it. Effie moved toward the table and it was like Jimmy could read her mind. He began pulling the chain even faster.

Not fast enough though.

Effie lifted a chair then ran forward and brought it down on Jimmy's head. Blood spattered and two of the legs broke off the chair. His head dropped to the floor. Even if he was not moving, Effie was not taking any chances this time. She tossed the mangled chair aside and picked up its broken legs. Her hands slid over the surfaces as she inspected one then the other. She placed the pointiest of the two about where she thought his heart would be.

"Bastard!" she screamed as she stabbed with every ounce of energy she had left. She fell to her knees in a pool of blood.

Tears poured down her cheeks but Effie would not be beaten. She picked up the frying pan and began pounding on the chair leg and Jimmy and anything else she could reach. "You are never going to hurt me or anyone else ever again," she shrieked and pushed herself away from the body.

With that, Effie got up and gave the chain a few good yanks so it was as far from Jimmy as possible. Even if he really was dead this time, she was not going to leave the frying pan by his side. She picked it up then went over and began digging through the pockets on the jeans.

At first, she thought she was mistaken. Effie dug through the pockets a second and then a third time. And each time she came up with the same thing. Nothing. She could not believe her eyes. How could that be?

Then it hit her. Jimmy must have added the padlock keys to a key ring and that meant one of two things. Either they were on her key ring and now in the outhouse or they were on the key ring for the truck and they were now in Destry's possession. Either way, it didn't matter. The keys weren't in the cabin, plain and simple and there was no telling where Destry was.

Effie's heart sank. She was stuck in a cabin with two dead men and no way to get free. Why had she believed that Destry would come back and help her escape? What a waste.

She gave the chain a good tug. If only she had the key. If only Destry would come back and unlock her cuff. Effie frowned. Forget him—with or without the key. It was time to put everything out of her mind and start figuring out a way to break the chain off her ankle. There was no way she was going to spend another night in that cabin.

Chapter 31

Every time Effie heard the slightest creak or even imagined a sound, she stopped what she was doing and stared at Jimmy to make sure he was not moving. She had spent several frustrating hours trying to pick at least one of the locks on her chain. Nothing she could find was quite small enough to slip into the keyhole. The longer she sat there trying, the more she was sure that Jimmy or Harry might not really be dead and they would get up and torture her to death.

For a brief time, Effie thought that it would not be such a bad thing to sleep in the cabin one last night. At least then, she could travel in the daylight. Then she thought about the two dead men. She just couldn't do it.

It wouldn't have bothered her as much if it had only been Harry's body. He was out of sight and therefore, easier to put out of her mind. Sitting across the room from Jimmy's body was another thing. Not only was it a constant reminder of what she had done, but there was also a pungent aroma beginning to waft into the room. Or maybe it was just her imagination suggesting the sickening scent. Either way, she decided that it was best to leave as soon as she could get free. If she could just find a way to get a lock off…

Effie looked around the room. Knives did not work. There were no tiny screwdrivers or anything of the kind. Maybe she could break it somehow. Everything breaks if you hit it hard enough. She just had to find something hard that she could use to hit it.

The first thing that came to mind was an old hammer that Effie had seen in the bottom of the chest in the corner. She hurried over and began digging through the pile of things Jimmy had thrown on the floor when he was looking for the rope. When she did not find the hammer there, she opened the chest and dug in. In no time at all, she found what she was looking for.

She hurried to the middle of the room and before she thought about what she was doing, Effie was sitting down. One look at the cuff around her ankle and the lock and she realized she might not be able to swing the hammer hard enough to break the lock. It was at least worth a try. Anything was worth a try.

Effie raised the hammer and swung as hard as she could. As it hit the lock, she squeezed her eyes shut. A piece of metal flew off, hit her, then landed a few feet away. Was it really that easy? She slowly opened her eyes and looked. The lock was still intact. Unfortunately, the same could not be said for the hammer. The impact had caused the head of the hammer to break off the handle. All she was left with was a useless piece of wood in her hand.

"Why?" she screamed. "Why me? Why can't anything be easy? Why can't anything work for me?"

She slumped over then laid her head on the floor and began crying again. All she could think about was surviving that long only to die of starvation or thirst. It just wasn't fair! Some people sailed through life on a cloud—people like Rich Hale. And then there was Effie. She had to fight for everything, including her life. She couldn't even do that anymore, she thought, shaking her head.

Who was she kidding? It was very probable that no one even missed her. Even if she did escape, the outcome would probably be the same. It did not matter when it happened, she was going to die alone. No matter how hard she worked or what she did or even who she knew, in her mind, Effie St. Martine was going to die alone. Why bother prolonging the pain?

She laid there, staring at a black blob through tears. After a while, she ran out of tears, the cast iron frying pan came into focus. The frying pan. Why hadn't she thought of it sooner. It was heavy, it was really hard metal and if it was strong enough to knock Jimmy silly, it was strong enough to beat the hell out of one of the locks. Effie got on her hands and knees and crawled over to pick it up.

The pan had to work better than the hammer. With something as big as the pan, she was definitely going to have to break the lock off the other end of the chain. She could get more power behind it if she did it that way and if she missed the target, it was much better to hit the floor or the post than her ankle. This was good. She could do this.

Effie moved over next to the post then positioned the chain so she would not have to work with her back to Jimmy. With her hands cinched around the handle, she brought the frying pan up to eye level studied it for a moment. True, it had not killed Jimmy when she hit him but this was going to work. It just had to. This time she would go slow, focus and aim.

A trickle of sweat ran down her brow as she sat on her knees, eyes frozen on the padlock. If she had to sit there all night, beating the lock, Effie was going to get free. She had survived Jimmy and Harry and now she was going to break that damn lock and regain her freedom.

Effie let loose a blood-curdling scream and as she did, she brought the frying pan down on the lock. There was a loud clank and for a moment, the pan continued to ring. When she lifted it away, she frowned. The lock was unscathed.

She lifted the heavy frying pan and slammed it down again and again. It did not matter if it was working or not. The lock was not going to beat her! She let the pan rest on the floor for a moment. If it was the last thing she did, she was going to break that lock off the chain.

For a little while, Effie sat with her hands covering her face, thinking about life in general. It hadn't been a bad life, yet she hadn't been very happy either. All of the things that upset her had built up and she never let them go. That is what put her in the situation in the first place. It was like she wasn't just a prisoner in the cabin, she was also a prisoner in her mind. She assumed that she wouldn't be able to break the lock just like she assumed the worst in other aspects of her life. Maybe it was time to get over everything bad and start believing in herself.

Nothing in the past mattered anymore anyway and that meant she could just forget about all of it. It was time to put the old Effie in the past and leave her there. The new Effie could do anything. After all, she had beaten Harry and Jimmy, hadn't she? Anything.

Effie wrapped her fingers around the handle of the pan again, telling herself that it was going to work this time. Focus. On the count of three, she brought the pan down. When she lifted it up, she couldn't believe her eyes. It worked! The lock was laying in two pieces! It was like the triumph radiated right through her soul. She could do anything. The last thing keeping her there was no longer an obstacle. She practically leapt to her feet and danced around the room as she looked for some kind of clothing she could put on.

Even the fact that she could not find anything to put on could not bring Effie down. She was finally free. For a second, she thought about going under the cabin and getting some of the clothes from down there. The thought of seeing (or not seeing) Harry again was more than enough to change her mind. There were enough blankets around.

She found the remains of the blanket Jimmy had used to tie her up and tore off a few more pieces. She found another warm blanket and wrapped it around herself then secured it with the strips from the other blanket. Effie looked around the cabin one last time then she picked up her chain and hobbled toward the door.

Chapter 32

Effie stepped out into the cool night air. The rain had stopped and the sky had cleared enough to let a little moonlight shine through. She was aware of every sound around her. There was no telling what sort of animal might be hiding in the shadows of the forest.

With each step she took, a sharp pain shot from the bottom of Effie's feet into the pit of her belly. Damn Jimmy for doing that! He knew that she was going to run if she had the chance. Even if he didn't, he was obviously bent on hurting her no matter what. That wasn't going to keep her there. Every step away from the cabin was a step away from her past. Nothing was going to stop her.

Now, her only worry was finding her way to town then locating the police. That could be a problem. She did not know how far it was to town or who might be sympathetic to Jimmy and Harry. As she understood it, they had been going to that cabin for years. If that was true, it was likely the people from town would be friendly with the men. They may have even told some of their sick friends about her. There was a chance they might not take too kindly to her. It was a chance she was going to have to take.

Effie suddenly froze. Her ears perked up and she could feel the hairs on the back of her neck stir. Slowly, she sucked in a deep breath and held it. Someone or something was moving off to her right. As much as she did not want to, she knew she had to search the darkness.

Her eyes narrowed as she peered into the shadows. She half expected to see one of the men waiting to attack her. There seemed to be nothing and after a few more minutes of studying everything around her, she began walking again. Perhaps it was only her imagination.

There was that noise. She stopped again, her heart racing. It had to be Jimmy. Who else would hunt her from the shadows like that? He must not have been dead. She hadn't checked for a pulse. She just assumed. After all, he just laid there through all the noise of breaking the lock then finding something to cover her body. She should have checked for a pulse or something. Why hadn't she checked? Now there was something in the shadows and Effie couldn't be sure that it was not Jimmy.

What was she going to do if it was him? Running was no good. He would easily capture her. If it came down to it, she was going to have to fight him off by hand and the thought of that was grim.

Effie jumped, a small gasp escaping. A prickly feeling ran up and down her spine. She was sure she had just felt something brush against the back of her leg. She spun around in a complete circle but there was nothing. Just shadows.

Maybe the noise and the sensation on the back of her leg were nothing more than her mind playing tricks on her. Yes. That was probably it. After all, she was a city girl out in the dark woods at night. It made perfect sense.

Thinking about it that way made everything better and she was about to begin walking again when a twig snapped. Effie stopped breathing and her eyes bulged as she stared in the direction of the sound. It definitely was not her imagination. She was sure of it this time.

"Screw this," she whispered under her breath and tore off down the two-track. There was no reason to stand around waiting for someone to attack her. She ran as fast as she could, ignoring the pain from her injured feet and the sharp rocks digging in with every step. She never even looked over her shoulder. That would only slow her down.

Through the darkness ahead, it looked like there was a clearing. Effie's body ached and she was out of breath but there was no stopping her. She hadn't survived that long for nothing. Giving up was no longer an option. She just kept pressing forward.

When she made it to the clearing, her heart leapt into her throat. It wasn't a clearing. It was the road!

Without even thinking about which way to go, Effie ran left, down the middle of the road. Every inch of her body was screaming at her to stop but she kept going, her bare feet slapping on the pavement. She had to find town—the police—a house with a telephone—something—anything.

Things were beginning to get fuzzy and Effie was gasping for air. She couldn't stop. She just couldn't. There was something shining in her eyes and at first, she did not realize what it was. Then it came to her. Headlights. And they were getting closer.

Effie stopped when the headlights were almost upon her. She began waving her arms—or at least she thought about it. They felt like dead weights. The headlights belonged to a truck. It seemed to be slowing. Had it stopped?

There was something...The thought disappeared. Effie glanced around. She wanted to say something or at least finish her thought. Maybe later. She was suddenly aware of only one thing: The ground was racing toward her. And then there was nothing.

Chapter 33

Effie opened her eyes. Everything was a blur of lights and shadows. There was a silence in the air that seemed to make everything cold. Was she dead? There was no more pain and it felt like she was floating on air.

She blinked a few times. No, she couldn't be dead. But if she wasn't dead, where was she? This couldn't be what happens when you die. It was like being lost in a fog.

Her eyes darted around, searching. The haze began to fade. There more she blinked, the clearer things became. A pale green wall melted out of a shadow. Effie blinked again and again, willing everything to come into focus. Lights appeared. She wasn't floating on anything. She was laying on a bed…a hospital bed…hospital…

How did she get there? She tried to think back. It was all in her memory. It had to be. All she had to do was find it.

Darkness. Dark shadows. She was running away from something. But what? There were tall trees all around. She was in a forest. A noise? That's what it was. She was running away from the noise because someone was going to hurt her. Then there was a road and headlights. The headlights belonged to a truck. She wanted to make it stop and it looked like it was going to. Then something happened. The road didn't stay where it was supposed to. It just flew at her and that was it.

"How did I get here?" she whispered. Her throat was parched.

Something moved in the corner of her eye. She turned. There was a man in a chair next to her bed and he had obviously been sleeping. He looked at her for a moment as he rubbed his eyes. He looked so familiar. She knew that face from somewhere.

All of a sudden, it was like a light clicked on in his head. His eyes widened and he jumped out of his chair. He ran to the door and began yelling into the hallway. "Nurse! Nurse, she's awake! Come quick! She's Awake!"

That voice! She knew it. It was…Destry.

Hurried footsteps came down the hall and Destry stepped back as a middle-aged nurse rushed into the room. Within moments, she was joined by a younger nurse. Everyone seemed so frantic. Effie was so stunned by the static air of excitement that all she could do was watch in silence.

"I called Dr. Hemley and let her know she was awake. She said she was on her way. She also said not to let the police know until after she had a chance to look her over," said the younger nurse.

"Well that's to be expected Jessica," said the older nurse. "Can you imagine the mess if they got in here and started with their questions? Right after that, those darn news crews would be in here too. They'd disrupt the entire wing."

The nurses began chattering back and forth as if they were repeating a conversation they had been through before.

"I still think it was Brianna Nicholes who let them know that she was here in the first place."

"Who else could it have been?"

"She's the only person I can think of."

"Well for God's sake, don't let her know that our star patient is awake!"

A woman in her mid-forties, wearing a log white jacket sped into the room. Immediately, the two nurses became more serious. "How long has she been awake, Samantha?" she asked.

The older nurse spoke up. "Only a few minutes, Dr. Hemley. Mr. Clare told us she was awake just before we called you." She hesitated for a moment. "I checked her stats while we were waiting for you. It looks like everything is normal."

"Thank you, Samantha. I still need to check a few things myself. Mr. Clare?" Destry was still standing near the door. "Would you please excuse us for a moment. You can come back in as soon as I am finished. It will only be a short while. You can step into the hall or wait in the lounge," Dr. Hemley said as she pulled the privacy curtain around the bed.

"Yes, Ma'am," Destry said reluctantly before being ushered out by the younger nurse.

The moment the curtain was around the bed, the doctor smiled. "I'm Dr. Hemley," she said. "You're welcome to call me Crystal." She held a tiny instrument up and checked Effie's pupil dilation. Satisfied, she looked at a chart, hanging on the end of the bed then began making comparisons.

"It looks like you've been through quite an ordeal," she said. "You weren't conscious the night Mr. Clare brought you in." She paused and looked over the top of the clipboard for a moment before going on. "We cleaned up your cuts and scrapes and got you on an I.V. to get you rehydrated. Considering the shape you were in when you were brought here, you seem to be doing pretty good."

"How long…"

Dr. Hemley smiled. "How long have you been here? Just two days. You've been in and out of sleep quite a few times but you haven't been quite lucid." Effie gave her a confused look so she went on. "What I mean is, you've had your eyes open but the painkillers haven't been kind to your cognitive functions. It's normal. You weren't able to recognize where you were. You did a little talking but no one could make any sense of what you were saying."

"But I was OK up until I saw a truck," Effie said. "Did it hit me? Is that why I can't remember?"

"No, you weren't hit by a vehicle. You were just mentally and physically exhausted," the doctor said, nodding her head. "Stranger things have happened. I'm willing to bet that the entire ordeal was just too much for your body. You've obviously been through some serious trauma."

"But—"

Dr. Hemley interrupted. "I'm sure you have dozens of questions and I promise, we will get to them. I have a few questions and small tests that I need to do first."

"I'm sorry," said Effie.

"Now," the doctor said, poising her pen over the clipboard, "can you tell me your full name?"

"Euphamia Mae St. Martin," she said, causing the doctor to raise her eyebrow. She quickly added, "Euphamia was my great-grandmother's name."

"Age?"

"Thirty-two."

"Date of birth?"

"April 22, 1972."

Dr. Hemley asked several more questions, checking each one against the chart. When she was done, she laid the clipboard down on a table and pulled a little light out of her pocket. As she began checking Effie's pupil dilation again, she said, "I imagine that the police will be here as soon as they hear that you are up and about." Satisfied, she put the little light back in her pocket and began a series of other little tests. "We can keep the media out but I'm afraid you're going to have to go through a questioning by the police. We can only keep them at bay for so long."

Effie gave her a funny look. "The media?" she questioned.

"You're famous Ms St. Martin. Apparently the police were looking for you for several days. When you didn't return to work, your employer contacted them."

"People missed me," she muttered, causing Dr. Hemley to give her a questioning look. When Effie realized that she had said it out loud, she blushed. "I'm sorry," she said. "Can I ask you a silly question?"

The doctor smiled. "Sure," she said. "Anything for my celebrity patient."

"Where am I—besides a hospital. That's obvious."

"Canyon City, Colorado." It was Effie's turn to give Dr. Hemley a confused look so she added, "It's southwest of Denver quite a ways."

Before Effie could digest the words, the privacy curtain was yanked back, revealing a thirty-something woman in a blazer and jeans accompanied by a younger man in a nice polo shirt and khaki's.

Dr. Hemley was obviously angry. "You can't just come busting in here Detective Dillard!" she said. "This patient just woke up and I still have quite a few tests I want to complete. She's been through a lot and she needs her rest before being put through the third degree by you." She reached up to slide the curtain closed but the other woman motioned for the man to prevent it.

"Can it, Crystal," the woman said. "You were supposed to call me as soon as she woke up. That was the deal."

"No, Christie, I said that I would call you as soon as she was ready to answer your questions."

"Same difference."

Effie just looked from one woman to the other as they argued back and forth. It was obvious that they were well acquainted. Neither one bothered to hide their annoyance with the other.

"Excuse me," Effie interrupted. Both women stopped arguing and looked at her. "I'll answer the detective's questions." Detective Dillard gave Dr. Hemley a smug look. "I want to talk with that guy that was in here—Destry—

first."

It was the detective who spoke first. "I don't think that's such a good idea. Talking to anyone could make you fill in things you can't remember clearly with the wrong details."

"I remember everything except coming here quite clearly. I'll tell you every last detail but first I want to talk to Destry."

The detective gave her a grim look. Effie sighed. "Look detective, if it wasn't for him, you may never have found me. That man saved my life, not you. I am not going to answer a single question until I get to talk to him!"

"Fine," Detective Dillard said, throwing up her hands. "Go down and get him Ron."

The man nodded then stepped out of the room without a word.

"Thank you," said Effie.

The detective looked rather unhappy—Perhaps even more so than the doctor. "Detective Charles and I will be waiting in the hall. As soon as you're done, we'll talk," she said.

"Agreed."

Detective Dillard stepped out of the room but Dr. Hemley stood beside the bed with an unhappy expression on her face. Effie raised her eyebrows as if to say that she was sorry and the doctor turned to leave, shaking her head. Moments later, Destry walked in and just stood at the foot of the bed, looking at Effie, tears in his eyes.

"It was you in the truck," she whispered and he nodded his head. "You came back for me." Tears spilled onto Effie's cheeks. "Close the door and come here."

Effie raised her arms to draw Destry into them when he came near. She held him to her, shaking uncontrollably.

"I'm so sorry," he cried. "I wanted to come right back. I wanted to kill Jimmy for what he did to you but I knew he was serious about killing you if he ever saw me again. I went to Ahanu Webb and told him everything. We knew we couldn't just leave you there so we hid out in the woods at night, waiting to make our move at the perfect moment. I saw what he did to you. I wanted to storm the cabin right away but Ahanu stopped me. He said your position was too vulnerable. You had no way to defend yourself and Jimmy would have killed you before we got in there."

"Why didn't you just go to the police?"

"Are you kidding? The local cop has been friends with Jimmy and Harry since they were kids. I'm surprised they didn't have him out there to join in the abuse. Bobby would have just covered everything up I'm sure of it."

"Oh," said Effie.

"Ahanu and I were on our way back the other night when we saw someone in the road. It turned out to be you and as soon as we got near, you just collapsed. I panicked. I figured that Jimmy would be on your tail in no time so I just picked you up and pulled you into the bed of the truck with me. You wouldn't talk or open your eyes or anything so I held you in my arms all the way here, praying that you wouldn't die."

Effie clutched his hand in both of hers and brought it to her heart. "I don't know what to say, Destry. Thank you."

"Listen, Effie," he began. "I'm really sorry about everything. If I could go back and change it so none of this ever happened, I would. I'm just so sorry."

They were both sobbing and Effie tried to tell him that everything was OK but he hushed her. "Please," he said, "let me finish."

Effie shook her head in silence, brushing the tears away.

Destry took a deep breath and went on. "I would be lying if I told you that I didn't have any feelings for you." He looked into Effie's eyes then leaned forward to gently kiss her. She wanted more. He hadn't abandoned her.

"I haven't told the police everything yet but I'm going to, Effie. I was part of it and I'm prepared to pay the consequences for my actions."

"Don't," she said.

"Even if I don't say anything, Jimmy and Harry will as soon as the police catch them. It would look worse for me—like I'd lied. I don't want to be like them."

Effie studied his face. "They won't say anything," she said. Destry looked at her in confusion. "They're dead—both of them. I killed them."

Destry's face went pale and he just gawked.

"I'm sorry," she whispered, "but Jimmy was all set to kill me. They went fishing in the afternoon one day and somehow Harry talked Jimmy into letting him keep me. He said it would be like I was his wife. The two of them would take turns spending time with me and trucking. I was horrified. There was no way I could spend the rest of my life like an animal in that cabin. I knew I had to do something."

He shook his head. "No."

"There's more. You were just a pawn in all of this. I got Jimmy to talk and it wasn't just me and Angie that he's done these things to. He bragged to me about luring women up there by himself for some time. I believe him that they are up there. I don't know how many more there are but I think there's a lot.

I noticed that nails were missing from some of the floorboards so I pried some of them up. I saw my bag down under the cabin but there was so much more that I didn't recognize. I think he kept little trophies from each woman he kidnaped. And Destry, he said there are more graves out behind the cabin— About 50 yards out, I think."

"But how?"

"He said he picked up runaways and prostitutes at rest areas and truck stops."

Destry sank into the chair beside the bed, his hand still on Effie's. Suddenly, it was like a light clicked on in the back of his mind. His face lit up with an expression of instant recognition. "It all makes sense," he said, shaking his head. "There were so many times when he was gone longer than it should have taken him to make a haul. Perfect sense."

"See? None of it was your fault. It was Jimmy all along."

"Was it? I was there right from the start. He didn't hold a gun to my head and make me do anything. I did it on my own and that makes me just as bad as him."

"That's where you're wrong, Destry," Effie said, frowning. "Don't you get it? He's been playing the same game with you since you were kids. Anytime you didn't want to follow his lead, he reminded you of the time he saved your life—Probably the only time he ever did anything good. The man had no conscience and he dragged you along. He probably figured when he killed Angie that he had to get you involved really deep. Otherwise you were a witness to his crime."

"It doesn't matter—"

"It does," she interrupted. "One of the first things I recognized when I saw you in that ally behind the Coon Pit was that you didn't want to go along with Jimmy. I *saw* you hesitate and walk away. I knew you didn't want any part of it but Jimmy just sucked you into the mess."

Destry looked at the floor. "I don't know Effie," he said, shaking his head. "I want to do what's right. And I'm sure by now, the cops have found proof that I ran with those two."

His eyes connected with hers and for a moment, there was silence. "Why are you doing this," asked Destry. "Why are you trying so had to keep me out of trouble?"

Effie pulled her hand from his and raised it to brush his cheek. "Because," she said, "I'd be lying too if I said that I didn't have any feelings for you."

215

Chapter 34

Effie stood next to her hospital bed, packing up dozens of gifts people had sent from across the country. It was nice to be a celebrity for a while but she was looking forward to getting back to a quieter lifestyle. She knew the hounding reporters wouldn't go away quite yet as she still hadn't granted even one television or newspaper interview. Her first one would be with the *Lansing Sun Press*. It was the least she could do. Raymond Ludgreen had flown to Colorado to see to her needs personally. He'd even booked her a first-class flight back to Lansing out of his own pocket.

She wouldn't be going back to Lansing to stay, though. The experience had changed everything about her and it was time to start over with a clean slate. As soon as her affairs were in order and her apartment was packed up, that was it. She was leaving. .

A young girl who volunteered at the hospital had helped Effie load up dozens of flowers and plants onto carts earlier but she seemed to have disappeared. As soon as Effie put the last of her belongings into a bag, she stepped into the hall. "Excuse me," she said to a young man in scrubs. "Is there a candy-striper or a sunshine lady I could borrow for a little while? I received all these flowers and I can't possibly keep them. I'm flying back to Michigan this afternoon and rather than see them thrown away, I would like to have someone deliver them to patients who don't get many visitors or who might need a little cheering up."

The young man looked toward Effie's room. Four full carts sat against the wall and two more just inside her room. She could tell by his expression that he didn't want to be bothered with tracking down a volunteer but he could hardly deny her request.

He stepped into the nurse's station and placed his hand on a telephone. Effie stood watching until he raised his eyebrows as if to say he wasn't going to do it with her watching. As she turned to go back into her room, he punched in some numbers and requested that someone come up to take care of the plants.

Effie sat on the edge of her bed to wait. Because of all the reporters, the detective was supposed to send an officer to take her to the airport. As she closed her eyes and leaned back, she marveled at how much she'd changed. Somewhere along the way, she'd gained a new self-confidence. She had a feeling that she could do anything she wanted. She was going to, too.

When news of her abduction and escape had hit the airwaves, it was like the entire country was her friend. When people found out what business she was in, job offers came pouring in from every corner of the country. Many, she hadn't taken seriously. She knew they were just companies looking for that push to make their ratings a little higher. Everything was there, though, from television to newspapers to magazines to book offers. She'd even received an offer to make her story into a made for television movie. She turned them all down. All but one.

Chapter 35

Effie sat in Raymond Ludgreen's office, waiting for him to get off the phone. As she did, she stared out the window behind him. Somehow, she'd missed the great view he had of the Michigan State Capital Building before. Maybe the shades had always been closed. She couldn't be sure. Or maybe her eyes had just been closed to the rest of the world. There were so many things she'd overlooked that she was almost sad to be leaving them behind.

Finally, Mr. Ludgreen hung up the phone and smiled at Effie. "Sorry about that, St. Martin," he said. "It's great to have you back. Now, can I get you something to drink? Soda? Coffee?"

Effie smiled politely and raised her hand. "No thank you, sir, I'm here because I need to talk with you."

"Ok," he said. "Shoot. If it's about the cover story I promised you, I have several from which you can choose. All you have to do is take your pick. You're going to be a star reporter from now on."

"That's not really what I'm here to talk about, sir." She drew in a deep breath. "I don't know of any easy way to put this other than to just lay it right out there on the table for you."

Mr. Ludgreen gave her a questioning look but said nothing. He leaned forward, clasping his hands, and rested his elbows on the desk. His eyes rested on Effie.

The words were building up like water behind a dam. Effie was just going to have to say it or she would burst from the pressure. "I'm quitting, Mr.

Ludgreen—Sir," she blurted out.

He sat back and covered his mouth like he was trying to hide a laugh. "That's a good joke, St. Martin," he chuckled. "Your expression almost had me convinced. That's very good. Now come on and tell me why you really wanted to meet with me."

"I'm serious," Effie said, giving him a no-nonsense look. "I'm really quitting. I've had several job offers and I've decided to take one of them."

Raymond Ludgreen's face paled then glazed with shock as he realized that she wasn't joking. "If it's about the money, we'll give you a raise. Or— or if it's about the columns you've been writing, you don't have to worry about them. Like I said, you are going to be getting bigger stories. You're a great writer, St. Martin. We can't afford to loose you."

Sure they couldn't. He wanted to keep her there for the exact same reason that every other person wanted to hire her—circulation and sales. She gave him a knowing smile. "It's not about either of them sir."

"Then what is it? Is it Rich Hale? He won't be bothering you again. I let him go because of his actions toward you."

"No, it's not that either," she said, shaking her head. "I need a change. I'm not the same person I used to be and I think it's time for me to go somewhere and start over."

He studied her face for a moment. "Are you sure this is what you want?" he asked.

"Not only do I want it, I think I need it."

"And there's no talking you out of it?"

"No. I've made up my mind. I have a friend packing up the last of my apartment as we speak."

Mr. Ludgreen raised his eyebrows. "It sounds as if you've put some real thought into this. I guess there's nothing I can do to make you change your mind." He paused for a moment as if to ponder what was happening. "Do you mind me asking where you are heading?"

Effie smiled from ear to ear. "Montana. There's a little publishing company in a town named Missoula and they've offered me a pretty nice position editing books. It's what I've always wanted to do."

"I guess I have to say that I'm happy for you, kiddo. We'll miss you around here but if your mind is made up, there's nothing more I can do." Mr. Ludgreen looked like a kid who'd just had his balloon popped.

Effie leaned in. "I'm still going to grant the *Lansing Sun Press* my first interview, sir." That brought a smile to his face.

"We'll get the best to do it. I'll can call my top reporter down here right away."

"No!" she said shaking her head. "I have one condition and I think you will be more than happy to agree to it. If not, I'll take my interview elsewhere."

"Well?" he questioned.

She nodded toward the door. "There's a part-timer I've talked with a few times. She's just out of college and I think she even lives in my apartment complex. Her name's Rebecca Quaid. I think she has a lot of promise and this story is exactly what she needs to give her a jump on her career."

"Quaid," he said. "I don't know that she's ready for this sort of thing. I think we'd be better of with someone a little more experienced."

Effie shook her head. "That's my deal. I've had plenty of inquiries from other papers. Some of them have even offered to pay. Either Rebecca gets the assignment or I will take my interview, a*nd her,* elsewhere. Bottom line."

"My hands are tied on things like this, St. Martin, and you know it."

"No they aren't. You're the one who hands out the assignments." She shrugged. "It's your call, Mr. Ludgreen. Take it or leave it."

He looked more than a little annoyed. Raymond Ludgreen was not the type of man who liked to be pushed into a corner and told what to do. The problem was, Effie wasn't anymore either. This was her story and she wasn't about to let him hand it out to just anyone.

"You'll still have one of your reporters writing the piece, sir. It just won't be your star reporter. That won't change anything, though. Half the papers in this country will still want to run your column no matter who writes it."

Finally, Mr. Ludgreen sighed and brought his hands to his eyes and began rubbing. At that moment, Effie knew she had won. Rebecca Quaid was going to get the assignment!

"Can I at least ask what your deal is with Quaid?"

"Well sir, if you ever took the time to really read through her articles, you would see exactly how good she is. You are passing over real talent for someone who is tried and tested. I know of at least one other reporter you've done that to."

"Oh?" he said, raising his eyebrows. "Who?"

"Sir, I'm trying to see that she doesn't end up in the same place I did. Just tell her she can stop by my apartment tonight." He pulled out a pen and gave her a look she knew to mean that he wanted to write down her address. "River Ridge Apartments on Willow Highway. I'm in apartment 5-B. She needs to stop tonight or she'll have to wait a few days. I'm leaving for Montana tomorrow. She won't be able to call me out there for at least four days."

"She'll be there tonight."

"Fine," said Effie as she rose to leave. She walked toward the door then stopped and turned to look at Mr. Ludgreen. He was sitting with his hands covering his eyes. She smiled at him one last time.

"Good luck St. Martin," he mumbled without looking up.

"Thank you sir," she said. "It's been a pleasure."

With that, Effie St. Martin walked out of the *Lansing Sun Press* building for the last time. It felt good to know that she and Destry would be leaving for Montana in less that 24 hours. Every step she took down Michigan Avenue was a step toward her new life. Everything was going to be different and everything was going to go her way.

Printed in the United States
56684LVS00004B/231